DÌLEAS SECURITY AGENCY

fatal
MISSTEP

C.S. Smith

Fatal Misstep by: C.S. Smith

Published by: Jug End Media, LLC

Copyright © 2025 by C.S. Smith

Editor: Liana Brooks

Cover Design: Deranged Doctor Design

Publisher's Cataloging-in-Publication
(Provided by Cassidy Cataloguing Services, Inc.)

Names: Smith, C. S. (Cynthia S.)., author.
Title: Fatal misstep / C. S. Smith.
Description: [Charlotte, North Carolina] : Jug End Media, LLC, [2025] | Series: Dìleas Security Agency ; book
4.
Identifiers: ISBN: 9798998663901 (paperback) | 9798998663918 (ebook)
Subjects: LCSH: United States. Army. Special Forces--Fiction. | Bodyguards--Fiction. | Organized crime--
Fiction. | Drug dealers--Fiction. | Navajo Nation, Arizona, New Mexico & Utah--Fiction. | Women
physicians--Fiction. | Fugitives from justice--Fiction. | Psychic trauma--Fiction. | Ene-

mies--Fiction. |

Redemption--Fiction. | Opportunity--Fiction. | Special forces (Military science)--Fiction. | Arizona--

Fiction. | New Mexico--Fiction. | Suspense fiction. | Romance fiction. | LCGFT: Action and adventure

fiction. | Military fiction. | Detective and mystery fiction. | Romance fiction. | Thrillers (Fiction) |

BISAC: FICTION / Romance / Action & Adventure. | FICTION / Romance / Suspense. | FICTION /

Romance / Military.

Classification: LCC: PS3619.M55397 F38 2025 | DDC: 813/.6--dc23

Ebook ISBN: 979-8-9986639-1-8

Print ISBN: 979-8-9986639-0-1

CHAPTER ONE

THE WINTER SKY, ALREADY sullen with iron-gray clouds, dropped its curtain of starless night, coating everything in darkness. The rain stopped, the squeak of windshield wipers on dry glass setting his teeth on edge, so he turned them off.

Caleb Varella glanced at his rental Jeep's dashboard. *Eighteen-thirty*.

The smell of the funeral home he'd just left—antiseptic and lilies, sharp and sickly sweet—clung to his skin. He needed a drink. Not for pleasure, but for distraction.

Something acidic enough to dissolve the past clawing its way into his present.

His headlights bounced off wet asphalt, casting desert scrub in ghostly white. Up ahead, the desolate terrain gave way to the artificial glow of civilization as he entered the outskirts of Gallup, New Mexico, the closest place that would meet all his needs tonight—liquor, food, a warm bed, and anonymity. Even with a relatively meager population of twenty-one thousand, Gallup was the regional hub for tribal communities that straddled the northern Arizona–New Mexico border.

A weight pressed on his shoulders. Grit scratched his eyes. If he were smart, he'd find the nearest motel and faceplant on a cheap mattress. A month providing close protection for a silicon valley tech guru setting up a hub in Kenya's new Konza Technopolis and then, the phone call. His mother was dead. An overdose.

His mother, who'd been sober for over five years.

He turned onto old Route 66, passing budget motels, fast food joints, and a self-storage facility.

A glowing red neon sign caught his eye.

Lucero's Lounge.

First, that drink.

A square adobe squatter, the bar sat between two empty lots of dormant grass and scrub, as if quarantined from more respectable businesses. Between that and the weeds sprouting in the cracked pavement up front, this was no tourist hot spot.

On satellite radio, an 80s rock queen went full throttle about being alone. Caleb guided the Jeep into the gravel lot on the side of the building. A chain-link fence separated the property from railroad tracks, where a Burlington Northern Santa Fe train rumbled on, with no visible beginning or end.

A lone security light cast a dim yellow haze over the three parked vehicles. Given it was Tuesday, they likely belonged to a few diehard locals who wouldn't give him the time of day.

Perfect.

He wasn't good company right now, anyway. He killed the engine and stepped out, cutting the songstress off before her last lonely notes faded away. Chill, damp air muted the smell of diesel and neglect in his surroundings, and nipped at skin left exposed by his white t-shirt.

His phone buzzed as he strolled to the bar's entrance. He glanced at the message from Danny Mayhew, one of his colleagues at Dìleas Security Agency, and ignored it like he had the others. Condolences, even the well-meant ones, twisted his gut. He'd figure out what to say when he returned to DC.

His childhood wasn't something he talked about.

With anyone.

Five years. Last year, his mom had busted her knee but refused anything stronger than ibuprofen. Said she didn't trust herself around stronger pills.

Which made the way she died—fentanyl disguised as oxy—even harder to stomach. A new, deadly variant, according to the Phoenix police.

Where the hell had she gotten the pills from? His drug-dealing old man had been killed in a Phoenix back alley years ago. Eighteen, in fact.

A day of celebration as far as Caleb was concerned. Not his mother, though. She'd actually mourned the bastard.

Caleb gave the glass door a weary tug. He should have called her more often.

Should have gone to Phoenix during the holidays instead of accepting that protection job in Mexico City no one else wanted because it was over Christmas. He'd been meaning to visit her after.

Then the Kenya job came up.

Inside the bar, warm air leached the chill from his bones. Burnt tobacco invaded his nose. Stale beer stuck to his boots.

It was as expected for a dive. Dim lights, wood-paneled walls, beer brand placards and a mishmash of Americana and Native art. The bartender, stocky with a face weathered by desert sun and black hair streaked with gray, slouched near two old-timers with Desert Storm ball caps.

Veterans like him, but from a different war.

Three sets of eyes turned his way. Dark. Assessing. Caleb nodded. They dismissed him and resumed their conversation.

He took a seat on a cracked vinyl stool. Propped his elbows on a wooden counter that needed a fresh coat of varnish. Behind it, liquor bottles stood on glass shelves like soldiers in formation.

It had been a long day, escorting his mother's body five hours north from Phoenix to the Navajo reservation. He'd raise a glass to her tortured soul, curse his father's, and brace for tomorrow, when he'd bury his *amá* and face the family he hadn't seen since he was twelve.

Including his grandfather. President of the Navajo Nation.

"What can I get you?" The bartender eyed him with mild suspicion. Caleb's black hair, copper skin, and brown eyes broadcast his Native and Hispanic roots. Common in the Southwest. But in this bar, he was still an outsider.

Caleb scrutinized the liquor bottles. They all tasted the same—more medicinal than pleasure. He rarely drank more than an occasional beer.

"Johnny Walker." *Shit.* Now he'd have to choose. "Red. Neat. Got any food?"

"Navajo tacos are pretty good." The bartender jerked a thumb at the swinging door beside the counter. "Wife makes them."

"Perfect."

The bartender poured the whiskey, set it on a cocktail napkin, then vanished into the kitchen. A minute later, he returned to his spot with his buddies.

The liquor scorched Caleb's throat, igniting a fire in his chest. Harsh. Like the memories trying to push their way forward.

Lillie Blackwater Varella had made him promise to bury her among the Diné—the Navajo word for themselves that translated to The People.

Why, he'd never understood. Still didn't.

He'd been her only family. His grandfather hadn't reached out, not even after Caleb's father died, when Caleb was sixteen, and it had been just him and his mom struggling to survive. As soon as he turned eighteen, his paychecks from the Army had kept his mother housed and fed.

Now he protected high value individuals and got paid handsomely for it. He'd made sure his mother wanted for nothing.

Except his time.

He took another, larger swallow and observed the men in the corner. Navajo. Like her. The whiskey soured in his stomach. Maybe he shared their blood, but he didn't belong any more than the tourists who bought trinkets at the trading posts off the interstate.

Lifting the glass, he studied its contents. Honey gold. Not top shelf, but it did the job. Tomorrow, he'd do what his mother asked. Bury her on Diné land. Treat his grandfather with respect, undeserved as it might be for a man who abandoned his only daughter.

And leave with his past firmly in the rearview mirror.

Forever.

Maybe he'd head to the cabin in the mountains of North Carolina that he owned but rarely visited.

Or maybe he'd take the lead on the protection job coming up in New York so his boss, Ryder, could stay in London with his fiancée, Nathalie. She'd just started art school.

The door swished open. Cold air gusted in, cutting through the beer and cigarettes.

He sipped his whiskey and flicked his gaze to the mirror behind the bar.

A woman stood in the doorway.

Dark brown hair fell in waves just past her shoulders, brushing a burgundy hip-length leather jacket. Blue jeans molded long legs ending in brown ankle boots. The woman tucked a strand behind her ear. A diamond stud winked in the light.

Classy. Too classy for a place like this.

Tense shoulders. A careful sweep of her gaze.

Like she was searching for threats.

Caleb sat straighter. He knew that look. Had seen it too many times during his deployments in war zones, and even now, protecting people whose money, status, or celebrity made them targets.

"Hey, Doc," the bartender called out a greeting. He set a plate of tacos in front of Caleb and reached for a soda glass.

Caleb almost replied, then caught himself. The bartender hadn't been speaking to him. He'd been nodding at the woman.

"Doc" had been Caleb's nickname as the senior medic when he was an E-7 Special Forces Medical Sergeant in his ODA with the 3rd Special Forces Group out of Fort Bragg. But that was years ago.

He'd seen enough blood and trauma to last a lifetime.

The woman set a white paper bag on the counter. "Hey, Billy, I brought your medicine."

Her voice was a melody of hard consonants and drawn-out vowels—New York, if he had to guess. She greeted the old-timers, then launched into a hushed lecture about diet and exercise.

Billy the bartender nodded, looking like a man enduring a root canal, and promised to do as instructed.

Good luck.

Caleb smirked behind his taco. *Hell,* if she were his doctor, he'd hang on to her every word. Her voice—low, husky—vibrated through his chest, easing some of the pressure there.

He bit into his meal. Crispy fried bread, hot and greasy, crunched between his teeth, mixed with seasoned beef, beans, lettuce, tomatoes and cheese. His stomach growled in appreciation. He cleaned his plate while watching the show.

The doctor finished her speech.

Billy handed her a club soda with lime before taking Caleb's empty dish to the kitchen.

Full sensual lips stained a dusky pink covered the rim of the glass.

Lust punched Caleb, as unexpected as it was disturbing. He reined it in and tried to think of something to say that wouldn't spook her.

"Your patient?"

She studied him for a moment. Eyes the color of sapphires and filled with shadows.

"Yes."

Graceful movements. Unmarked golden skin.

But his father had never left visible bruises, either.

He extended his hand. "Caleb."

To put her at ease, he smiled, the gesture foreign to his facial muscles.

Her eyes grew large. Her hands stayed on her drink.

He let his fall to his thigh. Apparently, he needed more practice at appearing non-threatening.

Then she surprised him, stepping closer.

He caught a hint of desert flowers after rain.

Sweet. Lush.

Another surprise. He'd expected a cloying perfume to match her expensive-looking clothes.

"Are you from Gallup?" Her voice was wary. One wrong answer and she'd vanish.

"No. I'm here to bury my mother. I live in Northern Virginia, just outside of DC."

At least that was where his mail went and where he slept between jobs.

Her eyes softened. Sympathy replaced caution. "I'm sorry. Is she a member of the Navajo Nation?"

Simple question. Complicated answer.

"Yes." Caleb left it at that. "What about you?"

Doc—he still didn't know her name—glanced at the door and took another measured sip of her drink. "No. I work at a clinic about forty minutes away."

He did a quick mental calculation. Forty minutes in either direction was a whole lot of nothing. "On the rez?"

She flinched. Bit her lip. "Yes."

Truth. Reluctantly delivered.

"You said your mother was Navajo." She set her glass down. "Did you grow up around here?"

"Not really."

Her brows knitted together.

He elaborated. "We moved to Phoenix when I was twelve. I joined the Army after high school. Haven't been back much."

Why was he telling her this? He kept his business to himself.

You don't want her to leave.

He'd sit and talk all night if she wanted. It beat going to a hotel room alone and thinking about how shitty the next day was going to be.

He glanced at her hands. No rings, and no evidence a ring had made itself at home on her left finger.

"Another club soda, Doc?" Billy aimed a scowl at Caleb.

"No, thanks. I need to head home."

Billy nodded and sent another squinty-eyed glare in Caleb's direction before he returned to his buddies.

The door opened, ushering in more chill night air and a stranger.

Around five-eight. Dark eyes. Salt and pepper hair. A drooping Winnfield mustache.

Doc's fingers tightened around her glass, knuckles turning white.

A doe scenting a predator.

Caleb gave the newcomer his complete attention. With his faded jeans, worn cowboy boots, and a long-sleeve flannel shirt, he could have been a day laborer looking for a beer after a hard day's work.

Except his clothes were too clean, too tidy, and his demeanor was anything but casual. The flannel shirt hung loose, like it was concealing a weapon.

Caleb's fingers flexed, inching toward his concealed carry Glock.

Dammit.

Which he'd locked up in the Jeep while he was at the funeral home.

There was something familiar about the guy. Recognition teased the edge of Caleb's memory.

The man locked eyes with Doc, and the air in the bar shifted to something unspoken.

Dangerous.

"I have to go," she whispered. Fear overpowered her delicate perfume.

She slipped out the door.

The stranger followed.

Well, hell. Caleb's protective instincts kicked hard.

He slapped cash on the bar, shoved his wallet into his pocket, and went after them.

Chapter Two

Terror took hold of Gianna Barone's feet, propelling her from the bar. Frigid air stung her cheeks, and she shivered, the temperature having dropped another few degrees in the short time she'd been inside.

Get to the car. Get back to the reservation.

The man who'd walked into Lucero's Lounge was a stranger, but he'd recognized her somehow.

Idiot. She'd been so careful to stay under the radar. This was why she always made excuses to her friend, Jennie Tsosie, about skipping girls' nights.

She should have dropped off Billy's medication and left.

Shouldn't have lingered to talk to the attractive man—Caleb. Shouldn't have been drawn to him.

When he'd smiled, her heart had thumped so hard she'd almost bolted.

That would have been the smart move—run.

Instead, she'd let a handsome face and killer smile lower her guard when she, of all people, should know better.

She rounded the building's corner and skidded to a halt.

In the yellow haze of the security light, a lanky kid in his twenties leaned against the bumper of a black SUV. Stringy brown hair hung from beneath a pink knit beanie. His thin, sullen face and cold eyes didn't match the bright wool cap.

He glanced over her shoulder—at someone behind her. Straightening, Pink Cap tracked her approach with an intensity that made her pulse stutter.

Don't show fear.

Easy to say. Harder with adrenaline spiking and her vision blurring.

Maybe she could bluff her way to her car. Lock the doors. Call Zach Blackwater.

These goons might back off if a Navajo Nation Police officer showed up.

Or they might shoot him.

Then she'd have another death on her conscience.

She was only halfway through her twelve-week locum tenens contract at the Navajo medical clinic, filling in for a doctor on maternity leave. And she needed the money. If she left before her contract was up, she'd never get another job as a doctor.

Gia dug out her key and wedged the metal shank between trembling fingers. Next time she bought a car, it would be new enough to have a fob.

If there was a next time.

She started forward, chin high, sweat dampening her lower back despite the cold.

Gravel crunched behind her. No need to look.

She knew who it was.

Her steps quickened.

She would never go back to Miami.

Not to the man she'd almost married.

Not after what she'd seen.

The secret she carried like a stain on her soul.

"Señorita." The voice, high-pitched and rhythmic, came from behind.

Gia kept walking.

Pink Cap watched her approach, his stare flat, cold.

Her pulse thudded. She held her breath. Passed him. Shifted the key in her grip.

Blood thundered in her ears.

One more step.

The key lifted, her hand shaking like a leaf in a squall.

A shove from behind slammed her into the RAV4. A hard body pinned her against cold metal.

Stale breath bathed her cheek. Panic clamped down on her lungs. Pinpricks of light sparked in her vision.

"Señorita Winters."

The man with the mustache—the one who'd recognized her—appeared in her periphery. "You are far from home, no? I hear Señor Garcia has been looking for you."

Breathe.

Her life depended on it.

She flexed her fingers on the key. "My name isn't Winters." The lie slid out easily. "You've got the wrong person."

He laughed. Scrolled through his phone. Held it up. "This is you, no?"

The screen showed a woman in a red designer gown, her sleek hair straight, her makeup expertly done.

The night Vincente opened his Miami Beach nightclub.

"No. It's not," she said.

Not anymore.

If these men forced her to go with them, she'd never be free.

Her skin crawled under Pink Cap's touch. If he didn't release her soon, the screams crawling their way up her throat would break loose.

"I don't know anyone named Garcia. I'm just passing through Gallup. If it's money you want, I don't have much. You can take my wallet."

He had her photo, but Mustache Man had looked surprised to see her. Maybe they'd stumbled across her and didn't actually know where she lived. Or worked.

Her lids slammed shut. Why had she admitted to Caleb that she was a doctor at a clinic on the rez?

Stupid. Careless.

The only thing to do was continue to bluff.

"If I'm not back at the hotel in ten minutes, my coworkers will come looking."

Mustache Man grinned, showing nicotine-stained teeth. "You won't be here when they arrive."

"Let her go."

The voice was calm. Deadly.

Caleb.

Gia shivered. Her fingers clenched tighter on the key.

Inside the bar, he'd been friendly, disarming even. Now his voice carried a lethal promise.

Pink Cap spun her. Metal, razor sharp and warm from his body heat, pressed into her throat.

She froze. Her key slipped from nerveless fingers.

Only her eyes worked. She raised them to her would-be savior.

The light bathed Caleb in gold and shadow, an avenging angel. A scar she hadn't noticed earlier curved from behind his left ear down his neck. His t-shirt molded the toned chest and biceps she'd admired in the bar. Jeans hugged his hips and thighs like God meant them to. He seemed impervious to the winter chill.

Their gazes met. A hint of warmth lightened the gold flecks in eyes the color of melted chocolate under moonlight.

Then they flattened into the cold, emotionless stare of a killer.

Gia's heart plummeted. Not an angel.

But if this man could help her, she'd take her chances with the devil.

Mustache Man drew a wicked-looking knife from his boot. "Mind your own business, *pendejo*."

Caleb smiled—a slow, lethal smile that made her blink—and stepped closer.

Without warning, his palm struck out.

The knife flew.

He moved again, a blur of motion.

Mustache Man crumpled to the ground.

Pink Cap flinched. Gia hissed as the blade at her throat bit deeper.

"Back off or she dies." Fear leaked from his voice.

He was bluffing, like her. If Vincente's father had sent them, then yes. She'd believe it. But Mustache Man had said Garcia, not Lopez.

If Vincente planned to kill her, he'd make it personal, not farm it out to a low-level thug.

"He won't do it," she forced out, past the press of sharpened steel.

Pink Cap flung her aside. He charged Caleb, his knife slicing the air in fluid strokes.

A scream locked in Gia's throat.

Caleb side-stepped and parried the attack, sending Pink Cap's knife hilt-over-blade to ricochet off gravel.

The younger man didn't go down as easily as his older counterpart.

Time slowed.

Curses littered the air.

Flesh met flesh in a deadly dance of hand-to-hand combat.

Gia stood, feet rooted to the ground while her body jerked in sympathetic rhythm with every grunt. Caleb, a stranger, was risking his life for her. She should run inside, get Billy to call the police.

Except if Caleb lost, she couldn't risk the people inside the bar. And police meant an official report.

Attention she couldn't afford.

Leave. Now.

She'd have a head start. Back to the safety of the rez. Then she'd figure out what to do.

She dropped to her knees. Felt around for her key. Her fingers grazed metal.

Key in hand, she stood on shaky knees. Panic blurred her vision, along with an oppressive wave of guilt. Was she really going to abandon her Good Samaritan?

Metal scraped as she struggled to unlock her car door.

The key slipped into the lock.

A bloodied hand closed over hers.

She screeched, her heart nearly exploding.

Caleb raised his palms. Stepped back. Blood flecked his white shirt and swelled from his lower lip.

"I'm no threat to you." Despite the exertion, his voice was calm. Too calm.

"I have to go." Her voice shook along with the rest of her.

"You're in no condition to drive. I'll take you wherever you need to go."

She shook her head, unable to form words past the howling in her brain. *Go. Go. Go.*

"At least let me open the door for you."

Tremors racked her. Could she trust him? He *had* come to her defense.

Movement over Caleb's shoulder caught her eye.

Mustache Man got to his feet. Raised his gun.

Pointed it at Caleb.

Gia's eyes flew wide.

Caleb lunged, wrapping his arms around her.

The sky tilted as a shot rang out. Metal pinged.

Caleb grunted.

Gia hit the ground, pebbles digging into her back. Caleb's broad palm cushioned her head. His hard body covered her.

Gravel crunched beneath Mustache Man's boots.

She stared over Caleb's shoulder at the cold, black barrel of a gun, then tore her gaze from death to look into the eyes of her protector. This close, his breath, smelling of sweet whiskey and spicy chili, bathed her lips.

"I'm sorry," she whispered.

Her vision blurred. How damned unfair that a good man would die tonight because of her.

Another death on her conscience to mark her soul.

His thumb swiped her cheek. His lips grazed hers—soft as butterfly wings.

She waited for fear, revulsion. Instead, she felt the fleeting contact to her soul. A sense of comfort, of peace she hadn't felt for as long as she could remember.

Caleb's leg swept out.

Mustache Man sprawled backwards, the gun flying from his grip.

A chill blanketed Gia's body, bereft of Caleb's warmth as he vaulted to his feet, his boot connecting with Mustache Man's head.

Gia sucked in sorely needed air. Her lips tingled.

She licked them to find out if Caleb had left a taste of himself behind, then levered to a seated position, her thoughts scattering at the tableau of violence spread before her.

Blood.

Drops of it rimmed a neat round hole in her driver's door. More on the gray pebbles next to her hand. Another next to Caleb's boot.

He bent to pick up the gun. Crimson blossomed across the white fabric on his shoulder.

Her fear vanished. She scrambled to her feet.

"Come on." Grabbing his uninjured arm, she unlocked her passenger door with surprisingly steady hands. "Get in."

On the backseat, she spied the towel she'd thrown in the car with every intent of going to work out at the wellness center yesterday, but an emergency patient had kept her late.

Folding it into a neat square, she pressed it to his wound. "This might sting."

He didn't flinch. It was easy to believe he was no stranger to violence.

She wouldn't think too hard about that right now. *The enemy of my enemy is my friend.*

"Press your shoulder into the seat. The compression will slow the bleeding."

Pink Cap was stirring.

She jumped into the driver's seat. The RAV4's engine rumbled to life.

Gia thanked God, or whoever listened to her prayers, that the old clunker she'd purchased for cash seven and a half weeks ago hadn't chosen this moment to be temperamental.

She fishtailed out of the parking lot.

Her knight in shining armor reached for the seatbelt. "Try not to kill me after saving me."

"Ha ha." He wouldn't be in this situation if he hadn't played the hero. Of course, if he hadn't...Her grip on the wheel tightened.

Caleb.

A strong name. It suited him.

"Where are we going?" he asked.

Good question. Everything in her was screaming to get back to the rez, pack her bags, and flee.

But what did she do with him?

"Are you a tribal member?" He'd told her his mother was, so it stood to reason.

"No." Clipped. Flat.

Okaaay. Touchy subject.

She was a doctor. She couldn't drop him off on the nearest street corner and wish him luck. He wasn't safe now either, thanks to her. The main hospital in Gallup would notify the police. She couldn't take him to a tribal medical facility without there being questions she didn't want to answer.

"My place," she blurted.

What are you doing?

The steering wheel dampened beneath her palms. "I can treat your wound." She owed him. "You saved my life back there—thank you."

It would give her time to calm down. Think about what to do next. Make a plan.

Caleb's gaze met hers. "You're welcome, Doc. Now tell me who those men were."

CHAPTER THREE

"I DON'T KNOW. THEY were looking for someone else. Mistook me for her." Doc shot Caleb a nervous glance. "Crazy, huh?"

Her hands trembled on the wheel. Oncoming headlights lit the interior enough to catch the tension etched on her face.

A lie.

Maybe she wasn't as innocent as he'd assumed.

He'd expected her to live in Gallup. Instead, she sped north along the four-lane highway into Navajo Nation territory.

"Then why not call the police?"

"I just wanted to get away, okay?" Her voice climbed. "You got shot."

She bit her lip. "I told them I was just passing through Gallup on business, so it's not like they're going to come looking for me. They're probably long gone."

"Hmmm. Probably."

But that didn't mean they wouldn't come back. He recognized their type—low-level enforcers for a criminal organization. His father had been a *Halcón*—a Falcon—the eyes and ears of the Espina Negra drug cartel in Gallup and later Phoenix.

Maybe that's why the older guy looked familiar. Caleb had been too young to remember most of his father's associates, but that distinctive mustache sparked a memory.

Whoever they were, they hadn't tried to kill her. They'd tried to take her. Deliver her to someone.

And she knew it. With a knife at her throat, she'd given him permission to act, knowing the man holding her wouldn't actually cut her.

Caleb let it go. For now. But he wasn't leaving without answers.

If she was in trouble, he'd encourage her to seek help.

If his mother's family had helped her escape his father, maybe her life would've been different.

The SUV hit a pothole.

Pain jolted through Caleb's shoulder. He grimaced.

Doc threw him an apologetic glance. "Sorry."

"I've had worse." He needed a few stitches, maybe, and a bandage.

He repositioned the towel against his shoulder. This was a scratch compared to some of the wounds he'd dealt with as a combat medic, but if he was going to get shot playing the hero, at least he had a pretty doctor to patch him up.

The ribbing he'd take from his Dìleas teammates if they found out—the former Green Beret got winged rescuing a woman in peril. They'd joke he just met his future wife or some crazy shit.

His gaze slanted to the pretty doctor. *Classy. Caring. Brave.*

She'd fit in with the women at Dìleas: Lachlan's wife, Sophia; Nathan's fiancée, Emily; Nathalie, Ryder's fiancée. Even Penny—Dìleas's office manager and unofficial company mom.

Which was reason enough to keep his mouth shut.

They crossed into Arizona and drove through Window Rock. Some of the fear surrounding Doc like a shroud receded. Still, her knuckles stayed white on the steering wheel as she pulled into a neighborhood of mostly white and beige single-wides planted in rows of hard-packed red dirt and stone. Satellite dishes perched on the roofs.

Wooden electric poles lined the dirt road. The only actual color to be found was in the anemic green of the mesquite trees that dotted the neighborhood and the Russian thistle and kochia that grew as weeds in barren spaces.

Doc parked beside one of the trailers and offered a sheepish smile. "It's not much, but it's home."

His brows lifted. By rez standards, it was solidly middle class.

"You're not a tribal member, yet you have housing here? That's a privilege, even if you don't realize it." Many Navajo still lived in homes that lacked electricity and running water.

Hell, he hadn't even been inside yet and he could tell this place was a palace compared to the tiny shit-hole trailer he and his parents had lived in before they left Gallup. And the run-down apartment on the South Side of Phoenix after that hadn't been much better.

Doc opened her door, triggering the interior light. Pink bloomed on her cheeks. "I didn't mean it that way. I am grateful. And I know what people here live with. I see it every day."

She stepped out of the vehicle. "Wait there. I'll help you."

"I don't need help." He beat her around the front of the hood.

A huff of breath escaped her. "Another stubborn patient who won't listen to the doctor."

"It's in our DNA." He handed over the bloody towel.

"So I've noticed."

Inside, the trailer smelled like tomato sauce and melted cheese—out of place in his Southwest memories but oddly homey. A worn brown sofa and battered coffee table faced a double window with white metal blinds. Brightly colored Navajo patterned rugs in shades of red, blue, and gray softened the vinyl plank floor, and a flowering cactus added a feminine touch to the small space.

Basic, but neat and cozy.

A far cry from the beige walls and brown furniture in his apartment in Northern Virginia. He'd purchased some landscape paintings that caught his eye on his travels for work, but he wasn't around much to enjoy them.

Doc shrugged out of her coat and gestured to the dark wood table and mismatched chairs that separated the main room from the kitchen.

"Have a seat. I'll be right back." She disappeared through an open door to the left of the kitchen.

Caleb straddled one of the chairs, angling his body to give her better access to the wound. This wasn't his first rodeo.

Or his first bullet wound.

Moments later, she returned with a black medical bag. At the kitchen sink, she washed and dried her hands, then snapped on a pair of blue nitrile gloves and pulled scissors from the kit. "Some of the blood has caked. I need to cut the fabric away."

He gave a small shrug. "Do what you gotta do."

It was just a shirt. He had another one in his duffel in the Jeep.

Well, hell. He was going to need a ride back to the bar. The adrenaline rush fueling him subsided. Fatigue rolled in.

It had been a long day and tomorrow promised to be even longer.

Doc grabbed an unopened bottle of water from her cabinet. "I'm going to wet the fabric before I try to cut it off."

Room temperature liquid soaked his shoulder and trickled down his back. "Before you operate, don't you think you should tell me your name?"

When she didn't answer, he looked over his shoulder, holding her stare.

A flush stained her cheeks. "It's Gianna." She glanced away, then back again. "My friends call me Gia."

Gia.

Pretty name. No last name, but it was a start.

"Please to meet you, Gia."

Her snort was soft. "I doubt it. You almost got killed because of me."

"It's just a flesh wound." He wasn't a funny guy, but he did his best to sound like the Black Knight from Monty Python.

She wrinkled her nose. "Is that a reference to something?"

Damn. She looked cute when she did that.

"Monty Python?" At her blank look, he said, "I guess you're not a fan of classic British comedy."

A wry smile. "I was more of a *Gossip Girl* fan."

Gloved fingers slid beneath his collar. Even through rubber, her touch sent a current of awareness through him.

He shifted his gaze forward, focused on the tabletop, and willed his body to relax. The last couple of days had been a blur of travel and self-recrimination. And yet, being here with Gia—getting the bullet crease in his back tended to—was the first time since the phone call about his mother that he'd felt...content.

"Don't move." With careful hands, Gia worked the scissors beneath the fabric and slowly peeled it from his skin.

He tugged the rest of the shirt over his head and dropped it on the floor.

"So, Caleb...?"

"Varella. Caleb Varella," he supplied helpfully.

"So, Caleb Varella, what do you do when you aren't saving damsels in distress?"

She leaned in to inspect the wound. Her breath ghosted across his skin like a physical caress. Her floral scent teased his nose.

He smiled at the irony of her question. "Executive Protection."

At her confused expression, he clarified, "A bodyguard. I save damsels in distress."

She gave him the laugh he'd been looking for earlier. Humor and no small amount of relief lit her eyes and transformed her face. "Lucky for me."

Desire pooled low in Caleb's belly. He'd thought she was beautiful before, but when she laughed and the shadows disappeared?

Stunning.

Prickly pear.

That's what she'd taste like. It matched her scent.

Color crept into her cheeks. She looked away.

Caleb tore his gaze away and scrubbed a hand over his face.

His brain was zinging in all sorts of crazy directions. He'd barely touched his whiskey. It had to be leftover adrenaline.

Cool liquid stung his skin as Gia swabbed his shoulder with antiseptic.

"No bullet fragments and the wound is shallow enough to use glue instead of stitches." She applied Dermabond in smooth, even strokes. "You were very lucky."

"We both were." The pain he could handle, but when she leaned closer and blew on the glue to help it dry faster, his dick went half-mast.

He shifted in the chair.

"Sorry," she said. "I know it stings."

Not the problem.

"I'm fine." He grimaced at the rasp in his voice.

She taped a gauze pad over the wound. "Try to keep it dry tonight. You can take the bandage off when you shower tomorrow."

"Thanks." Caleb rose. "Mind if I use your bathroom?"

"Down the hall, first door on the right."

The bathroom was barely large enough to accommodate the white sink, toilet, and tub-shower combo. Caleb examined his reflection in the mirror. Lines on his face. Bloodshot eyes. Dark circles.

In short, he looked like hell.

When he returned, Gia sat curled on the couch in the main room. She raised her head at his approach.

The haunted look from earlier had returned.

Anger curled low in Caleb's gut.

Not haunted.

Hunted.

"Who's after you?"

Her gaze shuttered. "I don't know."

Another lie.

He crouched in front of her. "You may not have known those men, but you know who sent them. I'm trying to help—but I need the truth. I protect people for a living. That means I know how to identify threats and eliminate them before they become a problem. I'm leaving town tomorrow after my mother's funeral, but I can still make some calls. Find you some help."

He gave her what he hoped was a reassuring grin. "Consider it payment for patching me up."

She shook her head, not meeting his eyes.

He lifted her chin, and she flinched away from his touch.

Shit.

He snatched his hand back. Someone had laid hands on her.

The anger in his gut caught fire, spread. He buried it so it wouldn't show.

The last thing Gia needed was more violence.

"You knew they wouldn't kill you." He kept his voice soft. Measured. "If they'd mistaken you for someone else, how would you know that?"

Gia's eyes widened. "I didn't."

"You did," he reminded her gently. "You told me."

Fingers twisted together in a white-knuckled grip. Whatever fragile denial she'd been clinging to crumbled, her eyes going dull. "My ex sent them."

Ex.

"Husband?"

"No, thank God. Ex-fiancé." A bitter laugh slipped out. "I dodged that bullet."

She winced. "Sorry. Bad choice of words."

She was wound so tightly, he had the feeling that if he touched her again, she'd shatter.

Fiancé.

One who sent thugs to retrieve his prize.

How had a classy, educated woman like her ended up with a guy like that?

Probably the same way his mother had. A handsome, slick-talking liar suckered her into falling in love. Then used gaslighting and threats to keep her in line.

Unlike his mother, Gia had found the strength to leave.

Caleb suppressed a sigh. A restraining order wouldn't do much. *Hell*, she might already have one.

She needed to file a police report. Document the threat.

And she needed protection.

He'd make some inquiries before he left tomorrow. See if the Navajo police would help. If not, there might be a local agency in Gallup or out of Flagstaff or Albuquerque that she could employ for a reasonable fee.

But he couldn't stay.

Outside, headlights swept the front window.

A minute later, Gia's door rattled beneath an impatient fist.

CHAPTER FOUR

CALEB VAULTED ACROSS THE room in an instant, positioning himself beside the door. For the second time that night, instinct drove his hand to the shoulder holster beneath his arm.

Bare skin met his fingers.

His Glock was still in the Jeep. At the bar.

"Gia. It's Zach." A deep, urgent voice came from the other side.

"It's okay." Gia scrambled off the couch. "He's a friend. Navajo Police."

Friend or boyfriend?

Caleb's fingers curled. Not his business.

Still, he stepped aside as she opened the door. If the guy was a police officer, he'd keep her safe. Handle the two goons from the bar if they came back. Maybe he'd know some local agency that could help Gia.

The tall man who flowed into the room in a brown Navajo Nation Police uniform looked to be Caleb's age, and young for the lieutenant's rank pinned on his collar. An elastic tie tethered shoulder-length, straight black hair behind his neck.

"Billy called, said there was trouble—" The man halted when he spotted Caleb. Dark brown eyes swept over the room and narrowed. "Who the hell are you?"

His gaze dropped to Caleb's bare chest. "And where's your shirt?"

A jolt of familiarity zapped Caleb. Second time that day. First the mustached thug. Now this guy. He held the newcomer's stare, trying to gauge if the officer didn't like strangers in his territory or if he didn't like strangers with Gia.

Definitely personal. The guy puffed up like a jealous boyfriend.

For some reason, that made Caleb want to mess with him.

He cocked his lips in a taunting grin. "Shirt's in the kitchen where she took it off me."

A tick jumped in the officer's jaw.

Gia stepped in with a calming hand. "Zach, this is Caleb Varella. He helped me out of a bad situation—and got hurt. Caleb, this is Zach Blackwater. A friend."

Blackwater.

Recognition landed like a punch to the ribs.

Zach's eyes flared with the same realization.

His mouth twisted. "Varella." He extended a hand, the turquoise and silver bracelet on his wrist catching the light. "Welcome back. Cousin."

Caleb accepted the handshake. Brief. Tight. "Been a while."

They'd once been inseparable—chasing each other through sagebrush, hiding in arroyos until their grandfather threatened to tan their hides.

Caleb's throat tightened. After the move to Phoenix when he was twelve, he'd begged his parents to let him come back in the summers. To breathe air untainted by cigarettes, alcohol, and drugs. To escape a home trapped in the vicious cycle of toxic codependency.

The answer had always been no.

He hadn't seen Zach since.

The memory left a bitter trace. He kept it off his face.

Zach's posture remained stiff. "Twenty-two years. Since grand-mother's funeral."

"Cousin?" Gia's brows knit. "Like actual cousin? Not clan?" She glanced from one man to the other. "Got it. Now I see the resem-blance."

Zach turned to her. "What happened?"

When she hesitated, Caleb answered instead. "Two men tried to abduct her outside Lucero's Lounge. Cartel enforcers or gangbangers, most likely. No obvious colors or ink."

"You'd know, wouldn't you?" Zach muttered.

The words sliced through Caleb. His cousin didn't know the man he'd become. He'd spent his childhood judged by others because of his parents. But he wasn't a kid anymore.

And he had nothing to prove to Zach Blackwater.

Gia shifted on her feet, her gaze darting between them, clearly picking up on the tension.

Zach pressed the mic on his shoulder. "Lieutenant Blackwater. Contact Gallup PD—"

She touched his arm, her gaze pleading. "Is that really necessary?"

Zach's expression gentled. "Yes. I'm sorry."

He resumed speaking into the mic. "Request a patrol unit to Lucero's. Send out a BOLO for two individuals—" He cut his eyes to Caleb.

Caleb rattled off the men's physical descriptions, the vehicle make and model, and the Arizona plates he'd caught before getting into Gia's SUV.

"You in law enforcement?" Zach asked, his eyes narrowing. "That was a pretty detailed description."

"Executive protection. Before that, ten years in the Army. I'm trained to notice the little things."

Some of the tension eased from Zach's shoulders. He relayed the information to the dispatcher.

When he finished, he turned his focus back to Caleb. "I served, too. Marine Corps. Nine years. What unit were you in?"

"Third Special Forces Group out of Bragg." Satisfaction hummed as Zach's brows shot skyward. "You?"

"Third Battalion, Seventh Marines. Scout Sniper."

Now it was Caleb's turn to be impressed. His cousin would keep Gia safe.

Although, if her ex felt motivated enough to track her down when she'd clearly made an effort to stay hidden, Zach might need help.

I could help. The thought rose uninvited.

No. His part in this ended tonight.

Tomorrow, he'd bury his mother. Then visit the detective in Phoenix handling her case. After that, he'd pack up what few possessions of hers remained and head east. Maybe to his cabin in North Carolina for a few days to give his shoulder time to heal, then take the New York job for Ryder.

Right now, however, his concern was Gia.

Caleb ignored his cousin's aggressive posture and stepped closer. "You've had a rough night. Will you be safe here?"

She nodded, but her body said otherwise—arms curled protectively around her stomach, spine stiff.

"Of course she's safe here!" Zach snapped. "I won't let anything happen to her."

Protective and prickly. Caleb got it.

Gia was beautiful, intelligent, with a fragility that called out to his protective instincts. If he lived here, he might have competed with Zach for her attention.

But he didn't live here. Wasn't staying.

And Gia didn't need more men chasing after her.

The cell on Zach's hip rang.

"Blackwater," he barked, then listened. His features hardened. "Thanks. Let me know if they turn up. I'll get victim statements over to GPD."

He hung up and turned back to Gia. "Gallup police are at the bar. The guys who attacked you were gone by the time they got there."

"Cameras?" Caleb hadn't noticed any, but surely there had to have been one hidden somewhere.

"At Lucero's?" Zach shook his head. "The owner's never had a reason. It's full of old-timers who've been frequenting the place for years."

"What about the bartender and the two guys at the bar?"

"They saw the man come in. Gave the same description as you. When the gunshot rang out, Billy went for his rifle. By the time he got outside, Gia's car was gone, and a black Ford Explorer was leaving."

"Then the threat to Gia isn't over." Caleb instantly regretted his words when Gia flinched.

If looks could kill, Zach's glare would have been a shot to the head. "Law enforcement in New Mexico and Arizona are looking for the SUV. Gia's safe here, on the rez."

Zach shifted his attention to Gia. "I'll ask Naveah to stay with you after her shift."

"That's not necessary." Gia gave a stilted smile. "I'll be fine."

Caleb didn't buy it. He was close enough to see the tension in her muscles, the faint tremble in her body.

Fight or flight.

He had a feeling he knew which one she would choose.

He started to reach for her chin, then remembered her earlier reaction and dropped it. "Get some rest. Decide what to do in the morning."

Don't run.

"In the morning," he stressed.

She said nothing, just stared at him with wide, turbulent eyes that made him want to stay.

To watch over her.

To hold her until she felt safe again.

When he'd brushed his lips across hers on the ground outside the bar, it had been to distract her. Keep her calm while he planned his move against the asshole about to plug him with a round.

And because he'd wanted to.

She'd tasted as good as she smelled.

Prickly pear.

The hand he'd almost touched her with curled into a fist.

He'd had beautiful women as clients before and never once had his thoughts veered to unprofessional places. What was it about this woman that had him so off-kilter?

Maybe he should take a vacation instead of the New York job. He had plenty of time accrued. Make himself do something that wasn't work-related.

Get a life.

"Your car's still at the bar." The huskiness in her voice was as potent as if she'd stroked her palm over the front of his jeans.

His body tightened.

"I'll drive him back," Zach offered, his tone laced with irritation.

Caleb snapped back into himself and checked his watch. *Nine pm.*

His mother's funeral was in the morning.

"Thank you," Gia whispered. A butterfly touch to his arm that he felt all over. "For being my knight in shining armor."

He nodded, unsettled by the thought he might not see her again. "Take care."

The deadbolt clicked behind him and Zach.

Only then did he release the breath he'd been holding.

She was safe.

But for how long?

The chill night air cut through his bare chest. Still, he lingered.

He could stay. One more night. Just long enough to be sure.

But the thought was dangerous—his training, his instincts on overdrive from the events of the night.

He shoved it down hard and forced his feet toward Zach's white Tahoe, marked with the yellow and green emblem of the Navajo Nation Police.

Khaki colored cotton hit him in the face.

"Put that on," Zach muttered as he slid behind the wheel.

Caleb sniffed. "Is it clean?"

"Beggars can't be choosers," Zach growled. "Yes, it's clean."

Caleb pulled the shirt over his head, wincing at the snap of pain in his shoulder. "Thanks."

Silence stretched until Zach turned onto the highway.

"Lucky you were in the right place at the right time." Accusation clung to Zach's words.

Caleb bristled, then let it go. "What do you know about Gia?"

"She doesn't talk about herself."

"What about her ex?"

"Nothing." Zach cut his eyes in Caleb's direction. "She's been here six weeks. Grandfather met with her. Whatever she said satisfied him, so I didn't probe further. He helped her get a twelve-week contract job at a clinic that's short-staffed. Found her housing. She rarely leaves the rez."

"Whoever this asshole is, he found her anyway. His errand boys drove an SUV with Arizona plates. Think he's local?"

Zach shook his head. "Her car had a temporary Arizona plate when she arrived. All she'll say is she's from the East Coast."

"We need his name. My colleague can run a background check."

"I'll ask her. Maybe with what happened tonight, she'll be more forthcoming." Zach pointed to his badge. "And I can run a check."

He pulled into Lucero's. The neon open sign was no longer lit, the building dark. Only Caleb's rental remained in the lot.

Caleb climbed out of the Tahoe. Something else occurred to him. "What's Gia's last name?" She hadn't offered it up when he asked.

Zach's eyes narrowed. "If she didn't tell you, why is it your concern?"

"She's not safe here anymore."

"She's also not your problem. I'll take care of her. See you at your *amá*'s ceremony tomorrow."

Caleb blinked. "You're coming?"

A shrug. "*Shinálí* expects it."

When your grandfather was president, his word was law, apparently

The Tahoe's tires spit gravel as Zach sped off.

The temperature had dropped some more. Caleb's breath billowed out white as he made his way to the Jeep. He shrugged into his black leather jacket, then removed his Glock 19 from its case and set it on the passenger seat. His shoulder burned and his body ached from the blows the younger thug had landed.

He'd been planning to spend the night at a hotel in Gallup. Instead, he retraced the route back to Window Rock. The funeral and burial would be held on the rez, so he might as well spend the night there.

It had nothing to do with the fact it was closer to Gia.

The lone hotel in the town center was basic, but clean. The off-white walls, framed photos of local landscapes, and brown patterned carpet were typical of a two-star chain anywhere in America. Beneath the window, the A/C unit hummed noisily, belching out warm, stale air.

Caleb closed the drapes and stripped down to his briefs.

Forcing himself to scroll through the messages on his phone, he read each one from his Dìleas colleagues—personal notes asking how he was holding up, condolences about his mother, a virtual hug from Nathalie accompanied by a photo of a watercolor lily she'd painted for him.

He considered texting Ryder about the night's events, but decided against it.

For now.

No sense alarming his boss over something that wasn't job-related—especially since, as Zach had pointed out, Gia wasn't his problem to deal with. He'd take a few extra days off when he got back and recover.

Instead, he tapped out a brief reply to everyone: he was fine, the funeral was tomorrow. Then he settled cross-legged on the bed.

Inhale. Hold. Exhale.

Despite his attempt to clear his mind, Gia lingered. Her eyes held a wealth of secrets. Where had she come from? Why hide here, on the largest Indian reservation in the US?

The need to protect her called to something deep inside him. His cousin felt it, too.

He'd seek her out tomorrow, before he left town. Give her his business card. Just to make sure she understood how to stay safe.

But he couldn't stay.

CHAPTER FIVE

Run.

The word pounded through Gia's head like a war drum, driving out logic, drowning reason in a flood of panic.

She waited until Zach and Caleb disappeared down the road, then bolted for the bedroom, throat closing as adrenaline surged.

How had Vincente found her?

She was an East Coast girl who liked the finer things a city could offer. How naïve to think changing her name and hiding across the country on the Navajo Nation would be enough.

His family had eyes everywhere.

Gia yanked the brown Louis Vuitton suitcase Vincente had insisted on buying her from the closet and hoisted it onto the bed, careful not to catch a wheel on the indigo, black, and red Navajo pattern bedcover.

The luxury brand, with its garish monogram and bloated price tag, looked absurd in her modest home. Once, the designer bag announced her status. Now, like the jewelry she'd brought with her, its only worth lay in what it could fetch at a pawnshop for cash if the need arose.

The one piece of jewelry she'd left behind was the five-carat princess-cut diamond engagement ring Vincente had slipped onto her finger. Taking it off had felt like removing handcuffs. Ones she intended never to be shackled by again.

Where could she go? The RAV4, paid for in cash when she arrived in Arizona, was too distinctive—metallic green, hard to miss. If Vincente's men had noticed her plate and traced it, they'd know her real name.

Gianna Lucia Barone. Born in Brooklyn. Daughter of a man serving life for at least three murders.

Vincente would savor the irony. He'd known her as Abigail Winters—Upper East Side heiress, orphaned at eighteen.

A true story, mostly.

Just not hers.

The real Abigail Winters would have been Gia's age if she hadn't died as an infant.

So she'd borrowed the identity, and Abigail Winters had been born. Again. This time as a fully formed adult with a backstory. College. Med school. A residency at a top hospital followed by a career catering to Miami's rich and powerful.

Then she'd fallen for a man who'd turned out to be as devious and dangerous as the world she'd fled.

Maybe the old saying *blood will tell* was true.

From the chest of drawers, Gia scooped up panties, bras, and socks, and tossed them into her suitcase. Then she stopped.

A copy of her twelve-week contract with the medical clinic lay on top of the chest. She unfolded the paper. Six more weeks to go, with a bonus at the end—a bonus she desperately needed in order to disappear again.

Farther this time.

Her patients needed her. The overworked nursing staff needed her. She and Jennie were organizing a wellness fair at the clinic in three weeks.

Jennie.

A nurse at the clinic, Jennie Tsosie was fast becoming a close friend. She didn't know what had brought Gia to the Navajo Nation—or why Gia always found a reason not to join her and the others for a night out beyond its borders.

If Gia left now, Jennie would be stuck organizing the fair on her own, on top of everything else already on her shoulders. Gia needed to find a way to say goodbye. To explain.

But if she told Zach she was leaving, he'd try to talk her out of it. Tell her she was safer on the rez.

President Blackwater had gone out on a limb for her. He'd intervened so she could live and work here. He'd trusted her when no one else in their right mind would have. Walking away now—leaving the clinic short-staffed with no notice—would betray that trust.

She set down the contract and glanced at her open suitcase.

Vincente's men had come across Abigail. A name she'd told them was passing through. Not staying. They didn't know about Gianna Barone.

If she stayed put until her contract ended, they wouldn't know where to find her.

Still, she frowned. If they started asking around, it wouldn't take much to discover an Anglo doctor matching Abigail Winters's description working on the rez.

With a rough exhale, she lifted a single pair of panties from the jumbled pile, folded it neatly, then placed it back in the suitcase.

For all her efforts to carve out a life of privilege, she'd never felt as at home as she did here. The Navajo had accepted her—not because of who she pretended to be, but who she was. They needed her.

She could see herself building a life here.

That is, if she was ever free of her old one.

"And that's exactly why you can't stay." Her eyes watered. She gave them an irritated swipe and turned to the closet.

Screw destiny.

She'd remade herself before. Would do it again.

Shirts and pants hung in order, next to her white doctor's coat. Her hand hesitated over the sleeveless black dress she'd packed when she fled Miami.

Elegant. Timeless.

Fit for a funeral.

"Caleb Varella."

She whispered the name aloud, the consonants flowing over her tongue like a lover's caress. It had weight. Strength. Protection.

And that terrified her.

Not because she feared him. Because for the first time, she wanted someone and felt safe wanting him.

A shrill ring shattered her thoughts. The sound came from her living room.

She hurried down the hall and found her phone in her jacket pocket. If it was the clinic, it might be an emergency. With Doctor Chee out on maternity leave and Doctor Lewis at a conference, there were no nights off anymore.

Another reason to stay.

Her patients and the staff were beginning to trust her, to believe she had their best interests at heart. If she up and disappeared on them now, what would they think?

What would that say about her?

An unfamiliar number lit the screen. It wasn't local.

Her finger hovered over the green button.

"It's not Miami." She'd recognize that area code.

Her hand shook. "He doesn't know this number—he can't."

She'd left the old phone behind. Bought this prepaid one after she arrived in Arizona. Paid for the phone and the minutes in cash. No trace.

But those men had found her at Lucero's.

Coincidence?

Or had they known where to look?

The phone went quiet.

Her stomach flip-flopped like a fish out of water.

A blinking message icon. Voicemail.

Her hand trembled as it hovered over the notification.

She pressed play.

If you owe back taxes, the government is offering—

A spam call. Her head swam. Never thought she'd see the day she'd be grateful for one.

She deleted the message with a jab of her thumb. "You're being paranoid."

Only tell that to her racing heart.

She made a quick call to the clinic's nurse on call—just in case. "Hey, Wanda. Everything quiet? Great. Let's hope it stays that way. I'm here if anyone needs me."

At least for tonight.

Guilt bored a hole in her stomach.

"Have a good night."

On her way back to the bedroom, her gaze snagged on Caleb's bloodied t-shirt lying on the floor.

She kneeled to pick it up. Held it to her nose.

Blood—copper and iron. But beneath that, sandalwood and spice.

Warmth unfurled in her belly. Just touching the shirt sent awareness brushing over her skin—the way his sculpted muscles flexed beneath her hands. The calm in his voice. The heat in his eyes.

He was dangerous—he'd proven that by the way he handled those men.

Yet she'd felt safe in his presence.

He'd looked at her with male appreciation.

And she hadn't been afraid.

His job was to protect people. What if she asked him to protect her? Then she could stay here. Make a real difference in people's lives.

Gia gave an unladylike snort. "Who are you kidding?"

Vincente was too powerful. Too many connections. Anyone who tried to help her would probably end up dead, just like...

Her brain shied from the memory.

If she wanted Caleb's help, it should be to drive her to the airport and drop her off without looking back. She'd throw an imaginary dart at the outgoing flights board and hop a plane to a random destination.

Her hasty idea died a quick death. Now that he knew where she was, Vincente would have eyes at every airport in the Southwest.

Flying was out.

Back to her original plan. Drive north. Stick to back roads. Trade the RAV4 for another vehicle at a used car lot across the state line. Then keep going. Utah. Wyoming. Montana. Maybe Canada. Then Alaska. Start over again. New name. A new life.

Again.

She dropped Caleb's shirt in the trash.

Back at the closet, her fingers brushed the black dress. Instead of packing it, she left it on the hanger.

As tempting as it would be to rely on Caleb Varella, she couldn't involve him.

Still, he'd saved her life tonight.

She owed him more than the weak thank you she'd offered up before he left.

The least she could do was attend his mother's funeral.

Although, given the trouble she'd brought him, he might be thankful never to see her again.

Her heart gave a strange twist. In a different life, she would have liked to have gotten to know Caleb better.

A yawn cracked her jaw. The adrenaline spike from the evening's events had burned out. Gravity pulled her exhausted limbs closer to the floor. All she wanted was sleep—deep, dreamless, and long enough so when she woke up, Vincente would have forgotten about her.

She could live in peace.

But real life didn't work that way.

Her gaze returned to the black dress.

Caleb planned to leave after his mother's funeral.

So would she.

CHAPTER SIX

VINCENTE LOPEZ GARCIA TOSSED his wallet on the foyer table of his Miami Beach penthouse, where it landed with a muted thud. His salmon-colored silk shirt reeked of cigarette smoke and perfume. He unbuttoned it and tossed it over his white leather sofa.

Pouring a glass of mezcal, he went to stand in front of the floor-to-ceiling windows overlooking the Atlantic. Moonlight, dimmed by clouds, barely touched the sea. Pinpricks from distant vessels dotted the water—the only sign of humanity in the vast gulf of watery obsidian. Though the thick glass muted the surf, his imagination filled in the rhythmic lull of the waves. Palm fronds rustled below, caught in the glow of the pool deck lights.

Abigail had loved this view.

And he loved watching her, ass bare beneath one of the neon thong bikinis he'd insisted she wear, her silken brown tresses brushing her mid-back. His hand tightened around the crystal tumbler, wishing it gripped a fistful of her hair instead, her bare breasts flattened against the glass, palms splayed in surrender while he took what was his.

The rooftop lounge had good memories, too. He loved fucking her there, ignoring her protests about privacy. His men could watch, but never touch, from a discrete corner out of Abigail's sight.

Maybe that would change.

His cousin Juan had proven his loyalty as they expanded their reach in the US through networks in Arizona and New Mexico. He did the dirty work, ensuring the gangs and dealers moved only Espina Negra product, while Vincente focused on the business side.

Still, Vincente hadn't missed the way Juan looked at Abigail. With his sun-kissed brown hair and hazel eyes, Juan had lighter coloring and stood taller than him—a fact that irritated more than it should. But they were as close as brothers.

Perhaps close enough that he would gift his trusted second a night with his woman. As a reward.

His cock hardened.

With him watching, of course.

A long pull of mezcal cooled the lust heating his body. Smoke, earth, and spices singed his throat. The burn softened his erection but did little to tamp the fury building in his chest.

What had Abigail thought—this life, these luxuries, came from nightclub and restaurant profits alone? Did she not understand who he was? His father, Diego Lopez Becerra—*"El Víbora"*—controlled one of the biggest cartels in Mexico. Publicly, Vincente distanced himself and used only his mother's name, Garcia, so he could operate with discretion.

He'd tried to keep Abigail separate from that world, but it couldn't be helped, and she'd needed to see the burden of leadership. The cost of betrayal. If she was to be his wife, the mother of his children, she had to accept that sacrifices were required.

In return, he would have given her everything—designer clothes, expensive jewelry, a beautiful home where staff waited on her, and most importantly, status.

As his wife. His queen.

Instead, she ran.

Vincente downed the last of his drink and set the tumbler beside the decanter for the maid.

Tío Ramón's voice echoed in his head.

Abigail is a liability. Make her disappear.

Always buzzing like a mosquito in *El Víbora*'s ear, trying to paint Vincente as reckless, driven by his temper and cock rather than business.

The reason Abigail had run was because he'd done what was necessary for the business. The man he'd eliminated had been a spy. And worse, had accused Juan of plotting betrayal, something his cousin would never do. This, he knew for certain, because he knew why Juan stood at his side instead of Ramón's.

Juan, he trusted. Juan's father? Never. If anything happened to *El Víbora*, Tío Ramón wouldn't hesitate to eliminate Vincente to become head of the Espina Negra Cartel.

Crossing into his bedroom, he stripped off his slacks and draped them over the nearest chair, then set his phone on the nightstand. The white silk sheets on the California king gleamed in the low light, hiding the restraints stashed under the mattress.

His hand dipped for a quick stroke as he pictured Abigail spread out for his pleasure, submissive to his needs. Unable to find her own release unless he permitted it.

If she didn't return soon, another woman would take her place.

He'd already forgotten the face of the brunette he fucked in the back room of his nightclub. It was Abigail's face he'd seen as he pounded into the woman. Her tits were larger, and the perfume was wrong, but she'd served her purpose and took the edge off so he could rest tonight.

It had been too long. Two months. The detective Juan hired still hadn't delivered results. Time to replace him with a more competent one.

Despite everything, Vincente still wanted his beautiful doctor. But when he got her back, he'd bring her to his father's compound in Mexico. There, he'd break her resistance. Once she carried his child in her womb, her loyalty to him would be absolute.

As he headed to the bathroom, his cell buzzed with Juan's ringtone. Irritation dissipated the pleasant buzz of the mezcal. Late night calls rarely brought good news.

"What is it?"

"Abigail has been located," Juan said.

His breath stalled. "Where?"

"Gallup, New Mexico. Two of my men were meeting our new distributer when they saw her."

"Tell me the nearest airport." Vincente was already moving. "I'll have the pilot ready the plane."

Silence.

The pause grated on his nerves. "What is it?"

"A man interfered—former military, my men think. Skilled. He and Abigail escaped before they could follow."

Vincente's temper soared, seeking release. "Your men?" Venom slipped into his voice. "The last time I checked, they worked for me."

"*Sí, primo. Perdóname.* I meant no disrespect."

A breath hissed between Vincente's teeth. He was tired. Too tired to fight with family tonight. "Find out who this soldier is. Reach out to our new business partners. See what help they can offer. And make that fucking detective you hired earn his pay."

If Abigail ran again, he wanted her alone and undefended. He was running out of time to bring her back under his protection before his father or Tío Ramón took matters into their own hands.

"No mistakes," he warned Juan. "If this soldier—this *cabrón*—surfaces again, handle it."

CHAPTER SEVEN

MORNING SUNLIGHT SWEPT AWAY the night's gloom, painting the Navajo Nation in bright yellow and azure blue. Caleb pulled into the Episcopal mission lot a half hour ahead of schedule. Stepping out of the Jeep, he shrugged into his black suit coat, the ache in the back of his shoulder a reminder of the previous night's events.

Crisp, clean air frosted his lungs.

The church was a study of right angles—flat-roofed, squared off, clad in red sandstone. An ornate white cross topped its bell tower. A white van from the funeral home sat near the end of the gravel strip. Two black Tahoes with official Navajo Nation plates took up the front spaces closer to the blue entrance doors.

His shoulders locked, muscles strung tight.

He hadn't arrived early enough—his grandfather was here.

Gravel crunched underfoot as he approached the covered entrance and pushed into the vestibule. The furnace belched out warm air, smelling of aged wood, worn stone, and old leather. The sanctuary beyond was bright and airy, white stucco walls lined with Navajo art, the ceiling high and crossed with weathered wooden beams.

He strolled down the aisle between white pine pews, his gaze drawn to the large silver and turquoise cross. White roses and Asiatic lilies spilled from pedestal stands on either side of the sandstone altar. Their cloying scent dragged him back to a different funeral. A teammate. Killed in combat. He understood that kind of death.

This? This was different.

Breathing through his mouth, he shoved the memory away.

Two men stood deep in conversation at the pulpit.

One of them, Floyd Parker, he recognized from the funeral home. Thick around the middle, thinning gray hair and a red flush to his pasty white complexion, he fit the stereotype in Caleb's head of a funeral director. He noticed Caleb's approach and hurried over, speaking in a hushed tone that was as much a part of his work ensemble as his black suit and tie.

"Mister Varella. Everything is arranged. Once again, I'm sorry for your loss."

The hollow ache in Caleb's chest tightened. "Thank you. I'd like to see my mother."

"Of course. If you'll follow me." Parker led him through a side corridor. "Your grandfather is with her now."

Caleb swallowed the curse forming. He'd hoped for a few precious moments alone with his *amá*.

No such luck.

Two Diné men in dark suits flanked a closed door—a security detail. Their alert posture, watchful gazes, and suit coats sized to accommodate vests and concealed weapons all added up to executive protection, like him.

Only it wasn't his mother they were guarding.

Opening his suit coat, he waited for the pat down. "I'm not carrying."

The older of the two gave him a full visual sweep, then stepped aside. "You can go in."

It was on the tip of Caleb's tongue to remind the man that everyone was a potential threat to a high-profile figure—even so-called family.

He shrugged instead. Not his client. Not his problem.

His hand closed around the doorknob.

An unexpected wave of grief punched him in the chest. He swallowed hard.

Lillie Blackwater Varella hadn't been easy to love. But she'd been his mother. From the time he was a small boy, he'd run interference between her and his father when his old man was high or drunk and looking to take it out on someone. After his father died, he'd kept his mother sober when he could, fed and dressed in clean clothes when he couldn't. At eighteen, he'd left for the Army, angry and with no small amount of guilt.

Because he'd known if he didn't leave, he'd never get out.

Still, he should have done more. Visited more. Checked in more. Not just money and phone calls. The last time they spoke, his mother had sounded good. Maybe a bit lonely, but clean and sober.

Squaring his shoulders, he entered the room.

An old man in a black suit stood at his mother's coffin. When he turned, Caleb's feet rooted in place.

Benjamin Blackwater.

Shicheii—his mother's father. President of the Navajo Nation.

The bodyguards on the other side of the door were for him.

The last time Caleb had seen his grandfather was at his grandmother's funeral, twenty-two years ago. Back then, the man had seemed larger than life—tall with shoulder-length black hair. A face carved of granite that softened when he looked at his family.

Or maybe that had just been Caleb's childhood imagination.

Now, the hair was short, mostly gray, though the thick black brows remained. The lines etched into his grandfather's face were new, but his bearing wasn't. He stood straight, a leader to his core, his gaze sharp as obsidian as it raked over Caleb.

Caleb's mother had followed her father's rise—from tribal council member to leader to president. She'd told Caleb stories about Ben Blackwater's achievements—stories she must have gotten off the Internet. She didn't use social media or, as far as he knew, engage with other Navajo living in the Phoenix area. Still, she'd been proud of her father. Loved him.

Even if he and the rest of her family hadn't loved her back.

"*Yá'át'ééh*, Grandson."

Ben's eyes carried a pain Caleb refused to acknowledge. His grandfather had no right to look grief stricken—not when he could have extended a hand to his daughter in her time of need.

"Hello, Grandfather." Caleb joined the older man beside the casket. "Thank you for allowing Mom to be buried in the family plot." The words tasted like ash on his tongue. Bitter but true. His grandfather had at least done that much.

"She was my daughter. Much loved, despite the distance between us." Ben's gaze centered on Caleb. "As are you, Grandson."

Keep your damn mouth shut. He wouldn't dishonor his mother by causing a scene at her funeral.

Ben gestured toward the sympathy floral arrangement—white lilies, yellow roses, and baby's breath nestled in greenery—on a stand beside Caleb's mother's coffin. "From your colleagues, I believe."

Caleb sidestepped and angled his head, his gaze narrowing on the card tucked into the arrangement.

With our deepest sympathies to Caleb and his family. Dìleas Security Agency.

A quick smile touched his lips. Sophia and Penny had to be responsible. The men might be the muscle at Dìleas, but the women were its beating heart.

He made a mental note to text Sophia later, then turned back to his grandfather, searching for neutral ground.

"Strange, isn't it? Mom and *Shima' Sani'* both died when they were fifty-two."

One from cancer. The other from fentanyl she probably thought was a pain pill. Five years clean. All it took was one bad day. One bad pill.

His grandfather sighed, the sound heavy with remembered loss. "Your grandmother foresaw her death. She prepared for it in the way of the *Tódich'íinii*—the Bitter Water Clan. She lived in harmony with her fate."

He touched the polished wood of his daughter's casket. "Lillie's path, too, was determined before she was born."

Caleb's jaw clenched. Fire crawled up his spine.

"Does it help you sleep better at night to believe that?"

Shit. So much for keeping his mouth shut.

"I don't believe in your traditions. I don't believe in fate. Grandmother died because of a lack of decent medical care. Mom died because her family turned their backs and let her waste her life on a good-looking loser."

His accusation landed like a grenade in the stillness.

Rather than anger, his grandfather's expression conveyed sorrow. And something else. Something Caleb couldn't quite decipher.

"We were very proud," Ben continued after a long moment, "to learn you served in the Army and had become a Green Beret."

The old man kept track of him?

The forgotten boy deep inside Caleb soaked in those words like needed rain.

He covered the emotional jolt with a sneer. "You mean you were shocked I didn't end up like my father."

His grandparents had despised Julian Varella and never hid it. Handsome. Charming. Manipulative. Drug dealer. He charmed Lillie Blackwater, got her pregnant when she was eighteen. From him, Caleb had learned what kind of person he never wanted to be.

Ben's eyes narrowed. "You have a warrior spirit. It has served you well. But now it's time to make peace with your family. I suspect there's much you don't know."

"I'm not here to make peace." Caleb's voice cut sharp. "I'm here to bury my mother. As soon as that's done, I'm gone. Back to my life."

He lifted his chin toward the closed door—and the armed sentries beyond it.

"Like your boys out there, I get to use my warrior spirit to keep people safe. Only I get paid a helluva lot more than they do—and I'm not stuck on the rez."

It was a childish jab. One his grandfather didn't react to. His expression stayed neutral.

But the boy Caleb used to be—the one with an emotionally fragile mother, the one written off as the drug dealer's kid—remembered the sting.

Silence. Then Ben spoke. "There is more to this life than money and status, Grandson."

Before Caleb could respond, the door opened.

David and Vanessa Blackwater stepped inside. Faces from his early childhood. Zach's parents.

His uncle was a younger version of Caleb's grandfather, dressed in a dark suit and white shirt with a bolero tie, his short black hair threaded with silver. His aunt's dark hair was swept up in a bun. A traditional Navajo red sash wrapped the waist of her long-sleeved black dress. Behind them was his cousin, in a navy suit.

The woman accompanying Zach made the rest of the room fall away.

Gia wore a sleeveless black dress that hit just above her knees, black ankle boots, and a gray scarf with turquoise clusters draped gracefully over her shoulders. She'd braided her hair in a French plait, the end curling over one shoulder.

When their eyes met, she offered a tentative smile.

He forced himself to look away. To ignore the sudden lightness in his chest.

She hadn't run. Instead, she'd come to his mother's funeral.

For him.

Her gesture mattered more than he wanted it to.

His aunt and uncle joined him and his grandfather by the casket.

"*Shidá'í*." He offered his uncle a firm handshake, then let his aunt lean in and brush his cheek with a kiss. "*Shimá yázhí*." No matter how long they'd been estranged, his mother had made sure he knew who he came from, and how to speak to them with respect.

Their movements were stiff. Expressions guarded. As if unsure how to navigate the grief that stretched tight between them. Was it his presence that made them uncomfortable? Or was it standing this close to his mother? Someone they hadn't spoken to in decades.

"You look well," his uncle offered.

Caleb nodded. "Thank you for coming." The words sounded formal, as if he were speaking to complete strangers.

In a way, he was.

His aunt reached for his hand. "Your grandmother and mother are gone, but you will always have a mother."

"*Ahéhee' shimá yazhí,*" he thanked his aunt, his voice stiff. The words rang hollow. "If I ever move back here, I'll keep that in mind."

Vanessa's face brightened. "Are you thinking of coming home?"

"This isn't home." The words slipped out before he could corral them.

Her expression faltered. His uncle's jaw ticked, but he said nothing.

A discrete knock broke the tension.

The funeral director poked his head in, speaking in his hushed tone. "Reverend Avery is here. If you are ready, we can begin the service."

Caleb cast a pointed look at his family, then at the door. "I'd like a minute alone with *shimá.*"

His grandfather gave a single nod. "We'll find our seats."

As they filed out, Gia glanced over her shoulder.

He managed a small smile to ease the concern in her eyes. Why was it easier to accept comfort from a stranger than from the people who shared his blood?

The door clicked shut, leaving him in a quiet room with only the empty shell of his mother for company.

It felt all too familiar, this aloneness.

As a boy, he'd known it well. He'd learned to read the signs of her spirals early. The slurred speech, the dilated pupils, the hollow laughter that meant trouble was coming. He'd watched her disappear into that world more times than he could count, and every time it took a piece of him with it. Then she'd pull herself together and be the mother he needed.

For a while.

He'd carried that sense of isolation with him when he left. He'd been a good teammate in the Special Forces—and he was a good teammate now at Dìleas. But a part of him always looked in from the outside, never quite belonging.

The only person who'd ever understood him was dead—and he'd abandoned her long ago, too angry, too desperate to escape the harshness of their lives to return.

To her credit, she'd never asked him to.

He drew in a breath and opened the casket.

His mother lay nestled in white satin, her long, dark hair coiled into a bun. Corn pollen dusted her face in the traditional way. Someone at the funeral home had dressed her in the nicest clothes he'd found in her closet—a deep purple velvet blouse and a three-tiered skirt in harvest gold. The few pieces of silver and turquoise jewelry Caleb's father hadn't pawned adorned her wrist. The squash blossom necklace around her neck was unfamiliar. A small leather bag rested between her folded hands—more corn pollen for her journey. Her face, ravaged from years of hardship and substance abuse, was pale and smooth.

She looked more like the beautiful young mother he remembered. Before life burned through her beauty and left her brittle.

At peace. Finally.

His chest burned with emotion he was trying so damn hard not to feel. He'd failed her, like her family had, and now, all anyone could offer her were prayers and a plot of dirt for her weary bones to rest.

He bent and pressed his lips to her cool forehead. "Walk in beauty, Mom."

There wasn't anything to do for her now except make sure the Phoenix police tracked down the person who'd given her the lethal drug and put them in prison or, better yet, in the ground.

He gently lowered the lid, then turned and walked out to join his family in the nave.

The Anglo minister, robed in white vestments, introduced himself and offered condolences before taking his place at the altar. In the corner, a gray-haired Diné woman settled at the upright piano.

Caleb sat alone in the front pew, separated from his grandfather, uncle, and aunt across the aisle. Zach and Gia had taken the row behind them. His grandfather's security detail stationed themselves discreetly nearby.

As the funeral staff wheeled the casket to the altar, a hymn rose into the high ceiling, echoing off white stucco walls. Caleb stood, eyes fixed straight ahead, the bulletin clutched in one hand, unread.

Movement to his right caught his eye.

Gia scooted across the aisle and whispered. "Can I sit with you?" Her voice was hesitant. "You shouldn't be alone."

His chest tightened. "Please." He shifted to make space.

Her bare arm touched his coat sleeve, and he swore he could feel the warmth of her touch beneath the fabric.

From the second row, Zach scowled.

Caleb almost grinned. Let his cousin stew.

He'd enjoy Gia's company while he was here.

By this afternoon, he'd be gone, headed to Phoenix. Once he'd cleaned out his mother's belongings and spoke to the police about her death investigation, he'd be on a plane back to DC.

Back to the life he knew and understood.

At the cemetery, the midday sun warmed the winter air. Red clay and dormant sagebrush surrounded scattered headstones. No flowers. No mementos. Only a barren landscape forgotten by the living. Traditional Diné avoided spending time with their dead, believing that severing all ties ensured their loved ones' passage to the spirit world.

Caleb's mother's casket was placed beside his grandmother's grave. Gia stood at his side, bundled into a black puffer jacket, hands buried in her pockets.

"You don't like the cold." he said as she shivered.

"I lost my tolerance."

He caught the faint edge to her voice and tucked the observation away.

As the priest delivered the final blessing, Caleb stood apart from his family. Gia stood with him, her presence grounding him.

His grandfather stepped forward first, scooping a handful of soil from the rocky earth. He scattered it over his daughter's casket and said a few words in the language of his people. Then his uncle, his aunt, his cousin.

When it was Caleb's turn, he crouched low and let the dry earth sift through his fingers.

She'd wanted to be buried here. The homeland she'd left behind.

He still didn't understand why. He dropped the soil onto the varnished wood and stepped back as the cemetery workers lowered the casket into the hard-packed earth.

Gia's gaze swept the land, her face drawn with a goodbye she didn't want to acknowledge.

Not for his mother, whom she'd never met. He was good at reading people. Had to be in his profession. But even if he wasn't, he would have known her intentions.

"You're leaving," He kept his voice low to keep it from carrying to where his family waited nearby.

Startled, she met his eyes.

"If you run, you're alone." He pulled his business card from his wallet and slipped it into her hand. "I can help. This is what I do. Your ex found you here—he'll find you again."

The flash of fear in Gia's eyes twisted like a knife in his gut. He cursed himself for putting it there.

"She has a life here." Zach appeared at their side, shoulders squared, chin raised. "I won't let anything happen to her."

Their graveside tête-à-tête had started to draw attention.

Caleb's grandfather stepped out from the back of one of the Tahoes. Waving off his security detail, he joined them, his sharp gaze moving from one to the other.

"This is not the place for conversation," he said firmly. "Zach told me what happened last night. Lucy has prepared food. Important decisions are best made on a full stomach and with reflection."

"I need to get to Phoenix," Caleb said. But strangely, his heart wasn't in it.

"You need to eat before you go, Grandson. Please."

It was the plea in the old man's eyes that got him. The child who'd adored his grandfather pushing his way forward again.

Or maybe it was the tension in Gia's shoulders. The way her lower lip trembled like she was holding herself together by sheer will.

It didn't matter if he left later than planned. His mother's belongings weren't going anywhere, and the police were still in the early stages of investigating where she might've gotten the fentanyl disguised as prescription oxycodone.

"All right," he said at last. "I'll stay."

His grandfather's approving smile sparked fresh irritation. "For lunch," Caleb added, a warning in his tone.

Gia's eyes lit up. Her fingers brushed the sleeve of his coat, and the flutter in his chest was impossible to ignore.

"I'm sorry about your *amá*." Her words were low, meant only for him. "And I'm glad you're staying. Even if it's just for lunch."

"Ride with me." He scrambled for an excuse. "I don't know the way to my grandfather's home."

Her lashes dropped, hiding her eyes. "Okay."

Zach's jaw flexed as he visibly bit back a retort. With a clipped turn, he stomped off toward his car.

Caleb held back a smirk.

He shouldn't enjoy needling his cousin. After years of no contact, he thought he'd put Zach and the rest of his family out of his mind and moved on.

Apparently not.

It must be memories of how competitive they'd been as young boys.

Memories that would fade as soon as he left.

He hovered a hand behind Gia's back, and when she didn't stiffen, kept his touch butterfly light as he guided her to the Jeep.

CHAPTER EIGHT

DESERT ROSE.

Warm, earthy and floral.

Caleb inhaled Gia's scent, tension easing from his body as she settled into the passenger seat. "You know, you still haven't told me your last name."

"Does it matter?" Gia kept her gaze on the passenger window, her voice distant.

He kept his tone light. "I told you mine. Fair's fair."

A quarter mile of silence stretched out before she answered. "Barone."

Gianna Barone.

It rolled through his mind like a song lyric. Delicate, but with a core of strength. Like her.

She cocked her head toward him. "President Blackwater said he'll observe the traditional four days of mourning. Will you do the same?"

He shrugged to loosen the sudden knot in his shoulders. "In my way."

Maybe he'd take a few extra days after settling his mother's affairs in Phoenix—let the shoulder heal. He could still get back in time to take the New York job.

"There." Gia pointed to a small single-story house—off-white stucco trimmed in gray stone.

His hands tightened on the steering wheel.

He knew this place.

His grandfather still lived in the modest home he'd built for his wife not long before she died. Caleb had expected the Navajo Nation president to have fancier digs.

Street parking was their only option. He stayed in the Jeep, seatbelt latched, as his grandfather, aunt and uncle, and Zach streamed inside, the security detail close behind.

Gia's hand slid over his.

"Caleb?" Her voice was gentle. "Are you coming?"

"Yeah." He forced a smile and unlatched his belt.

Memories buffeted him as he stepped inside. The black, wood-burning stove in the living room corner. The tan sofa and brown armchair around a wood coffee table. Even the oak dining table crowded with documents instead of plates looked familiar—a workspace rather than a place for communal meals.

In the kitchen, a silver-haired Navajo woman stirred a cast-iron pot on the stove. She was new—to him, at least. The smell of mutton stew and fry bread made his stomach gurgle. His grandmother had made stew like that. After they moved to Phoenix, his mother had tried—cheaper cuts of meat, fewer spices—but eventually, even that had stopped.

"Lucy, this is my grandson, Caleb." His grandfather's voice brought him back to the present. "Lucy keeps me fed and my house in order."

"*Yá'át'ééh*, Caleb." Lucy handed him a steaming bowl and a generous piece of fry bread.

"*Yá'át'ééh, shimá sání.*" He returned the greeting, adding my grandmother as a term of respect.

Meal in hand, he hovered, unsure where to sit. The small space made him claustrophobic. His family probably had seats they gravitated to after years of gatherings he and his mother hadn't been part of. Would he have grown up sitting next to Zach? Would his life have been different if they'd stayed?

A dull ache bloomed in his chest. His jaw tightened.

No use mourning what might have been. He'd survived and was doing just fine.

His grandfather settled into the armchair by the stove. His aunt and uncle carved out space at the dining table. Gia and Zach took the sofa.

"Come sit," Gia said, patting the cushion beside her. There was something in her expression—the way her gaze lingered on his family, that hinted at a longing Caleb recognized all too well.

He lowered himself next to her and set his bowl on the coffee table, then tore a piece of fry bread and scooped a bite of stew into his mouth.

The flavors—tender meat, spicy chilies, carrots, onions, and—exploded across his taste buds and warmed his stomach. His eyes fell shut, savoring the connection to a life that used to be his a long time ago.

"My grandson approves, Lucy." A smile hovered over his grandfather's lips, despite the sadness in his eyes.

The small boy inside Caleb leaned into the hint of affection. The grown man remembered the years of silence, the abandonment.

His jaw tightened.

Too little, too late.

He wiped his mouth. "We need to discuss Gia's protection."

Gia placed her bowl carefully on the coffee table with unsteady hands.

Straightening, she turned toward Ben. "I'm so grateful, President Blackwater, for all you've done. But I think it's best if I leave so my personal issues don't endanger anyone here."

"Gia—" Zach started.

Their grandfather silenced him with a lift of his hand. "You're safer here. And our clinic is short-staffed. You have a twelve-week contract, and we need you for every one of those weeks."

His gaze cut to Caleb. Calculating. "My grandson's job is protecting people. Perhaps he'll stay until we know the threat has passed."

"I don't work for you." "We don't need him." Caleb and Zach tripped over each other's protests.

Their grandfather's eyes darkened in rebuke.

But what made Caleb's gut twist wasn't that—it was the hurt flashing across Gia's face. The pink dusting her cheeks.

The stew turned to lead in his stomach.

He was being an ass.

Maybe if someone had stood up to his father, offered his mother a way out, she wouldn't have spiraled into addiction. Maybe she would have had choices. Opportunities.

If he'd stayed in Phoenix, instead of chasing freedom in the Army, he could have helped her. She wouldn't have died alone, abandoned by everyone she once loved.

Including him.

His fingers curled into his palms.

Maybe it was too late for his *amá*, but he could damn well help Gia.

Protecting people was his job. One he had a particular set of skills for. Could he look his Dìleas teammates in the eye if he didn't help? Lachlan, Nathan, and Ryder had all put their lives on the line at some point to protect a woman.

And had ended up married or soon to be married to those women.

Moisture beaded on Caleb's hairline. This wasn't the same situation, of course. He shifted on the sofa cushion, avoiding the gaze of the woman seated next to him, the smooth skin of her thigh inches from his.

"I'll stay another day or two," he kept his voice neutral, "to help Gia figure out the safest path forward. Then I need to get back to my job."

And the life he'd made for himself that wasn't here.

Gia had told the men who attacked her that she was just a stranger passing through, but Caleb didn't trust that her ex—whoever he was—wouldn't ferret out where she lived and worked, if he hadn't already. Until Caleb conducted a more thorough threat assessment and gathered intel on her former fiancé, he couldn't recommend she upend her life without solid reasons and a clear plan.

The Navajo needed her medical skills, and she had a contract he could tell she wanted to honor.

He carried his bowl to the kitchen.

"If you're ready," he said to Gia when he returned, "I'll take you home."

"So you'll stay?" Ben asked Gia.

She drew in a breath. "Yes."

But Caleb could see the *for now* in her eyes.

Ben turned to him. "Will I see you before you leave, Grandson?"

Caleb hesitated. The weary hope in his grandfather's voice twisted something deep inside him. "I don't know. Maybe."

Guilt prickled under his skin. He hated how easily these people had slipped beneath his armor.

"If Gia stays," he added, "I'll draw up a security plan. Zach can help her implement it."

She stood quietly at his elbow. Unlike his relatives, her presence calmed him. The fact she had stood physically close to him all day, unafraid, made his chest puff a bit.

"I've got to head into work." Zach shrugged into his jacket. To Gia he said, "I'll check on you later."

Gia stayed silent as she followed Caleb to his car.

"I'm sorry," he said. "I didn't mean for my response to sound like I wasn't interested in helping you."

She sighed. "You don't have to feel obligated. It's best if you don't get involved."

He opened her door. Watched her slide inside.

Too late. "I'm already involved."

The truth of that statement hit him like the concussive blast from a grenade. No matter how this ended, walking away from Gia wouldn't be easy.

He'd text Ryder. Take an extra week off. He could still take over the New York job if Ryder assigned one of the other guys to do the preliminary leg work.

They drove in silence, Gia staring out the window, arms folded tight across her chest. Caleb kept his hand loose on the wheel even as tension coiled tight through him.

She was shutting down. Retreating into herself. Like his mother used to do when life overwhelmed her.

"Tell me about him. This ex."

Her shoulders sagged. "The smart thing to do would be to leave. I don't want anyone else paying the price for my mistake."

A knot formed between his shoulder blades. "What mistake would that be?"

Was she protecting the bastard? His mother had always defended her husband, no matter what he did.

Silence stretched between them, thick and oppressive.

"What's his name?" he pressed.

"Please, you don't want to cross him."

He pulled to the shoulder. Killed the engine.

"What are you doing?" Tension radiated off her.

"His. Name." Caleb stared her down. Waited as emotions danced across her face like a highlight reel.

Finally, a whisper. "Vincente Garcia."

He leaned back, studying her closely. "What does Vincente Garcia do for a living?"

"Caleb—"

"Gia, Give me something to work with. You can make this easy, or make it hard, but I will find out what I need to know."

Her voice cracked. "He owns a nightclub and some restaurants."

"Where?"

"Miami."

Caleb narrowed his eyes. Not a lie, but not the whole truth, either.

He started the Jeep. Pulled back onto the road. Shifted to the on-coming lane to pass a horse and its rider on the shoulder. "Is that where you're from?"

"I did my residency there, then joined a practice. Concierge medicine." Her lips puckered, like she had a foul taste in her mouth.

Concierge medicine for the rich and powerful. A far cry from Gia's job at the clinic on the reservation.

"You meet him through your practice?"

She flinched, but said nothing.

Frustration was a low simmer in his veins. "Any idea why those men were looking for you?"

Gia's face flushed crimson. "He wants...me back." The admission dragged from her mouth, coated in barbed wire and regret.

Again, his internal radar jangled. Women didn't flee cross-country and bury themselves on a reservation because their ex still had feelings for them.

Unless the jilted lover was powerful. Dangerous.

"Did he hit you?" He kept his voice low, steady—even as rage filled him.

That frightened doe look shadowed her face, just like it had last night. He didn't want to add to it.

She looked startled. "Hit me?" A quick shake of her head. "Not that."

Again, a truth mixed in with unspoken layers.

Maybe he hadn't beaten her, but there were other forms of abuse. Emotional abuse. Gaslighting. His father had perfected gaslighting his mom.

Caleb pulled into her driveway and parked. "What scared you enough to hide?"

Hesitation. Then, "He wasn't the man I believed he was." She shoved the door open and bolted toward her house, her movements jerky.

Her voice rang with conviction that time.

"Hold up." He grabbed his Glock from the glove box and hurried to catch up. "Let me clear the place."

"I'm pretty sure they don't know where I live." Still, she unlocked the door and stood aside to let him enter first.

"How do you know?" He swept the living room and kitchen with a professional eye, then shut the front door and motioned her to take a seat on the couch.

"I think if they knew where I lived, they would have come here, not stumbled across me at a bar I never go to."

She was too sure of herself. Like she had been when the kid in the pink cap had a knife to her throat.

He moved down the hall. Bathroom clear. Bedroom—

A brown Louis Vuitton suitcase sat next to the bed. He hefted it. Full of clothes, as he'd expected. The closet was nearly empty—just a few stray hangers. Dresser drawers were bare, too.

She'd been planning to disappear. Maybe still was, despite what she told his grandfather.

Dammit. Caleb pinched the bridge of his nose to ward off a looming headache.

Running wouldn't save her. She'd spend the rest of her life always looking over her shoulder. Always having to guard her secrets.

Tucking his pistol at the small of his back, he found her standing stiffly by the kitchen counter, watching him with wary eyes.

"You were leaving."

Her chin lifted. "Why do you say that?"

"Full suitcase. Empty closet."

She retreated a step, bumping into the counter. Flustered, she grabbed a pitcher of filtered water from the fridge and poured some into the bright yellow teakettle on the stove. "Tea?"

"No thanks. Just water if you don't mind." He accepted a glass with murmured thanks. "Give me a few days. If I can't ensure your safety on the rez, I'll help you disappear. My colleague at Dìleas can give you a new name. A new life. Somewhere you'll be safe."

A hollow ache burrowed beneath his chest. If she stayed on the rez, he'd at least know where she was and how she was doing. If he resettled her, he wouldn't see her again. It wouldn't be safe.

She crossed her arms, leaned into the counter, her gaze wary. "Why are you helping me?"

Because I didn't help my mother.

He kept his tone level. "It's what I do."

Her eyes dimmed. Behind her, the kettle screeched, belching steam into the air. Gia got out a tea bag and added it to her mug with the boiling water.

He had the feeling he'd disappointed her somehow. "You don't deserve to spend the rest of your life looking over your shoulder."

"You don't know what I deserve."

What the hell did that mean?

The kettle shrieked, breaking the moment.

She turned her back to him, busying herself with the tea. Her hands trembled.

"I'm sorry." Her voice was rough. Weary. "I'm grateful for your help. I told your grandfather I'd stay, and I want to honor my commitment—to him, to the staff at the clinic, and to my patients."

Caleb nodded. A surge of protectiveness and something hotter, more dangerous, stirred inside him. "I need to make a few calls."

"I'll leave you to it." She scooted past him, brushing his chest with her shoulder.

The contact was slight, yet an electric current arced between them.

Gia froze. Her gaze locked with his. Wide and unguarded. Her tongue swiped across her lips.

His restraint snapped. *Fuck it.*

For once, he wasn't going to do the right thing. Slowly, giving her time to back away, he lowered his head.

Her eyes fluttered closed instead.

He pressed his fists into his thighs to keep from reaching for her.

Their mouths met, tentative at first. Just their mouths. Testing.

He savored the connection. Because that's what it was—a connection.

His tongue slipped out, caressing the seam of her lips.

She opened to him, and the taste of her—peppermint and prickly pear—made his head spin.

She had him off-kilter. And that wasn't good.

He drove his tongue deeper and stepped into her, unleashing the control he had over his hands to allow them to slide behind her back and haul her into his body.

Hands pressed against his chest.

Immediately, he pulled back. Dropped his arms and silently kicked his own ass.

"Sorry," he rasped. The vulnerability in her eyes tightened his throat.

She touched her lips, her eyes shimmering.

"Don't be." Her voice was the barest of whispers.

Before he could respond, she slipped away to her bedroom.

He stared after her. The only thing he had to offer Gia was his protection and temporary physical gratification. He wouldn't be around long enough for it to be anything more. And if he made it safe for her to stay, Zach was better suited for her.

Something green slithered through his veins and burned in his chest.

Caleb exhaled hard, running a hand through his hair, and stepped outside.

He pulled up Nathan Long's number.

"Yo, amigo." Nathan's Texas drawl rumbled over the line. Dìleas's VP of Corporate Security was a six-foot-six former SEAL whose ice-blue eyes, spiky hair, and perpetual five o'clock shadow made him look more like a member of a biker gang than a corporate executive. "You still in Arizona?" His voice lowered. "Sorry about your mom."

"Thanks." Caleb cleared his throat. "I need your help. It's not Dìleas business, so I'll understand if you say no."

"Well, now you've got me curious. What's going on?"

"I need everything you can dig up on a Vincente Garcia in Miami. He owns a nightclub and some restaurants." Caleb hesitated, then added, "And Gianna Barone, early thirties. She's a medical doctor. Practiced in Miami. Originally from New York, I think. As soon as you can get it to me."

Nathan's easygoing tone disappeared. "You good, brother? You know Lachlan, Ryder, and I have your six."

Caleb stared up at the endless blue sky, a curious lump in his throat. The three men who'd started Dìleas were as tight as blood brothers, but he'd never considered himself part of their inner circle.

"I'm good. Just trying to help out a woman with a problem that needs to be solved." His fingers tightened around the phone. "I'll be sticking around here for a few days, maybe a week. Ryder told me I could take the time."

"Do what you need to do, brother. I'll get back to you as soon as I can with the info you need," Nathan said.

"Thanks, man." Caleb ended the call.

With any luck, Nathan would dig up something useful he could use as leverage to get this Garcia to back off. Gia could stay on the rez and he'd return to the life he'd made for himself far from Arizona.

A vehicle approached. Caleb's hand instinctively brushed the butt of his Glock.

Zach's cruiser pulled up.

His cousin got out, striding towards him. "I just got a call from Gallup PD."

Chapter Nine

"AND?" CALEB GESTURED FOR his cousin to follow him into the house. Tossing his suit coat over the back of the sofa, he rolled up his shirtsleeves.

Zach's gaze dropped to Caleb's gun, then lifted. If he had a problem with Caleb being armed on Navajo land, he kept it to himself.

"They traced the license plate you gave them for the black SUV. Belongs to a guy named Manuel Ortega. Lives in Phoenix. Here's where it gets interesting. Ortega pops up in the ACJIS."

"English, Cousin."

"Arizona's version of the National Criminal Information Center." Zach braced against the wall, arms crossed. "Looks like he's originally from Gallup. Had ties to the Aztec Kings—a local motorcycle gang on the FBI's radar for guns and drug trafficking."

Caleb's jaw tightened. "What does he do in Phoenix?"

"He's a warehouse manager for Azamex Food Distributors. They import Mexican and Central American snacks and distribute them to stores throughout the Southeast."

Azamex. The name rang a bell.

Caleb searched his memories. His old man had worked there once, stocking their warehouse before he died. Sometimes he brought home boxes of individually packaged chips—a rare treat in a house where there hadn't been many.

Frowning, Caleb dug deeper into the memory.

Was that why Ortega had seemed familiar? Had he worked with his father?

"There's more," Zach said. He leveled a cool look at Caleb. "The tribal hospital in Gallup reported a fentanyl overdose last night. They're waiting for the toxicology results to confirm the analog ingested by the deceased, but pills found at the scene looked like oxy."

Caleb's teeth ground together to hold back a snarl. "Tribal hospital. The deceased was Navajo?"

Zach's lips thinned, his eyes darkening to black. "Yeah. Which is why it's now our problem. My buddy reached out to the Feds. They were very interested in the fact Ortega's back in Gallup. They think he might be meeting up with old crew—and given his rumored cartel ties..."

A chill skated down Caleb's spine. "Cartel connections?"

"Yep." His cousin's brow lifted, a hint of censure in his eyes. "Espina Negra. Sound familiar?"

"Son of a bitch." Ice flooded Caleb's veins, then caught fire.

He shoved his hand through his hair, trying to hold back the roaring fury, his body trembling with the effort to stay in control.

Espina Negra.

His father's former cartel.

The cartel responsible for his mother's death.

More innocent dead.

And Gia—where did she fit in?

She knew more than she was telling.

Pieces of a puzzle scattered before him, just out of reach.

But he would put them together. And when he did...

He hadn't realized he was pacing until Zach stepped in front of him, blocking his path. "That look on your face is making me nervous."

Caleb jerked his head toward Gia's bedroom, lowering his voice. "Why go after her? There has to be a connection."

Zach gave a restless shrug. "Maybe her ex hired Ortega to track her down. Paid local talent to send a message. Wouldn't be the first time some businessman didn't want to get his own hands dirty."

"Maybe." Caleb didn't believe in coincidences.

"You good?" Zach asked, his gaze too perceptive.

Slipping into mission mode, Caleb blocked the rising storm inside him. Focused on the job.

Which just became finding Manuel Ortega.

"I'm fine."

His cousin didn't need to know the truth—that he wasn't anywhere near fine.

This wasn't just about protecting Gia anymore.

It was about avenging his mother.

Ortega had answers.

Caleb would get those answers.

At any cost.

Gia's fingers kept drifting to her lips as she unzipped her suitcase.

Caleb had kissed her.

And she hadn't been afraid.

She hadn't kissed a man since Vincente.

Hadn't *wanted* to.

Her white medical coat hung back in the closet. A few shirts, a couple of work outfits, a handful of underwear—all back in her closet or drawers.

The rest she'd left packed, ready to go at a moment's notice. Because even though she'd said she'd stay—and wanted to stay—if Vincente's men tracked her down, she'd have no choice but to leave.

Her fingertips brushed the tight weave of her Navajo bedcovering, the rough texture grounding her. Bought at a trading post, the woman who'd handwoven the blanket had told her each pattern told a story.

If someone wove a blanket of her life, what would it say?

Unlike the Diné, she had no community, no culture, no symbols of her beliefs.

The thought of endangering them if she stayed turned her stomach.

The mistakes she'd made were her problem. Hers alone.

Running scared the hell out of her. She had no new identity to fall back on. Little cash left in her reserves.

If she ran, she'd have to cut ties. She'd never know the results of Florence Begay's CAT scan, and if she was getting the treatment she needed. Or if Billy Nakai would actually follow through with the diet and exercise recommendations he needed to get his blood pressure and diabetes under control.

No goodbyes to Jennie. Zach. President Blackwater.

And Caleb.

God, Caleb.

There was no denying the attraction. His dark eyes and quiet strength had drawn her from the first moment at Lucero's Lounge.

Then he'd appeared in the parking lot, handling those men with a ruthless efficiency that should have terrified her.

Only it had made her feel safe. Protected.

If Caleb ever knew the whole truth, he'd never look at her the same.

He'd see her for what she was—a liar, a coward, a woman who should've known better than to fall for a devil with a silver tongue.

She'd ignored the signs.

Until the night she couldn't anymore.

No amount of running would wash away the blood. She'd slept in the bed of a murderer. Trusted him.

Her gaze darted back to the closet. To the clothes she'd unpacked.

Fear seized her lungs in a viselike grip.

What was she thinking? She should never have agreed to stay.

She should never have whispered Vincente's name.

If Caleb actually confronted him, Vincente and his family would come for him, too.

They solved problems by eliminating them.

She shoved her suitcase deeper into the closet, then changed into jeans and a burgundy knit top.

Just her luck to find a decent man when there was no future in it.

Low, masculine voices drifted down the hall. Too low to make out the words, but the tension in every sharp syllable was palpable.

Her heart skittered.

Caleb wasn't alone—and whoever was with him had brought bad news.

Each step down the short hallway twisted the ball of nerves in her stomach tighter.

When she turned the corner, she found Caleb and Zach facing off near the front door.

Zach caught sight of her first. He straightened, dropping his arms to his sides.

She barely had time to register his sober face when Caleb turned.

Eyes, cold as a glacier yet alive with a suppressed fire, pinned her in place. His mouth was a thin line above a jaw rigid enough to shatter.

Unease crawled up her spine. "Has something happened?"

This wasn't the man who'd kissed her with tender heat.

This was the soldier. The one who understood violence and death.

The one that reminded her too much of the world she'd escaped.

"We got information on one of the suspects who attacked you." Zach peered at his black Cassio G-Shock.

Grimacing, he added, "Caleb can fill you in. I'm headed to Chinle on a missing persons case and won't be back until late. I'll assign an officer to keep an eye on Gia's home tonight."

"Do that." Caleb's tone was curt. "I've got some business to handle. I'll be back by morning."

Hello? She was standing right there. "I have my shift at the clinic."

Caleb spared her a glance. "I'll drive you."

"That's not necessary. I can drive myself."

Because if Vincente's men somehow discovered her real name and tracked her to her workplace, she might need a quick exit.

"Yes, it is." Both men said in unison.

Blood will tell.

Gia blew out a breath, exasperated but oddly warmed. Protectors. Both of them. To their core. "I can tell you two are related."

Truth was, it felt nice to have men who cared. Even if it was temporary.

"Contact me if the police locate Ortega and his buddy," Caleb told Zach, his voice cool.

Zach returned the stare, then gave a curt nod and left.

The door had barely closed before Caleb stalked toward her. His movements were fluid. Like the big cats she'd seen at the Miami Zoo.

But his eyes still burned with icy rage.

And suddenly, she felt like prey.

Her pulse tripped.

"What did Zach tell you?" She cursed the tremble in her voice. Caleb had to hear it.

Too many secrets.

Too many lies.

"Did you know those men who tried to abduct you?" he demanded.

"No." She stiffened her spine, injecting as much forcefulness as she could into the single word. "I already told you that."

She hadn't recognized them.

But she knew who sent them.

"You've never seen them before? Not even with your ex?"

This soldier interrogating her with his hard voice and cold, relentless gaze frightened her.

"No."

"Then why were you so sure they didn't know where you lived?"

Because they were looking for Abigail Winters.

Not Gianna Barone.

"They were strangers. Not from around here. And they were surprised to find me, remember?" A flimsy excuse. She knew it.

So did he. "Ever heard of Azamex? It's a food distributor. Maybe your ex has business with them?"

"Maybe." Gia wiped sweaty palms on her jeans. "He never discussed work around me."

He'd introduced her to men and women he referred to as business associates. They'd rarely spoken to her. She'd been Vincente's arm candy.

Dusk had settled. The soft glow of headlights cut across her windows.

Caleb strode to the glass, his hand moving over the gun at his back. When he turned to face her, his features had shuttered.

No anger.

No suspicion.

Just a chilling remoteness.

"Zach's officer is here, stationed outside." His voice was flat. "I have to go."

A sudden chill peppered her flesh. "Where?"

"Hunting."

"No." She shook her head hard enough to make her hair fly. "Not for me. I'm not worth it."

His eyes narrowed, searching hers.

Looking for a truth she didn't dare give him.

Finally, he spoke. "The guy with the mustache knew my father. He might have a connection to my mother." His voice roughened. "Lock your door."

He turned to leave—then paused. "And for what it's worth, you *are* worth it."

Warmth bloomed in her chest.

"Caleb," she blurted, halting his exit. "Be careful."

She shouldn't worry about him. He'd proven he was more than capable of handling himself.

Still...the thought of something happening to him.

His eyes thawed, just a little. "I'll be fine."

The door clicked shut behind him.

Closing her eyes, she pressed trembling fingers to her lips, where his kiss from earlier still lingered.

He was hunting for the men who had come for her.

What would he learn if he found them?

After he left Gia's, Caleb called Nathan.

"How fast can you locate the clubhouse for the Aztec Kings, a motorcycle gang based in Gallup?"

"Locate it?" Nathan asked. "About two minutes. Identify the security setup and its strengths and weaknesses should you decide to pay a visit that wouldn't be welcomed, about thirty to forty-five minutes or more, depending upon how good of a setup they have."

"I just need the address. This is a reconnaissance mission."

"What's going on, amigo? First you ask me to dig up information on a woman and her ex. Now you want to spy on a motorcycle gang? I thought you were in Arizona to bury your mom?"

"That's done. But there's someone I need to talk to about my mother's death, and he's in town visiting the Aztec Kings."

"Don't do anything stupid where we have to come haul your ass out of trouble," Nathan growled.

Caleb's dark mood lightened a shade. "You know you'd have fun doing it."

Nathan chuckled. "Yeah, I would, but I'm getting married soon, and you've met Emily. If I get shot again she'll finish the job."

Now it was Caleb's turn to laugh because yeah, he did know Emily, and he wouldn't cross that feisty blonde daughter of a Navy SEAL admiral, either. "How are the final wedding preparations going?"

"I am keeping my head down and mouth shut other than to say yes, dear."

"Smart man. Text me as soon as you have the address." Caleb hung up.

Ten minutes later, Nathan had sent him the location—an address, a satellite photo of the area, and a message:

> *Friendly group of guys. They make the Hells Angels look like a knitting club. Unconfirmed rumor, a Mexican gang's been sniffing around, looking to become a player in the US drug pipeline—Los Coyotes.*

> *Don't get caught in a turf war.*

Caleb drove to the location and staked out the clubhouse from a distance through binoculars.

He didn't have to wait long.

Bingo.

Manuel Ortega and his young sidekick slipped out and drove off in a battered Ford sedan—burgundy, with enough dings and scratches to be forgettable.

If the Kings had police informants, they'd already dumped the black Explorer at a chop shop.

Oblivious to their tail, they drove to a budget motel, entered one of the rooms, and left ten minutes later.

Caleb parked his Jeep behind a fast-food taco restaurant across the street, tucked deep in the shadows.

He pulled the hood of a plain gray sweatshirt over his head, waited for a break in traffic, and dodged across the road.

Everything he'd learned as a Green Beret and as an executive protection specialist screamed to call Zach. Sit tight. Let the authorities handle Ortega.

He knew better than to do what he was about to do.

And he didn't care.

Every second wasted meant another trail gone cold.

Another mother buried. Another son left with nothing but grief and regret.

His gut told him Ortega knew about the fentanyl that had killed his mother—maybe he'd even been the one to hand it over.

If the police grabbed him, he'd clam up, lawyer up.

Or Espina Negra would silence him.

Strike first, strike fast, no mercy.

Caleb needed answers.

About his mother. About Vincente Garcia.

And Gia.

A healthy dose of fear might loosen Ortega's tongue.

The motel was a two-story L-shaped structure that looked every bit as low rent as its thirty-five-dollar a night rate suggested. Room 102 was tucked at the far end of the building furthest from the lobby.

Keeping to the shadows, Caleb jogged to the far corner, avoiding the harsh light thrown off by the cheap security lamps.

At the door, he knocked. "Maintenance."

Silence.

He knocked again, then picked the outdated deadbolt with practiced ease.

Unholstering his Glock, he twisted the knob, and used his foot to push open the door, then swept the room.

So far, his only adversaries were two queen beds that looked like someone barfed Kool-Aid on them. A battered heating unit wheezed musty air.

He riffled through two black backpacks on the particle board desk.

Clothes, toiletries. No IDs.

Nothing useful.

Dragging the lone chair to the opposite corner, he sat and waited.

Forty-five minutes later, two male voices drifted through the air.

Coming closer. Joking in Spanish. A few beers in from the sound of it.

He got one piece of intel out of the exchange as they argued about who had the key—the kid's name was Emilio.

Caleb rose silently and positioned himself behind the door.

Emilio sauntered in, Ortega a step behind.

Caleb's arm clamped around the kid's neck, ignoring the stab of pain from the wound on his shoulder. He pressed his Glock to Emilio's temple and kicked the door shut.

"Don't do anything stupid."

Ortega's hand twitched against his thigh.

"You'll be dead before you clear your weapon," Caleb warned.

The older man's hand fisted.

"You should have left town, *pendejo*," Ortega spat. "Kept your nose outta someone else's business."

"Nosy's my middle name." Caleb gestured with his chin. "Sit on the bed. Hands in the air."

He kicked the back of Emilio's knee, sending him to the stained carpet with a grunt, then disarmed the kid.

"Up. Slow and easy. Go join your friend—hands where I can see them if you don't want a bullet in your head."

Caleb let the cold ruthlessness he'd honed as a Green Beret show on his face as he faced Ortega. "Been renewing old acquaintances in Gallup? On behalf of Espina Negra?"

Surprise flickered in Ortega's eyes before he masked it with a sneer. "What fucking business is it of yours?"

Caleb gave a nonchalant shrug. "I heard Espina Negra's peddling fentanyl through the Aztec Kings. And you're the middleman."

Ortega barked out a humorless laugh. "What, you looking to sample the goods? Smoke a blue?"

Rage detonated in Caleb's chest.

Before Ortega finished the insult, Caleb pistol-whipped Emilio across the temple and shoved the barrel of his gun hard against Ortega's skull.

"Someone important to me is dead because of that new shit." He grabbed Ortega's chin. Twisted the man's head so their eyes met. "My old man was a *Halcón* for Espina Negra. Bastard's dead, so it wasn't him. But whoever it was…"

His voice dropped to a deadly growl. "I'm going to end them."

He cocked his head, narrowed his gaze. "Maybe it was you. You look familiar."

Recognition widened Ortega's eyes. "Varella. You're his brat."

Caleb tightened his grip on Ortega's face. He'd been right about the connection to his father.

"Did you give my mother those pills?"

The question came out in a guttural snarl, fueled by rage and grief. The urge to put a bullet through Ortega's brain was so strong he had to move his finger off the trigger.

Ortega tried to shake his head, but Caleb hadn't loosened his grip.

"No man. I swear—I don't know nothing about your mother!"

Liar.

The scent of Ortega's fear was a sickly sweet perfume.

Caleb leaned closer, whispered into the man's ear.

"You two are expendable."

He let the words sit with Ortega and his sidekick for a moment.

"And when the boss finds out the Aztec Kings are looking to cut a side deal with another cartel…"

He tsked softly.

"I bet that won't sit too well with *El Víbora*."

Sweat beaded on Ortega's forehead. His gaze darted from the Glock to Caleb's face.

"You're lying," he wheezed. "The Kings are solid."

One motto of the Green Beret was "Improvise, Adapt, and Overcome." And Caleb had just thought of a way to throw Espina Negra into disarray.

He eased back, arching a brow in cold amusement.

"Am I? I hear one of the Mexican motorcycle gangs is looking to push north, into Arizona and New Mexico. They'll need local partners. Who better to connect with than the Aztec Kings?"

Fear flared in Emilio's eyes, his Adam's apple bobbing on a swallow. Ortega's fists clenched helplessly.

"If I'm right," Caleb continued, "*El Víbora*'s going to blame someone—might as well be you."

Time to twist the knife.

"Look at you, old man," he sneered. "All these years with Espina Negra and you're still an errand boy. "Once Lopez guts you, he'll go after the Aztec Kings. No one double crosses Espina Negra and lives to tell about it."

He slid one foot back.

Then another, keeping his gun trained on the men.

Before he left, he delivered one final promise.

"And tell that prick in Miami, Vincente Garcia, that the woman is under my protection. He sends anyone after her again..."

Caleb let a feral grin curl his lips.

"...he'll answer to me. This is desert country, where the wind and the sand steal your screams—and secrets stay buried forever."

Palming the doorknob, he slipped into the night.

CHAPTER TEN

THE SUN PEEKED OVER the mesa, gilding the frost on the sagebrush in gold as Caleb drove Gia to work the morning after his mother's funeral. The air was crisp but clean, with the promise of new beginnings.

Which Caleb needed. Tension knotted his shoulders. Last night, he'd let his grief and rage get the better of him. In the light of day, he could see how recklessly he'd waved a red flag in front of the cartel—while he was supposed to be protecting the woman sitting next to him.

Gia wore navy slacks and a pale blue blouse beneath her white doctor's coat, her long hair confined in a twist. The small navy backpack she used as her work bag sat on the floor between her feet. The aroma of cinnamon-laced coffee in the travel mug she gripped drifted toward him, rich and spiced. Her posture was too rigid, her glances in the side mirror too frequent.

Half-truths, evasive answers. Her past a mystery she refused to share.

It wasn't paranoia—he'd honed the ability to read people in the Army.

Gia's fear came wrapped in secrets.

And now that he'd confirmed Manuel Ortega's ties to Espina Negra, he needed answers.

Protecting her served a purpose now—finding out who was responsible for his mother's death.

Bullshit.

If that were all it was, he wouldn't notice every time her hands trembled, or her breath hitched. Wouldn't dream of her scent or the way she tasted when he kissed her.

If she were just a means to an end, he wouldn't have the urge to bury Vincente Garcia in a remote desert canyon every time fear darkened Gia's eyes, or she glanced over her shoulder.

No, this was personal now. In more ways than one.

And that was dangerous.

His muscles began to loosen as they drove deeper into the rez. The medical clinic sat tucked in a sparsely populated valley, far enough off the highway that outsiders wouldn't go unnoticed.

"There's the clinic. Up ahead." Gia pointed to a single-story metal building with a ramp leading up to glass doors.

Caleb parked in a space marked for staff and glanced down at his black suit trousers—the only pair he'd packed that weren't jeans. "As far as your coworkers are concerned, I'm staying a few days to reconnect with family and offered to help out at the clinic given you're short-staffed."

His white dress shirt still looked passably clean. He'd packed light, because he hadn't planned on sticking around. "I'm a trained Army medic."

She pivoted to stare at him. "Army medic, huh? You neglected to mention that."

He shrugged. "Special Forces train for a lot of roles. And it's a decent explanation for my presence—keep people from asking questions."

"So many layers to you, Caleb Varella," Gia murmured, stepping from the Jeep.

Inside, a middle-aged Diné woman with short, black hair and oval, rose-tinted glasses greeted them from behind the white reception counter.

"Morning, Susan." Gia greeted her warmly. She indicated Caleb. "This is Caleb Varella, President Blackwater's grandson. He's volunteering at the clinic for a few days."

Susan's eyes lit with curiosity. "*Yá'át'ééh*, Caleb. It's been a long time since you've been home. I'm sorry about your mother."

He kept his expression politely neutral. "*Yá'át'ééh*, Susan. Thank you."

"There you are!" A slender woman in blue scrubs hurried toward them, her long dark braid swinging.

She wrapped Gia in a hug—one Gia didn't flinch from. "I heard what happened the other night at Lucero's. I'm glad you're okay."

A friend, then.

Gia's face tightened. "Word travels fast, huh, Jennie? This is Caleb Varella."

"So, you're the long-lost grandson." Jennie Tsosie, RN, according to her badge, offered her hand with a friendly smile. "Nice to meet you."

Shorter than Gia by an inch, she had high cheekbones and long lashes over expressive brown eyes that studied him with open curiosity.

"Not lost." He held her fingers gently before letting go. "Just not here."

Gia was right. Despite the vastness of the reservation, gossip rode the wind.

"Jennie's my head nurse and a good friend," Gia said.

"Galina Wauneka's back, room one." Jennie handed Gia a clipboard. "Her arthritis is flaring again."

Gia skimmed the chart. "Is she following the anti-inflammatory diet I recommended?"

"I'm sure she did her best." Jennie's mouth curved with a soft smile. "Fresh vegetables are expensive and not always easy to come by."

A delicate flush crept up Gia's neck.

Caleb kept quiet, silently approving of Jennie's tactful reminder.

Gia was still adjusting to a lifestyle and culture far removed from her own. The Navajo Nation was a vast, open territory with few population centers. More accessible trading posts and convenience stores often carried cheaper, highly processed, less perishable foods.

He followed her down the hall to a small office. Inside were a dark laminated desk, a black faux leather high-backed swivel chair, and two metal-framed chairs. Wedged into the corner was a set of tan filing cabinets. A black computer monitor and keyboard sat on the desk.

No diplomas. No framed family photos. Nothing that gave away personal information.

"The doctors on staff share this office."

Gia must have noticed him staring at the bare walls.

She set down her mug and slung a stethoscope around her neck. "This way."

The scared woman he knew disappeared, replaced by the calm, focused professional.

She led him to exam room one. "Wait out here. We need Galina's permission for you to be in the room."

Through the open door, Caleb glimpsed a tiny, wrinkled elder perched on a chair. Pain grooved her face and shadowed faded brown eyes.

She greeted Gia with a nod, her gaze latching onto Caleb.

"Hello, Grandmother," he greeted her in the manner of the Diné.

"Hello, Grandson. You look like your mother."

He quelled a sigh. Before he could even introduce himself, everyone already knew who he was.

Gia explained his role.

Galina nodded her permission and waved gnarled fingers toward the exam table. "I can't get up there."

Caleb stepped into the room and offered his hand. When she took it, he lifted her with gentle strength onto the table.

A small whimper escaped her.

"I'm sorry," he murmured, grimacing.

She patted his cheek with a wrinkled palm, and for a moment, memory blindsided him.

Sweet, grainy blue corn cakes. The smell of sheep's wool and dung. His grandmother's kiss.

He stepped back, breaking the connection to his past, and watched Gia work from the corner.

"Galina." Gia had stooped to examine her patient's feet. "How long have you had this dark streak on your toenail?"

Galina peered down and shrugged.

"I'd like to get you an appointment with a dermatologist, if you don't mind." Gia's lips pursed. "It could be nothing, but it could also be a sign of melanoma."

Caleb waited until Gia finished her exam, and they'd left the room to speak. "Good catch, Doc."

He still wasn't sure how she'd spotted the small streak beneath Galina's pinky toenail—something anyone else might've passed off as a bruise unless they were looking closely.

A hint of color touched Gia's cheeks, but her eyes lit with quiet pride. "I did some reading on signs of skin cancer in the Native

American population. Did you know Native Americans have the second-highest rate behind the White population?"

"My grandmother died of cancer," he told her. "By the time they discovered it, it was too late."

Maybe if a doctor like Gia had been around back then, his grandmother would still be alive—and his mother wouldn't have agreed to move to Phoenix.

Every patient that morning allowed him into the exam room, their curiosity outweighing caution. It gave him the chance to observe Gia in her world—respectful, caring, patient. She made recommendations she'd likely made more than once.

Between appointments, she called specialists. Researched affordable medication options. Battled systems bigger than herself on behalf of patients who had no one else.

Caleb's admiration for her grew.

She only stopped for lunch when Jennie intervened, for which Caleb was grateful. His stomach had been growling for hours.

After eating, he let Gia return to her patients while he commandeered the conference room. He had tasks of his own to accomplish—a facility risk assessment for the clinic to keep Gia safe at work, and phone calls to Camila Richardson, his mother's friend, and to Phoenix PD's Drug Trafficking Bureau.

Scrolling through his phone, Caleb found the phone number for Camila.

Her voice, warm and soothing, flowed across the line. She'd offered to clear out his mother's apartment—donating what she could, boxing up any personal items she thought Caleb might appreciate having.

She'd been the one to call and break the news of his mother's death.

"I won't be back in Phoenix tomorrow as planned," he told her. "Something's come up here."

"No worries," Camila assured him. "I found a box with some journals in it. I didn't want to pry, but they're in your mother's handwriting." She paused. "I think you're going to want them."

Journals?

"Yeah, sure. Thank you." He didn't know his mother kept journals. Maybe someday he'd read them. Not now.

Not while his grief was still fresh.

After hanging up, he placed a call to Carson Elliott, the detective in charge of his mother's death investigation.

"How can I help you, Mister Varella?" the detective answered, his voice impatient.

Caleb tamped down the irritation skating across his neck. "There's a man named Manuel Ortega. Warehouse manager for Azamex. I need you to find out if he had contact with my mother before she died."

"What was Mister Ortega's relationship with your mother?"

"I'm not sure. He knew my father." A familiar childhood shame burned in Caleb's chest. He stared blindly at the round analog clock on the wall. "Ortega has ties to both Espina Negra and a motorcycle club in Gallup that may be distributing the cartel's fentanyl products."

"Look, Mister Varella," weariness edged the detective's voice, "I've got thirty open cases besides your mother's. I'll pass the information along to the DEA, but you'll have to be patient."

In other words, don't expect much.

Caleb worked his jaw to loosen the tension. "I'll be in touch."

He shoved his phone in his pocket and stood.

If he wanted justice for his mother, it looked like he'd have to get it himself.

Chapter Eleven

Gia finished notations on her patient's case file at a computer behind the nurses' station, its monitor framed with stickers of colorful hot air balloons. The fluorescent lights cast a pale glow over the keys as her nails clacked across them with the efficiency of years in practice. The sharp smells of disinfectant and burnt coffee hung in the air.

"You always use the same computer," Jennie said as she returned from escorting an elderly man into room two.

Gia smiled. "I love the balloons. They're fun to look at."

"You should come with me to the hot air balloon festival in Albuquerque this October."

October. She'd be long gone by then. Gia's smile faltered. "My contract's up in six weeks. October feels like a long way off."

"Maybe you can stay." Jennie passed her the chart for the next patient. "God knows we need the help."

She glanced around. "Where's your hottie escort?"

"He had calls to make." Gia logged out of the computer. "I think he got tired of being the object of curiosity."

She quirked an eyebrow at her friend. "And for the record, that's President Blackwater's grandson you're drooling over."

Jennie snorted. "I'm not the one undressing him with my eyes."

"I'm not—" Gia sputtered. "We're not—it's not like that." Her face burned hotter than a day at the beach without sunscreen.

Sleep had eluded her, the memory of their kiss replaying in her mind—along with a wish she'd had the courage to take it further.

"Uh huh." Jennie's knowing look said it all. "You're blushing. And I've seen the way you check him out when he's not looking. Plus"—she gave a mock shiver—"I've seen the way he stares at you. He's a sexy, still-waters-run-deep kind of guy. A warrior. Zach must hate him."

Caught off guard, Gia blinked. "Why would Zach care?"

Not that Jennie was wrong. Tension crackled between the two men.

Jennie's brows arched nearly to her hairline. "Zach has a thing for you. Surely you've noticed." Her gaze darted away. "Everyone else has."

Gia's stomach dropped. "Zach's a friend. Nothing more." Had she somehow given him the wrong idea?

Vincente had accused her often enough of flirting if she so much as smiled at another man. She'd learned to suppress herself to keep the peace.

"And Caleb?" Jennie pressed.

She thought again of their kiss. The rush of need that had her wanting more. The feeling of safety she wasn't sure she could trust.

Restless, she shifted her shoulders. Caleb was a good man. One she didn't deserve.

"He's leaving soon."

Even if he wasn't, nothing could come of it.

If Vincente found out, Caleb wouldn't live to regret it.

She'd never have the chance at another relationship until Vincente was out of her life for good.

"What about you?" Concern replaced teasing in Jennie's eyes—another weight added to Gia's already heavy shoulders. "There's talk you might leave. Who were those men who attacked you?"

Guilt pressed on Gia's lungs, making it hard to breathe. She didn't want to lie to her friend. Only President Blackwater and the clinic's medical director knew the truth behind her move to Arizona, and that had been a necessity to explain the name discrepancy on her medical license. If they hadn't been so desperate for a doctor who could start immediately, they probably would have tossed her application in the trash.

The words hovered on her tongue. That it was a random attack. A case of mistaken identity. But she was tired of building relationships on lies. If she left, she didn't want Jennie's memories of their friendship sullied by deceit.

Shoving trembling hands into the pockets of her doctor's coat, she forced herself to say, "They work for my ex. I left without telling him, and let's just say, he didn't take it well."

Jennie's eyes widened. "Does Zach know?"

"Zach and Caleb both know. They're helping me figure out what to do." Gia slid into her doctor persona, offering Jennie a confident smile at odds with her tripping pulse. "Don't worry. I'll be fine."

Judging by Jennie's pinched features, she wasn't buying it.

Rosenda Golden, one of the other nurses, approached before Jennie could press further. "Doctor Barone, President Blackwater is here." Her voice brimmed with curiosity. "He'd like to speak with you."

Gia exchanged a puzzled glance with Jennie, who waggled her eyebrows. "You've become a favorite of the Blackwaters, it seems."

I don't want to be anyone's favorite.

That never worked out well for her.

"Can you bring him to the conference room?" she started to say, then caught herself.

Caleb was in there.

"No—wait. My office, please."

She wiped sweaty palms on her coat.

Maybe her decision to stay—or leave—was about to be taken out of her hands.

President Blackwater entered her office with his security detail. He motioned for them to wait outside.

The door shut behind them with a soft click that sounded more like the crack of a gunshot to her frayed nerves.

"President Blackwater." She gestured to one of the metal chairs and took a seat next to him, her throat dry as the dust swirling outside. "To what do I owe the honor of your visit?"

"I need your help."

She blinked. "My help?" That wasn't what she'd expected.

"My grandson, Caleb." Ben's gaze was steady. "He's formed a connection with you."

She leaned back, nonplused. "We hardly know each other."

"And yet, he's stays for you."

Warmth fizzed in her veins—one she immediately tried to drown in cold reality.

"He protects people for a living. He's just...helping me figure out what to do about my situation."

Ben nodded, his expression knowing. "I understand the circumstances are not ideal, but without you, Caleb would have been gone the second we buried his mother. Probably for good."

It wasn't her place to ask, but... "Why?"

A heavy sigh escaped him. One loaded with so many layers Gia couldn't even begin to decipher.

"My wife wanted our children to follow the traditional ways. Lillie—Caleb's mother—rebelled. She wanted more than the life we could offer. They fought constantly—but the bond between them never broke until my wife died. Something in Lillie died that day as well. She took our grandson. Moved to Phoenix with Caleb's father. Cut all ties."

Pain lined the older man's face. "Caleb believes we abandoned them. The truth is more complicated."

Gia's heart twisted.

No wonder Caleb carried such deep wounds. So did the man seated beside her.

"How do you think I can help?" she asked quietly.

A sly smile lit the president's eyes. "I haven't had the opportunity to visit your home since you settled in. I have some free time this evening."

Her brows drew together.

Ben elaborated, his voice mild. "Perhaps I'll get lucky, and you'll have a visitor when I arrive?"

Ahhh. Understanding dawned.

Gia made a quick mental inventory of the contents of her cupboards and fridge.

"Dinner? I make a mean lasagna."

"Seven p.m.?" Ben rose. "What may I bring?"

Gia stood as well. "Just yourself. I'll make sure I have everything else."

Including your grandson.

He nodded, looking pleased. As he reached for the door, he paused. Looked back.

"The day before you came to us, a dragonfly visited my yard. A Western Red Damsel. They're found near water, so the sighting was unusual. I took it as a sign and told it my wishes."

She had no clue where this was going, so she kept silent.

Ben patted her shoulder. "More tradition. I believe Caleb is ready to hear the truth about why he's been apart from his people all these years."

"I hope you're right," Gia whispered.

She knew what it felt like to be estranged from family. Even if the reasons were valid, it left a piece of your soul missing. The least she could do was facilitate a meeting that, with any luck, would lead to reconciliation between Caleb and his family.

"We'll see you tonight," she added.

After he left, she found Jennie tapping away at a nurse's station computer. "Has Caleb come out of the conference room yet?"

"Not that I've seen." Jennie glanced up. "Why?"

"Good."

Jennie's eyes narrowed. "You don't want him to know his grandfather was here."

"It's complicated."

If Caleb knew, he'd ask why. He wouldn't like the answer, and she didn't want to lie.

Her life was already a series of lies and she was tired of it.

"Here." Jennie lifted a file folder. "Last patient."

Gia glanced at the clock. *Four-thirty*. "I'm heading out after I see—" she took the folder, glanced inside—"Mister Shirley."

"Hot date?"

"I've got lasagna to make."

"For Caleb?"

Gia leaned in and whispered, "And President Blackwater."

Jennie's laugh bubbled up. "Let me guess—Caleb doesn't know that part?"

"I hope I'm not making a mistake by getting into the middle of this family feud."

Jennie squeezed her hand. "For what it's worth, I think you're doing the right thing." She smiled. "Caleb's Diné. He needs to know his family."

Caleb drove Gia home in silence.

The winter sun dipped toward the western horizon, the shadows growing longer and the moon showing promise of the radiant glow it would give off once the sun took its final bow for the night.

He kept a sharp eye on the road—wildlife and errant livestock were a constant hazard—but he kept just as close an eye on Gia, sitting stiffly beside him, hands folded tight in her lap.

Something happened earlier that had her skittish, but when he'd asked, he'd gotten a breezy smile and a non-answer that set his teeth on edge.

A glint of light flared in the rearview mirror—too bright, too close.

Gia's posture snapped even straighter.

Glancing at the speedometer, Caleb noted their pace. The car behind them had to be doing at least seventy—gaining fast. Slowing the Jeep to forty-five, he eyed the glove compartment where he'd stashed his weapon.

With a roar, the other vehicle veered into the opposite lane, surged past them, and vanished over the next hill.

Beside him, Gia's shoulders sagged with a long exhale.

"Something wrong?" he asked casually. Just to see what she'd say.

"No."

Lie.

Her body language screamed otherwise.

He waited a beat, then said, "Does Jennie know the truth?"

She paled. "The truth?" Her throat worked. "About what?"

Another dodge.

He took his eyes off the road long enough to pin her with a look. "About who's after you. And why."

Because she hadn't told him everything. His intuition rarely let him down.

She turned to stare out the window. "I told her my ex sent those men to harass me."

Caleb ground his molars together. Her vulnerability yanked hard on his protective instincts. He admired her compassion, her internal strength in the face of fear.

But if Manuel Ortega and the young punk with him had ties to Espina Negra, where exactly did Gia's "ex" fit into the picture?

He pulled up in front of her house, where a Navajo Nation Police cruiser sat parked in the street, the silhouette of a female officer visible inside.

"That's Naveah, my neighbor," Gia said.

"Good." Zach had come through.

"Caleb..." Gia licked her lips, and suddenly, that was all he could focus on.

Pink tongue, full lips.

He really did like that color she wore.

"...dinner. As a thank you. For all your help."

"What?" He'd missed something.

Her cheeks flushed. "I said I'd like to make you dinner. I make a really good lasagna—family recipe. It's better than hotel food and..." she shrugged awkwardly. "I feel like I owe you."

"You don't owe me anything."

But he wasn't about to turn down a home cooked meal—especially Italian. Or more time around her.

There were still too many questions he needed answered.

Gia reached for the door handle.

He caught her wrist before she could bolt.

She froze, a sharp inhale raking his ears.

Shit. He let go immediately. "I'm sorry." The last thing he needed was to scare her when he was trying to earn her trust. "What time?"

"Time?" she echoed.

"Dinner."

"Oh. Six-thirty?"

"I'll be here."

Relief brightened her face. "Thank you for bringing me home," she murmured.

He watched her until she disappeared inside, then waved at the officer and drove away.

Gia had been afraid he'd say no to a meal?

You need to work on your people skills.

On the drive back to the hotel, he called Nathan. "Tell me you have the information I asked for."

"I do," Nathan drawled. "Was gonna call you earlier but I got stuck working a security system retrofit for a client."

His tone sharpened to a deadly edge. "Vincente Garcia's shiny on the outside, but under the hood? Rotten. Reminds me of Jules Mirga."

Caleb's hands tightened on the wheel.

Mirga—the Parisian crime lord who nearly made Nathan's fiancée, Emily, a victim of his sex trafficking ring.

Nathan continued, "Guy operates some legit businesses in Miami. Runs with the celebrity crowd. Works hard to keep certain family connections out of the press—uses his mother's maiden name, Garcia. She's a prominent figure in the Cuban community—best buds with the mayor."

Dread curdled in Caleb's gut. "What family connections?"

"Our boy's Miami-Dade birth certificate lists his full name as Vincente Lopez Garcia. His daddy is Diego Lopez Becerra. Also known as *El Víbora*—head of the Espina Negra cartel."

Air rushed from Caleb's lungs like he'd taken a punch straight to the solar plexus.

Everything made sense now.

Nathan kept going. "*El Víbora* runs the cartel from a heavily guarded compound in northwest Mexico, along with his brother Ramón. Rumor has it Vincente heads up the cartel's US fentanyl trafficking operation, but the guy's like Teflon—nothing sticks. DEA got an agent inside his Miami nightclub, but the man went missing a couple months ago. Hasn't been seen or heard from since."

Gia's ex-fiancé was Espina Negra royalty. Head of their US fentanyl trafficking operation.

The man ultimately responsible for his mother's death.

Son of a bitch.

"What about Doctor Barone?" His voice came out a rasp.

He forced the emotions down. Focused.

"Even more interesting. You sure you got the name right?"

His chest tightened. "Gianna Barone. That's what she told me."

"There is no Gianna Barone, doctor or otherwise, in Miami. Closest matches were a few social media profiles. None seemed a good fit, but you didn't give me much to go on, so I'm sending those leads to you."

Caleb's phone dinged. He pulled over to the side of the road and opened the file Nathan sent him. Photos of three different Gianna Barones. "None of these are my Gianna."

Heavy silence filled the Jeep's interior.

Shit.

After a moment, Nathan responded. "Didn't think so. You said you thought Doctor Barone was from New York. So, here's where it gets interesting. I found a Gianna Barone from Brooklyn. Age lines up. Father was mobbed up. Doing life for multiple hits. Mother divorced him, remarried inside the family if you know what I mean. At age eighteen, Gianna Barone disappeared."

Caleb's fingers flexed around his phone. "What do you mean, she disappeared?"

"Just that. She dropped off the grid. No addresses, no employment, credit records, death certificate. Nada. But funny thing—same year Abigail Winters pops up. Attended college and med school in New York. Did her residency in Miami."

"Family?"

"Martin and Rachel Winters. Upper East Side. Died in a car accident when Abigail Winters would've been eighteen. No children mentioned in the obituary."

A beat of silence crackled over the line.

"I did a little digging," Nathan went on. "Turns out they had one child—a daughter. Died of SIDS at three months old. Any guesses what her name was?"

"Abigail."

"Bingo. You sure are smart for an Army guy."

Caleb couldn't even muster up a half-hearted fuck you. "Do you have a photograph of this Abigail Winters?"

"I can do you one better." Nathan's amusement faded. "The photo is from Miami's society pages. Guess who Doctor Winters is pictured with?"

"Vincente Lopez Garcia."

"Give the man a cookie."

Caleb's phone dinged again.

In the new photo, Gia—no, Abigail—wore a red gown that molded to every tempting curve. Diamonds glittered on her ears. Her hair had been straightened and hung over her shoulders like liquid night.

Next to her was a good-looking, dark-haired man in his thirties. *El Víbora's* son, Vincente, stood in a custom black tuxedo, his hand possessively at her waist.

"Is that your Doctor Barone?" Nathan asked. "She's a looker."

"Yeah."

She *was* a beauty.

She was also a liar.

CHAPTER TWELVE

"THIS IS THE SECOND major shipment lost to the Americans this month." Diego Lopez Becerra—*El Víbora*—glared at his son through a sixty-five-inch monitor in the secure room of Vincente's Miami Beach nightclub, Club Turquesa. The other monitors in the room displayed real-time feeds from the security cameras throughout the club.

"*Papi*, the DEA and Homeland Security are cracking down." Vincente kept his voice level. In the background, the main dance floor's thumping bass pulsed, although the pale gray acoustic panels lining the walls kept most of the club noise out.

He sat at the long oval table of smoked glass and brushed steel. "Border crossings are up. Precursor chemical shipments from China are under scrutiny. They're sending a message."

"Where are your informants? What are they doing besides collecting large sums of money from us?"

Pain stabbed behind Vincente's eye. "Tío Ramón killed one of my informants, remember?" He massaged the burn in his chest and leaned back into his sculpted white leather chair. If he'd known he'd be dealing with his father tonight, he'd have skipped the heavy meal and the whiskey.

"Maybe my brother did what you should have, no?" Diego's silver-threaded black hair glinted in the Baja California sun as he reclined on a chaise in nothing but a Speedo. "Maybe you should spend less time partying and more time running our business."

Vincente bit back a retort, waiting until the scantily clad woman—his father's latest mistress—handed him a tequila cocktail and retreated from view. "Tío Ramón overstepped. He interfered in my territory. I've grown this product line by over sixty percent in the US. *Sixty percent!*"

His uncle never missed a chance to undermine him. His father might be the Viper, but the real snake in the family was Ramón.

Diego waved a dismissive hand. "Yes, yes. With your fancy degree. But sometimes, a man must get his hands dirty."

"I have," Vincente ground out. "Or have you forgotten what I had to do a few months ago."

It had cost him Abigail.

No. Not Abigail. Gianna. His lover hadn't been who he thought she was, either.

Gianna Barone. He liked the sound of the unfamiliar name on his tongue.

After the sighting in Gallup, Juan's private investigator finally unearthed some interesting information about the woman Vincente had known as Abigail Winters. She'd taken a job on an Indian reservation under a different name—her real name, as it turned out.

No fancy pedigree. Just the daughter of a mafioso.

And she'd turned her back on her family.

His Gianna liked pretty things. Hadn't he treated her like a princess? Given what he knew of her background now, she should have understood his world. He'd trusted her enough to show her a glimpse of his reality—and she'd run.

At least she hadn't gone to the police. It was the only reason she still breathed.

"Ramón tells me your woman was spotted in Gallup." Diego's words rang with an almost sadistic glee. "Have you dealt with her yet?"

Damn Tío Ramón and his spies.

"She hasn't gone to the police, *Papi.* I know where she is. I'm handling it."

"Hmm, like you're handling your new distributor?" Diego's tone sharpened. "I hear the Aztec Kings are talking to Los Coyotes. They want our territory."

Vincente kept his face blank, but not before a flicker of triumph in his father's eyes told him he hadn't hidden his surprise quickly enough. Juan had informed him only yesterday of a rumored meeting between the Kings and a middleman for Los Coyotes.

"Maybe it's time you visit the Southwest." Diego's voice hardened. "Take care of both problems personally, *hijo.* Or I'll let Ramón handle them for you."

The screen went black.

Vincente exhaled heavily. Sparring with his father had only gotten worse since Gianna's disappearance. Rising from his chair, he crossed to the glass-and-steel bar console, stocked with fine liquors and imported Cuban cigars, all tucked beneath a climate-controlled humidor. From the crystal decanter on the bar tray, he poured two fingers of whiskey.

Amber liquid caught the light as it sloshed against the sides, the glass cool and heavy in his hand. The tremble in his fingers was a small betrayal he couldn't afford. Not with Juan watching.

"Your father enjoys meddling in my business."

Juan stepped away from the wall, arms folded. "As he meddled in mine. Let my Carlita die in a raid just to prove I wasn't ready for more responsibility."

"Which is why you came to me." Vincente downed his whiskey in one swallow, the harsh burn spreading to his chest. "Someone in our crew reports to Ramón. Find our spy and deal with them."

He locked eyes with his cousin and closest confidant. "Your father and I will come to blows eventually. You know this."

"You promised me a future. Loyalty." Juan's hand swiped across his mouth. "My father gave me neither."

"Good." Vincente slapped his cousin's back. "Let's go home."

But Juan moved to block the door, one hand braced against the frame. "My father's not known for his patience. He's positioning himself. If he convinces *El Víbora* you've lost control—"

"I haven't," Vincente snapped. The burn in his chest intensified.

Instead of responding, Juan shrugged. "Then do as your father suggested. Visit the Aztec Kings. Show him you're still in control."

Heat flared at the tips of Vincente's ears. "You think I look weak."

"No, primo." Juan gripped his shoulder. "My father is trying to make you look weak and you must not let him. Handle the Aztec Kings. Retrieve Abigail yourself."

"Not Abigail—Gianna," Vincente corrected. "Any news?"

Juan hesitated.

Vincente stilled. "What is it?"

"The man who interfered the other night? He tracked Matteo and Emilio to their hotel. Was waiting for them. He had a message for you. *Leave the woman alone, or deal with me.*"

Vincente blinked, then gave a sharp laugh. "Who is this man who threatens me?"

A dark, possessive emotion coiled inside his chest. Was Gianna fucking him?

She'd regret it if she was. No one touched what was his.

"He's either very brave or very foolish."

Juan shrugged. "His name is Caleb Varella. His father worked for Espina Negra before he was killed. Matteo kept in touch with the wife. Kept her quiet. Said she talked about her son—the Green Beret."

Green Beret?

A soldier. Skilled. Maybe even for sale. If he was anything like his father, the answer was probably yes.

It also was possible this Green Beret had ties to Los Coyotes, and his involvement with Gianna was just a distraction—a cover for a deeper betrayal inside Espina Negra's territory.

Vincente pinched the bridge of his nose as a headache loomed. "A dangerous man whose loyalties we don't know is a threat."

Juan gave a silent nod.

"Tell your men to deal with this Caleb Varella." Vincente's voice iced. "Permanently."

CHAPTER THIRTEEN

FIRST, MEAT SAUCE—DARK RED and heavy with garlic, the scent rising with each spoonful. Then noodles. More meat sauce. Then béchamel, pale and silky, the scent of nutmeg just barely rising as it hit the warm pan.

Gia repeated the layers with steady hands, though her chest felt tight. The rhythm helped. She'd been on edge all afternoon, every hour ticking closer to tonight.

A chill crept across her skin. How would Caleb react when his grandfather showed up?

Shredded mozzarella fell from her fingers, the cold white strands drifting like snow. The undercurrents at Lillie Blackwater Varella's funeral hadn't just been about grief.

The empty mozzarella bag crinkled in her hand as she tossed it aside and reached for the dollar-store grater, fingers closing around its flimsy plastic grip. Warm air carried the sharp scent of parmesan as she worked the wedge into a small mound, each movement precise, controlled—because everything else felt anything but.

Despite Caleb's belief, she couldn't reconcile Ben Blackwater—who had welcomed a stranger in need into his community—as a man who would abandon a daughter and grandson.

There was more to the story. Had to be.

The plastic handle snapped beneath her grip.

"Crap." She stared at her handiwork in disgust. Too much pressure and it snapped. Broken beyond repair.

Kind of like her life.

The shards hit the trash with a hollow clatter. She scattered parmesan across the top of the lasagna and slid the pan into the oven. Despite her mess of a past, she recognized Caleb's goodness. And Ben's. And Zach's.

Whatever had torn this family apart could be mended.

She could help. One last gift before she had to leave—a thank you for all they'd done for her. For how welcoming they'd been.

If the medical clinic offered her a permanent position once her contract was up, she'd gladly stay and make this her home. Despite the hardships, this was a true community—people who looked out for one another. A part of her envied that. Wanted to belong.

But it would never happen. Because Vincente would never let her go.

Her nerves jangled. Not for the first time, she wished for a glass of wine. Or two. But she followed the rules of the rez and kept no alcohol in the house. She'd had to find healthier ways to cope—ways that didn't involve drowning fear and guilt in a bottle.

Wiping her hands on a kitchen towel, she glanced at the clock and hustled to the bathroom to freshen up. The makeup she'd applied before work had long since vanished. She cleaned her face. Added foundation. Blush. Smoky eye shadow that accentuated the blue of her irises. Kohl liner and two coats of mascara.

Armor.

She had a feeling she'd need it tonight.

A swipe of fiery red lipstick.

Done.

Her Miami face stared back from the mirror.

She shuddered, her stomach cramping.

Without another thought, she smeared on cleansing balm and scrubbed. Each stinging swipe of the washcloth, punishment. When she finished, she applied a sheer layer of tinted moisturizer to mute the redness.

A swipe of lip gloss. That was enough.

With a final mirror check, she brushed out her hair until it gleamed, changed into jeans and a blue knit top, then went to check on the lasagna.

Her doorbell rang. Six-thirty on the dot.

She wiped sweaty palms on the kitchen towel and opened the door.

Caleb stood on the steps. He'd swapped out his black trousers for jeans. His white button down opened at the collar beneath the black suit coat he'd worn to his mother's funeral. Gia mapped the firm line of his clean-shaven jaw, the strong tanned column of his throat, his broad chest—and the bouquet of yellow, orange, and purple flowers in his hand.

"These are for you." He thrust them at her, then dropped his gaze to his boots, hands shoved into his pockets.

She barely hid a grin. *How sweet.*

"Thank you. They're lovely." She stepped aside to let him in.

Vincente used to flood her with flowers—orchids, lilies, and roses delivered daily. Their sweet, overpowering scent still haunted her dreams.

These flowers were different. Desert blooms. She didn't know their names, but had seen them growing wild in the area.

Caleb smelled like clean skin and sandalwood and spice. More intoxicating than the wine she'd been longing for.

Her body flooded with warmth. She buried her nose in the flowers, to hide the flush heating her cheeks. They carried a faint perfume of orange blossom and—she sniffed the spike of vibrant purple blossoms with yellow and white markings—grape soda?

"I'll put these in water." Rooting through her cabinet, she found a tall plastic lemonade cup from the Navajo Nation Fair, filled it with water, and placed the flowers on the table.

He bent to peer through the oven glass door. "Looks and smells incredible."

She caught herself admiring the taut muscles of his backside. "My mother said it was her lasagna that had men lining up to marry her."

Too bad her choice of men sucked.

Gia's hadn't been any better.

He glanced over his shoulder. Caught her staring. Straightened. "Don't look at me like that."

That sexy rasp in his voice was new, but it carried a trace of anger she didn't understand. Even so, it sent heat skittering through her body. Her bra felt too tight, her skin too sensitive.

She couldn't stay here as much as she wanted to. Vincente would find her again, and she'd be forced to run.

Again.

But if she couldn't escape, why couldn't she at least have the memory of another man's arms around her to keep as a treasured secret? Arms that would make her feel protected instead of used.

Just once.

She stepped closer. Close enough for the heat of his body to brush her skin. Close enough to see his pupils darken, and his jaw go rigid.

"Please."

The word slipped out. Desperate. Her breath hitched. Her face caught fire.

His gaze dropped to her lips, and for a heartbeat, she thought he might kiss her, even as his fingers curled into his palms.

"Gia, there's—"

His head jerked. "Someone's here." His voice hardened as he crossed to the window and peered through the blinds.

Where had the gun come from?

"Wait!" Panic surged in her chest. "It's—"

"My grandfather." Caleb holstered his weapon, his scowl sharp as a blade.

Her stomach dropped. *Please let me have done the right thing.*

He yanked open the door.

President Blackwater's lead security agent met him with a flat stare and held out his hand. "Weapon."

"I'm not going to shoot my own grandfather."

Gia bit her lip. The snarl in Caleb's voice probably didn't help his case.

"Are you licensed to carry?"

"I do the same job as you. Of course I'm licensed."

The bodyguard merely lifted a brow. "On Navajo Nation land?"

"Joseph." Ben Blackwater waved the man off and climbed the steps. "I'm confident my grandson won't abuse the privilege."

He smiled at Gia. "I thought I'd check in on our newest doctor."

"What a lovely surprise," Caleb said, voice dry as desert dust.

He stepped aside. "Gia's made lasagna."

She'd set him up.

The knowledge sank like lead in Caleb's gut.

Gia avoided his gaze, hurrying to set the table.

For three.

Pretty little liar.

He cursed himself for the flowers—an impulse buy he should've known better than to make. And for the nerves that hit the moment she opened the door in those designer jeans and a knit top the same deep blue as her eyes. Her hair spilled around her shoulders, the ends brushing the upper curves of her breasts.

Lust had gut-punched him hard enough to make his hands shake.

He'd fought for control. Until he caught her staring. Then she'd said please in that sexy, throaty voice.

He didn't stop to think about all the reasons he couldn't trust her—his body responded to the unspoken invitation.

Hell, he ought to thank his grandfather for the interruption. Another minute, and he'd have been in Gia Barone's bed, making her scream his name while cursing himself for letting desire overrule every ounce of judgement he had left.

This would've been a good time for that whiskey he had the other night. He could almost feel the harsh burn of it down the back of his throat. The fire in his chest. Instead, Caleb poured three glasses of water and put them on the table.

He thought back to his earlier conversation with Nathan. Gianna Barone was an accomplished liar, and he wasn't leaving here tonight until he knew everything about her. He watched her slice the lasagna and plate it with quiet precision.

Or was Abigail Winters who she really was, buried beneath all the layers?

He carried the plates to the table.

Still... the fear in her eyes when he mentioned her past had been real. And the way she'd looked at him tonight hadn't felt like a lie.

The longing in her voice when she whispered that single word *please*.

It shouldn't matter.

But it did.

His grandfather waited for Gia to sit, then took a seat while his security detail faded into the background, as they'd been trained to do.

As Caleb was trained to do.

Only now, he was front and center. The main attraction.

He took the chair next to Gia. What to do about her would have to wait until this charade was over.

"Let us give thanks," Ben said.

Caleb sat with his head bowed, silent through his grandfather's blessing. As a boy in Phoenix, he'd prayed his grandfather would come for them. Bring them home. But he never did.

When his grandfather finished, Caleb dug into his meal. A perfect blend of cheeses, firm but supple pasta, and meat sauce with a symphony of spices lit up his taste buds.

Damn. He swallowed and tried not to fork the rest down like he was scarfing an MRE on patrol.

"This is excellent," Ben said, complimenting Gia.

"It is," Caleb added.

A flush of pleasure colored her cheeks. "Thank you. It's an old family recipe."

Family.

The pasta turned to ash on Caleb's tongue. "A Winters family recipe?" he asked bringing the water glass to his lips.

Gia's fork landed on her plate with a loud clank, her face pale.

He grimaced. That was a dick move.

But she'd lied. Manipulated him. Then she'd gone behind his back with this quaint family gathering he had no interest in.

And worst of all?

He still wanted her.

Tension rolled over the table like a heavy mist.

Ben's brows knit as he glanced between them. "I came with an offer for Gia. The clinic has a full-time position available when your contract ends."

Surprise flickered across Gia's face, followed by a flash of happiness so pure it nearly blinded Caleb.

Then came the crash. Her expression shuttered like someone had blown out a candle. "I'm honored—and I'd love to stay," she said quietly. "But I can't."

"Because of the man you left?" Ben asked gently.

"It's not safe."

"We'll make it safe," Caleb said.

He shut his eyes as the realization of what he'd just committed to hit him.

But it made sense. She needed to be rid of Vincente Lopez if she was ever going to live in peace, and he wanted justice for his mother.

He could help her and himself at the same time.

She turned to him, startled. Wary. But a flicker of hope lit her eyes.

One that had him rubbing his chest as guilt burned a hole in his esophagus.

She didn't know what he wanted in return.

A smile hovered on Ben's lips, as if everything had turned in his favor. "Grandson, this job protecting others fulfills you?"

"Yes," Caleb said, guarded. Where was this going?

"Your cousin feels the same way. Only he chose to return home after his time in the Marine Corps."

Was that a hint of censure in the old man's tone? A slow, decades old resentment writhed behind Caleb's ribs. "Zach's family didn't shun him."

Ben's sigh was weary. "We never shunned you or your mother. I tried for years to get her to come home and bring you with her. She refused."

It was on the tip of Caleb's tongue to call his grandfather a liar. "My mother died believing her family abandoned her."

Pain briefly seared Ben's eyes. "You and my daughter were always welcome. Wanted. It was your father I wouldn't welcome."

He glanced at Gia, then back at Caleb. "Perhaps you would prefer we have this conversation in private."

Bitter memories of Caleb's childhood—of his mother's pain—closed in fast. He wasn't in the mood to be the polite dinner guest and wipe away unpleasantries with his napkin.

"Gia can hear whatever it is you have to say." His grandfather took a slow sip of his water. "Very well," he said, his voice low. "I apologize for speaking ill of your father."

"No need to sugar-coat your opinion. He was a bastard."

Resentment simmered beneath Caleb's words. "But he's been dead for years. Where have you been? Mom needed you."

Pressure built in his hand—unnoticed until pain flared in his fingers. He glanced down. The fork was bent, metal warped from the force of his grip.

Jaw tight, he set it aside.

"Who do you think paid for your mother to receive treatment when you were in high school? And again, while you were deployed?" Ben pushed aside his plate and steepled his fingers. "It was the only help she would accept, and only because she didn't want you to get a message while you were overseas that your mother was dead."

Caleb shook his head. "If what you say is true, then why did she tell me you abandoned us?"

Despite her struggles, Caleb's mother had never lied to him.

At least he hadn't thought so.

"That, I can't answer, Grandson." Ben placed his napkin on the table and stood. "But I can show you this." He reached into his suit coat and withdrew folded papers, which he handed to Caleb.

Caleb hesitated, then accepted the documents. Rehab admission forms for a facility in Phoenix. His mother's name. Payment records. Benjamin Blackwater listed as the responsible party.

What the hell? Why hadn't he known about this?

Why hadn't his mother told him?

He handed the papers back to his grandfather without a word, unsure of what to say.

Ben placed a hand on Caleb's shoulder.

Caleb stiffened.

"You've always been in my heart," Ben said. "So was your mother. All I ask is that you consider the possibility that what you believe...isn't the whole truth."

He turned to Gia. "Thank you for the meal. It was an honor."

"I will think about the offer," she said softly. "You accepted me into this community when I had nowhere else to go. I won't forget that."

"You belong here." Ben patted her on the cheek, then cast another long look at Caleb. "Both of you do."

Belong? His grandfather dangled belonging in his face like bait on a hook.

What would it feel like to have a family? Roots? A place to call home that meant more than where he rested his head at night?

He told himself it didn't matter. But deep down, the boy who'd once played with his cousin, ate his grandmother's corn cakes, and looked up to his stern but loving grandfather knew the truth.

It mattered more than he wanted to admit.

And now, with everything shifting under his feet, he couldn't help but wonder what else he didn't know.

What had been kept from him.

What Gia hadn't told him.

Something cold coiled in his chest.

It wasn't just the past he couldn't trust.

It was the present.

CHAPTER FOURTEEN

THE DOOR CLOSED BEHIND Ben Blackwater and his security detail with the finality of prison bars, leaving Gia trapped in the silence that followed.

She'd felt the change—a subtle shift in the air, the kind of stillness that came before a storm.

Had been expecting it, ever since Caleb had asked if her lasagna was a *Winters* family recipe.

Winters.

Only sheer force of will had kept her rooted in her chair through the rest of the meal. That, and the fact that the conversation between Caleb and his grandfather had grown deeply personal and tense, shifting the spotlight away from her.

"We need to talk." His voice came from behind her, low and tight.

And beneath it...betrayal.

She steeled herself and turned. The eyes that had stared at her earlier—dark, hungry—were now flat and cold.

His stare cut through her. "Or should I say, Abigail?"

Her breath caught. The lightness in her chest turned jagged, pressing against her ribs like glass.

Abigail? I don't know who you're talking about. The lie hovered, instinctive.

But it was too late for that.

"You've been researching me." She barely heard her own words over the rush in her ears.

"Yes."

Of course he had. She'd given away too much—Vincente's name. Miami. All it would take was one image search on the Internet.

A weary sigh hissed from her lungs. Defeat. "What do you want to know?"

Caleb stood rigid, arms crossed, his jaw flexing with restrained fury. "Everything."

She needed something for her hands to do while she considered what to say.

Giving him her back, she walked past the dining table—past the brightly colored flowers he'd brought. False hope that her evening would be a memory to cherish instead of the nightmare it was becoming. In the kitchen, she pulled the coffee can from the fridge and held it up in silent question.

He gave a curt nod.

She filled the glass carafe with unsteady hands, spooned in the grounds, and started the brew cycle. The machine hissed, dark brown liquid entering the carafe in a slow, steady stream.

How much could she tell him? How much did he already know?

When the coffee was ready, she poured two mugs, passed him one, and curled up on the couch, her grip on the mug a lifeline.

Caleb set a dining room chair across from her—not too close. His mug sat untouched.

She couldn't tell him everything, but she could be truthful about herself. "Gianna Barone is my real name," she said. "I grew up in Brooklyn. My father was a hitman. When I was fifteen, he went to prison for murder." A sour film coated the inside of her mouth. "Murders. Plural. My mother divorced him and quickly picked up a new husband. One with a wandering eye."

Gia paused. Took a sip of coffee to calm her nerves. "Unfortunately, it wandered in my direction."

Caleb's low growl cut through the quiet.

She gave him a grateful smile. He might be angry, but his protective instincts ran deep. That mattered.

"When I turned eighteen, I leaned on some of my father's old connections to create a new identity."

"To escape your family." Caleb nodded as if he understood.

Given what she now knew of his family history, maybe he did.

"Escape my family. My lower-class, criminal existence." She took another sip. "I worked, went to college, studied everything about my classmates who came from money—how they spoke, behaved, their hobbies, where they ate—everything. When I graduated from medical school, I *was* Abigail Winters from the Upper East Side of Manhattan."

He leaned forward, elbows on his knees. "You put yourself through school and became a doctor. That's something."

She laughed, the sound brittle. "And then I fell for someone worse than the people I left behind. Only he disguised it with pretty words and expensive gifts."

Shame burned a hole in her stomach. She set down her mug, her gaze fixed on her hands rather than see the disgust on Caleb's face. "He made me feel chosen. For a while at least. Until I realized what living in Vincente's world meant."

Caleb's voice gentled. "What did it mean?"

It had meant blood on a pristine white boat deck. A lifeless gaze frozen in fear. Her lover's cold, dark eyes when he told her, calmly, that he'd had no choice.

She gathered her mug and took it to the sink. Motion to ground her and shatter the waking nightmare.

A shiver ran up her spine—her only sign Caleb had followed.

"You can't keep running." His voice was still soft, but a cold, deadly note had crept in. "Your ex is the son of Espina Negra's leader. That changes everything."

The mug slipped from her nerveless fingers. Porcelain shattered in the sink.

Caleb muttered a curse. His hand landed on her hip, spinning her to face him. This close, sandalwood and spice wrapped around her. His broad chest and shoulders blotted out everything else.

She licked parched lips. Stared at the tanned column of his throat instead of his eyes. "I guess I shouldn't be surprised."

"You should have told me the truth from the beginning."

No. Not when it was the only thing keeping her alive. The only leverage she had.

"I didn't want you involved. Vincente is dangerous."

His fingers tightened, eyes blazing. "He's the one bringing in the fentanyl that killed my mother."

Gia's knees buckled. The force of his pain—raw and unfiltered—hit her like a blow.

"I'm sorry," she whispered. "I'm so sorry."

His body thrummed, rage held barely in check. He caged her against the counter. "Why does he want you back so badly."

"I told you, he's possessive."

"There's more to it."

He didn't know what he asked of her.

She shook her head.

Caleb released her and stepped back, hands lifted as if only now realizing he'd touched her. "I need your help to bring him down. It's the only way you'll ever be free."

"You'll never be able to touch him in Miami. Don't you think the police have tried?"

It's why she'd abandoned her life and run. There would be no justice. Espina Negra's pockets were too deep, their tentacles everywhere.

"I'm not going after him in Miami. I want him to come here."

Her pulse skipped. "How would you get him here?"

As soon as the words left her mouth, she knew.

"Me. You want him to come for me." Her flat tone matched the pain knifing her heart.

Which was silly. She hadn't known this man long enough to let him breach her defenses.

To assume he was different from the other men she'd known.

Her protector was gone. In his place stood the Green Beret—the steely-eyed soldier with a mission of revenge—and she was a means to an end.

A casualty of his personal war.

Numbness crept in. She welcomed it. "You don't know what you're asking of me." Her flat tone matched her insides.

If Vincente found out she'd told anyone what she'd witnessed—what he'd done—she wouldn't survive. And neither would they. She refused to be responsible for another death.

He dragged his fingers through his hair, a plea in his eyes. "Then tell me."

"I'm sorry about your mother." Sadness, the weight of it rife with a thousand regrets, crushed her chest.

Maybe she couldn't stay after all. Not even to fulfill her contract. Her work on the reservation was the first time she'd put the welfare of others ahead of herself, and she liked the feeling. It was as if she'd been breathing pollution her entire life and the clean, desert air stripped away layers of the persona she'd created in Abigail Winters so her true identity could emerge from hiding.

Caleb exhaled a rough breath. He paced the room, then stopped in front of her. "I'll set you up somewhere safe until Lopez is no longer a threat."

Confusion furrowed her brows as she looked up. "Even if I can't help you?"

His gaze turned unreadable. "I won't hold your safety over your head to get you to cooperate."

Don't cry was all she could think, even as her vision blurred.

"Thank you." She reached out, her palm flat on his chest, feeling his heartbeat—strong and steady. His warmth seeped into her chilled skin. "You're a good man, Caleb Varella."

His expression shuttered. "Am I?"

He stepped back, and the air between them turned cold. "You work tomorrow?"

She gave a mute nod.

"I'll pick you up in the morning."

The door closed behind him, the silence left behind pressing against Gia's ribs like a phantom hand, squeezing the breath from her lungs.

The next morning, dawn spilled across the hills to the east, chasing away the darkness and setting the rocks ablaze in a fiery orange glow that contrasted with the icy wind in the air. Caleb checked his GPS, then turned off the main road north of Fort Defiance onto a narrow dirt track that led to his cousin's home.

A hogan came into view, Zach's police cruiser and a sleek black Dodge Charger with red rims and red upholstery parked beside it. Caleb got out of the Jeep, surveying the octagonal structure—stained log siding, asphalt shingles, a stovepipe curling smoke into the frigid air from the center of the conical roof. The hogan's door faced east to welcome the day. The traditional way.

He snapped a photo of the Charger and sent it to his colleague, Danny Mayhew. Danny had been a Navy SEAL—DEVGRU—under Nathan Long. Nicknamed Chaos for his role as the team breacher. Caleb had known his background when Danny hired onto Dìleas. The nickname he'd learned over beers one night.

Danny was also a motor head. He babied his blue Ford Mustang GT when he wasn't breaking the speed limit on the DC Beltway. He'd even given the damn car a name, after some woman he once met in a San Diego bar who, in Danny's words, was "built like a high-performance machine."

Caleb texted:

> *How does this compare to Consuela?*

Before he could knock on the hogan's door, it opened. Heat spilled into the cold as the scent of wood smoke wrapped around him, stirring memories of tribal gatherings from his childhood.

Zach stood barefoot and shirtless, sweatpants low on his hips, a flicker of surprise in his eyes. "*Yá'át'ééh*, Cousin. Come in."

Caleb stepped inside and shrugged off his leather jacket. The layout was traditional, but the interior contained modern amenities. He made a slow clockwise circuit—past a square pine dining table, a galley kitchen, a walled in bathroom, Zach's bed covered with a red and blue

Navajo wool blanket, and a brown cowhide sofa. At the open center, a black wood-burning stove radiated warmth.

"Nice place."

Zach chuckled. "I see you remember Grandmother's rules about entering a Diné home."

Caleb smiled faintly. He hadn't given it conscious thought. Patricia Blackwater had been determined to teach her grandchildren the old ways. "Maybe I'm afraid she'll come to me in a dream and scold me."

"Coffee?" Zach pointed to the percolator on the stove. "Mugs are top left cabinet."

"Thanks." Caleb draped his jacket over a chair and retrieved two mugs. "You want one?"

"*Ahéhee'*." Zach pulled on his uniform top and tied back his hair.

The percolator hissed. Caleb poured the coffee and handed over a mug.

"Oatmeal should be ready," Zach said. "Want some?"

As if on cue, Caleb's stomach growled. "If it's not too much trouble."

Zach scooped generous portions of creamy white porridge into two bowls and set one in front of Caleb with a spoon. "Did you come to tell me you were leaving?"

Caleb looked up, a retort on his lips, but paused at the twinkle in Zach's eyes.

Progress, of sorts. Yesterday, his cousin might have given him a police escort off the rez.

He quirked a brow and let his own amusement show. "Trying to get rid of me, Cousin?"

Zach sobered, his eyes taking on a distant quality. "Remember the year before Grandmother died—when Grandfather took us to the Navajo Fair?"

"I remember." Caleb's lips twitched. "We talked him into buying us cowboy hats, then tried roping sheep."

"We sucked at it." Zach chuckled. "But it was a good day."

"Until we ate too much fry bread and candy," Caleb reminded him. "We spent the night at their house on the floor with a bucket between us, whimpering like babies."

They shared a quiet laugh.

Caleb's chest tightened. Somehow, he'd buried those good memories.

Zach looked down at his bowl, then back up. "You should take time to reconnect with your people while you're here." He looked away, as if the display of sentiment embarrassed him. "What brings you to my home at sunrise?"

Caleb set down his spoon. "I had my colleague at Dìleas dig into Gia's ex." He paused. "And Gia."

A muscle twitched in Zach's jaw, a silent protest building. "And?"

"Her ex is Vincente Lopez. Son of *El Víbora*. Head of the Espina Negra cartel."

Zach blew out a harsh breath. "Hell."

Caleb shifted, the oatmeal sitting heavy in his stomach. "Yeah. She's not the innocent we thought. But," he lifted a hand, "I'm not saying she isn't afraid. Or undeserving of protection."

His cousin wouldn't like what came next.

"There's more. I tracked down Manuel Ortega and his sidekick the other night."

Zach's mug hit the table, coffee sloshing over the rim. "What the hell were you thinking?"

The censure in Zach's voice hit a nerve, but Caleb deserved it.

"Espina Negra's using the Aztec Kings to expand their fentanyl distribution." His training emphasized being part of a unit. A team.

He'd let anger drive him—anger and grief. "Ortega knew my father. Might've given my mother the pills that killed her. Or he knows who did."

The memory of that call from Camila cut through him.

Caleb, I'm so sorry. Your mother...she's gone.

His hands curled into fists beneath the table. He shoved his emotions in a mental box and slammed the lid. What he was about to propose required a clear head.

He'd had all night to think about Gia's lies. About the lives Vincente Lopez destroyed as he lived the high life in Miami.

"We could deal a serious blow to the cartel if we take down Lopez." Even as the words left his mouth, his gut twisted.

A heavy silence blanketed the room.

Storm clouds gathered behind Zach's eyes. "How do you propose we do that?"

"He wants Gia back."

"Fuck." Zach shot to his feet. Circled the small space with restrained fury, then came back to face Caleb head on. "Is that all she is to you? A mission objective? You planning to use her as bait and hope she survives?"

"That's not fair." Caleb shot back, then winced at the defensiveness in his tone. "She'll never be safe until Lopez is in prison or dead. You know that."

Using Gia to draw out Lopez felt too damn close to crossing a line that would leave a permanent black mark on his soul. She'd already sacrificed so much simply to survive. If he lost sight of that, he was no better than the man she was running from.

He rubbed the tension in his neck. His argument was sound, even if it left a taste like ash in his mouth. "I can help her start over, but she'll always be running unless we stop him here, where we have the upper hand."

"Have you discussed this with Gia?"

"Yes." He should tell Zach everything—what Nathan had found, what Gia had confessed. But something held him back. "She's...hesitant."

More than hesitant. Terrified.

A slow tilt of Zach's head, and Caleb found himself pinned by a stare sharp enough to draw blood. "Why come to me?"

"She trusts you. Considers you a friend. Maybe she'll listen if you back me up."

Zach scoffed. "A friend." His jaw set. "What does she consider you?"

Caleb looked down, remembering Gia's soft lips, her whispered plea. The quiet betrayal in her eyes when she'd realized his plan. It had felt like a dagger to his heart.

And his conscience.

"Someone who won't be around long enough to matter."

The job in New York waited. And after that, the next job.

He carried his mug and bowl to the sink. "Thanks for breakfast."

At the door, Zach called after him, "I won't agree unless Gia does."

Caleb turned. "If she still wants to leave, I'll relocate her myself. Somewhere safe."

He'd be frustrated as hell, but he'd do it. As long as she didn't practice medicine, Nathan could bury her identity deep enough that not even the cartel would find her.

But at what cost? She'd never again be able to do what she clearly loved—use her medical skills to help people.

And he'd never see her again.

"And Grandfather?" Zach asked.

Caleb's spine stiffened. "Did you know he showed up for dinner at Gia's last night?" His mouth twisted. "Funny, I didn't get the memo he was coming when she invited me."

And what he'd shown Caleb. The rehab papers.

Caleb was still processing that.

"No. But he wants to know you." Zach held his stare. "Give him a chance."

A chance to be a family.

"Why did you never reach out to me after I left?" The question burst from Caleb, or rather the boy inside Caleb who'd missed his cousin desperately.

Surprise flared in Zach's eyes. "I did. I wrote you letters. Why didn't you ever respond?"

Caleb frowned. "I never got any letters. I wrote some to you, too."

"I never got them."

They stared at each other, the past an arroyo still too wide to jump over.

Caleb shook his head, a silent dismissal of a wound deeper than any he'd received in combat, and stepped outside.

Every answer only raised more questions—and distracted him from his new mission.

Bring down Vincente Lopez.

For that, he'd kiss his grandfather's ring if he had to.

But first, Gia had to say yes.

CHAPTER FIFTEEN

AFTER LEAVING ZACH'S, CALEB drove Gia to the clinic.

She hadn't said much—not since the night before, when he'd asked her to help take down Vincente Lopez and she'd refused.

He hadn't pushed. Not then.

The tension coiled between them like a live wire—charged with everything unspoken and too dangerous to touch.

She needed time. But he could only give her a day or two at most before he needed to act.

With or without her.

Still, dropping her off alone at the clinic left a knot in his chest he hadn't been able to shake.

He hit the road to Gallup, picked up a few changes of clothes, extra rounds of ammo, supplies to supplement the go-bag he'd brought from Phoenix.

By noon, he was headed back.

Back to Gia.

Three days had passed since his mother's funeral, yet the weight of everything that happened since made it feel like a lifetime ago—like the grief belonged to someone else. The dissociation was familiar. He'd felt the same shift during combat deployments. Missions didn't pause for mourning, other than a brief solemn acknowledgment before a rifle planted barrel-first into empty boots.

He checked the time in London and placed a call to Ryder Montague. His boss at Dìleas was the son of an earl who'd traded privilege for service, refined manners for a gun. He'd served in the British Special Air Service under Dìleas's president, Lachlan Mackay.

The UK double ring tone pulsed in Caleb's ear before Ryder picked up. "Back in DC, mate?"

"Not yet. I'm taking you up on that offer of more time." Casual. As if they were discussing the weather. "There's something I need to handle."

"This wouldn't have anything to do with the woman you asked Nathan to investigate?" Ryder's voice stayed calm, but Caleb caught the edge of concern. "He told me what he found."

"Doctor Barone might need relocation. A fresh start." Caleb hesitated. "She can't afford it, so I'll personally cover the cost."

Ryder made a dismissive sound. "We'll handle it. But if this is personal, Caleb, I need to know."

Shit yeah, it was personal, but he wasn't about to admit that to his boss when he couldn't even explain it to himself.

"I'm trying to do the right thing," he muttered. "Even with a new identity, she'll never be safe if Lopez isn't stopped."

Vincente Lopez Garcia. Cartel royalty. Power, privilege, and impunity were his birthright. He could have whatever he wanted.

And he wanted Gia. Because he loved her?

Or was it about control.

Didn't matter. He couldn't have her. He'd never have the opportunity to get close to her again. To lay his filthy hands on her delicate skin. To get off on the fear that still shadowed her eyes.

"What precisely do you intend to do?" Ryder's voice had sharpened.

"Lopez oversees Espina Negra's fentanyl trafficking in the Southwest." Rage tightened his throat. "My mother died because of it."

"Caleb." Ryder's voice softened. "Pick the winnable fight. Doctor Barone is within reach—Lopez isn't. Not yet, anyway."

Anger surged, hot and acidic. "Law enforcement can't touch this guy. Lopez parades around Miami spending blood money, and no one lifts a finger. Did Nathan tell you about the DEA agent who went missing?"

Ryder's tone turned guarded. "If the DEA's involved, they may have an interest in your doctor."

The puzzle pieces Caleb had been trying to fit together snapped into place. He should have seen them sooner. "Because if she knew he was a leader in Espina Negra, it stands to reason that she also knows things that could send him to prison."

"So maybe she's running not only from an abusive situation..." Ryder began.

"But because of what she knows," Caleb finished. "She played me. Told me just enough." Doling out only the information she wanted him to have—that she was fleeing an abusive relationship.

Once he discovered Lopez's true identity, he should have known there was more to the shadows in her eyes, the evasiveness of her answers. Her lies made a mockery of his instincts, made him question his own judgment. The realization settled like a stone in his stomach.

"What are you going to do?" Ryder asked.

"I intend to find out the truth."

"Watch your six," Ryder warned. "If you don't, one of you will end up in someone's crosshairs."

"Understood." Caleb ended the call.

The highway unspooled ahead, a stretch of empty asphalt hemmed in by high desert. Towering in the distance, sandstone outcroppings marked the foothills of the Chuska Mountains, part of the Colorado Plateau.

Caleb's knuckles whitened around the steering wheel. The memory of his confrontation with Gia last night still clung like smoke—gray and suffocating.

She'd called him a good man. He wasn't, really. He'd try to protect her, but if she could help stop Lopez...

Leather creaked beneath him as he shifted, restless. He wouldn't force her. Too many men had failed her already. While he might not be a saint, he could show her that some men were trustworthy.

Near the Arizona line, a low-slung, red Mustang filled his rearview mirror, its distinctive rumble reminding him of his colleague Danny Mayhew's GT.

Military age male. Shoulder-length dark hair. Mirrored sunglasses.

Caleb kept to the right lane, waiting for the more powerful car to pass.

The Mustang slid in behind him.

A white pickup passed and cut in front of him—too close.

Single occupant. Mid-thirties, beard, sunglasses, bandana.

The license plate was caked in mud, but Caleb could still make out part of the motto: *Land of Enchantment.* New Mexico.

The hairs on the back of his neck lifted.

In the left side mirror, a silver GMC was closing in.

Pink cap. Winnfield mustache.

Ortega and his buddy, Emilio.

"Son of a bitch." Caleb's gut clenched.

Emilio, smirking in the passenger seat, extended his middle finger toward the glass.

The pickup ahead braked. Ortega blocked him on the left. The Mustang closed in on the rear.

A kill box.

Adrenaline hit like a lightning strike. Operational readiness 101 and he'd failed the test. Thinking about a woman instead of being alert to his surroundings.

He hit the hands-free button. "Call Zach Blackwater."

Emilio's window dropped. Sunlight glinted off the barrel of a 9mm. Caleb ducked.

His window exploded, showering glass over his jacket and seat.

He yanked the wheel right, blasting over the shoulder, through scrub and gravel, clipping the pickup when it veered to force him further off-road.

The window behind him cracked in a starburst.

"Caleb?" Zach's voice barked through the speaker. "What's going on?"

"I'm almost to Tse Bonito." Caleb rattled off a mile marker. "Ambush. Under fire."

He floored it, weaving around traffic. "Three vehicles."

"I'm on the way."

Crack. A bullet punched into the back windshield.

"I need to get off the highway. Now." Heading into town would endanger innocent people.

Zach gave him directions. "There's a dirt road three miles ahead, on the right. Can you make it?"

"Not like I have much choice."

"Turn in, follow the road. When it forks, go right."

Caleb gunned the engine and slid between two semis. Three miles felt like thirty.

There. The Jeep's tires skidded, scrambling for purchase on loose gravel before rumbling over the cattle guard.

He barreled past several single-wides terraced up the hillside. "Am I leading these guys into a populated area?"

"Keep coming," Zach said.

Fork. Caleb went right.

Onto a rutted dirt road, more narrow than the last one. No homes, only junipers and rocks the size of a Humvee.

The Mustang would never make it.

One down.

Caleb reached the clearing. A natural rise with a view of the road. Cover available behind sandstone boulders, junipers and sagebrush.

Up ahead, three long guns trained in his direction behind Zach's Tahoe and a black pickup.

Perfect.

One way in. One way out, and they controlled it.

His respect for his cousin shot up—and he didn't know how Zach had rounded up two more gun-toting friendlies in such a short time, but he could kiss him right now.

He hit the brakes and slid to a stop next to the pickup, diving for cover just as the GMC burst into view.

Caleb slipped into battle mode. Slowing heart rate. Heightened senses.

He trained his gun on the driver's side—Ortega.

Surprise, assholes.

"Navajo Nation Police," Zach bellowed. "Put down your weapons and exit the vehicle, hands raised where I can see them."

The GMC screeched into reverse. Tires spun, churning dust clouds. Caleb could read the fury on Ortega's face before he sped back down the road.

"You good?" Zach called. He leaped into the Tahoe.

Caleb's world narrowed to a single, visceral thought.

Gia.

"Hold up!" He sprinted over. "We need to get to the clinic."

"One of my officers is already there."

"Armed?"

"Yes. I'll tell her to be on alert." Zach threw the Tahoe into Drive.

Caleb gripped his cousin's shoulder through the open window. "Don't go after them alone. There were three vehicles. At least four men. Probably all armed."

Zach's lips pulled back in a snarl. "They attacked you. On Navajo land."

"And they're probably headed for the interstate. Alert the Arizona and New Mexico state police." Caleb gave his cousin a description of all three cars and, as best he could, descriptions of the men. "We need to get to Gia in case they've discovered where she works."

Zach gave him a furious stare before barking into his police radio.

Caleb returned to his Jeep. Pieces of tempered glass littered the inside and the ground. His leather jacket had shielded him from most of the flying shrapnel.

He found a bullet embedded in the driver's side passenger door, and another in the back passenger seat. Hollow points. Meant to expand on impact and cause more damage.

"You got lucky." The elder of Zach's friends, dressed in jeans and red flannel, and sporting a Gulf War Veteran cap, pointed to a round hole in the driver's door, then to the armrest on the interior door panel. "It stopped the bullet. Doesn't always happen."

"No. It doesn't," Caleb said with a grimace.

He shook hands with the man, then with his younger companion in faded jeans, a white Henley and Phoenix Suns ball cap. "Caleb Varella. Thanks for the assist."

"Roy." The older man said, then gestured. "My son, Ford. He served in the Marines with Zach. We live down the hill. Don't usually get this kind of excitement on the rez."

"Not the kind of excitement I wanted to bring."

Zach joined the group. "Not even here a week and already you've got people trying to kill you." He arched his brows. "Your visit with Ortega must've rattled someone."

"I doubt Ortega had the balls to come at me on his own." Caleb slid into the wrecked Jeep. "If Lopez wants me dead, he'll need to come himself."

The man was dangerous. But he let his minions do his dirty work for him.

I'm willing to get my hands dirty.

"The hotel isn't safe for you anymore," Zach said. "It's too exposed."

"I've got to get to the clinic." Caleb cranked the engine and sent up a silent thank you when the Jeep purred to life. "I'll worry about my sleeping arrangements later."

"You gonna show up in this?" Zach pointed to the battered Jeep.

"I need her to see. Understand the only way she'll be safe is by helping us."

Ford was crouched by the rear of the Jeep. "Your tire's toast."

Caleb stuck his head out where the window should have been. "Fuck."

The bottom half of his rear tire was nothing more than a black crease of rubber folded in on itself.

"Leave it here." Zach thrust his chin toward his cruiser, his voice steel. "I'll drive."

Chapter Sixteen

"This is the last one." Gia slid a carton of blue nitrile gloves beneath a storage shelf and wiped her forehead, drying her fingers on the hem of her doctor's coat. She unclipped her hair, finger-combed the damp strands, then secured it in a twist again.

Jennie sliced open another box and pulled out adhesive sterile gauze. "You didn't have to help. Reggie and I could've handled it while you grabbed lunch."

"I'm not sitting in my office eating while you two do all the work."

"You need to learn to act like a doctor." Jennie grinned. "Did you see the hottie delivery driver? He must be new."

"I noticed he was a flirt." The man had been attractive—late twenties, Hispanic, charming. He'd chatted up everyone as he hauled in boxes. "Did he ask for your number?"

"He tried you first, but you were oblivious. I told him you had a boyfriend."

Gia's cheeks heated. "I do not."

Any chance she'd had with Caleb died when he found out the man she'd once loved was the man he held responsible for his mother's death.

The fact your ex is the son of the head of the Espina Negra cartel changes everything.

A strange melancholy dragged on her chest. It was absurd, really—worrying more about Caleb's opinion of her than staying alive and one step ahead of Vincente.

"Uh-huh." Jennie shot Gia a knowing look. "So where's your handsome bodyguard? And how'd dinner with President Blackwater go? You've been off today."

"He had errands. And, dinner was…strained."

For too many reasons to explain.

"But it was a start." She glanced at the clock. *One p.m.* "He should have been here by now."

Reggie, the clinic's lab technician, poked his head in. "Lieutenant Blackwater and his cousin are here, Doctor Barone."

His brows lifted. "Came barging in like they expected to arrest someone."

Jennie clucked her tongue. "Eager to see you, no doubt. Two hotties. You need to start sharing." She laughed, but something in her eyes—warm, wistful—lingered.

Gia rolled her eyes, but couldn't help the smile tugging at her lips. College and med school had left little room for close friends, and Miami? The few girlfriends she'd had drifted away as Vincente monopolized her time.

Having Jennie in her life was…precious. Something she wanted to protect.

Something else Vincente threatened to take from her.

Zach and Caleb waited in the lobby—Zach in uniform, Caleb in his jeans, white t-shirt, and leather jacket from earlier.

The look of relief on their faces when they saw her made her stomach somersault. "What's happened?"

"We need to talk. Privately." Caleb's voice vibrated with restrained tension.

Zach's stance was cool, unreadable. But the fire in his eyes told her everything she needed to know.

They were in warrior mode.

The butterflies in her stomach turned to lead.

"Let's go into the conference room," she said, already moving. Her legs felt rubbery. Her pulse pounded against her throat.

She took a seat at the table. "Tell me what's going on."

Zach leaned against the wall, arms crossed, face set in grim lines.

Caleb sat beside her, close enough that their knees brushed, the contact oddly intimate.

"The men who tried to abduct you came back. And they brought friends." Caleb's jaw tightened. "They followed me from Gallup."

"Followed." Zach snorted.

He shook his head. "What my cousin meant to say was they ambushed him. Shot up his Jeep."

"Oh my God." She launched from the chair, her gaze raking over Caleb, searching for evidence of fresh injuries.

He wrapped his fingers around her cold ones, his palm warm and rough. "I'm fine."

No, you aren't.

Because Vincente's men wouldn't have acted without orders.

Which meant Vincente considered Caleb a threat.

She'd been a fool even to entertain the idea that she could stay here and not endanger everyone around her.

"This is my fault. You need to leave. Go back to DC before he—"

"It's not your fault." Caleb, his voice a growl, interrupted her. "Sit."

He tugged her back to the chair. "This may not even be about you. I sent a message to Lopez through his errand boys to stay away from you. But I also planted a seed that their new partner might be cutting a side deal with a rival cartel."

Zach glared. "My cousin waved a big red flag in front of the bull."

Caleb glared back. "Lopez started this. I'm going to finish it."

"Oh my God." Gia dropped her face into her hands. "I don't know what's worse—threatening Vincente over me or interfering in his business."

She lifted her head and met Caleb's steady gaze, her voice rising. "Do you want to die? You won't win. He's a dangerous man."

If anyone knew exactly what her former lover could do and get away with, it was her.

"So am I." Steady. So damn sure of himself.

"You're insane." She looked to Zach. "Tell him he's insane. He'll get himself killed."

Zach's dark eyes regarded her steadily. "Lopez sent men to kidnap you and tried to kill Caleb. He won't let up until he gets what he wants. If we lure him here, we have the advantage. I know this terrain. Caleb and I know how to fight."

"Trust us—trust *me*. The people here need you, and I know you want to stay. It's the only way you get your life back." Caleb's quiet voice carried a confidence she clung to with the desperation of a drowning woman.

She stared at him. *Her life.*

But at what cost? Losing Caleb would haunt her forever.

Damn you, Vincente.

Not a day went by when she didn't think about that night on the yacht. She'd promised Vincente she'd never speak of it. That it would die with her, even as it left a black stain on her conscience.

But Vincente wasn't letting her move on. He was burning every safe place she found to the ground.

Caleb's phone rang. His mouth tightened when he glanced at the screen. "Dileas. I'll be right back."

"Exam room two when you're done." Gia hadn't missed the wince when he stood. "I want to see for myself that you're," she used finger quotes, "*fine.*"

His grin sent her heart in a spiral. "Yes, Doc."

She tracked him as he slipped out the door, not wanting to let him out of her sight.

"You're attracted to him."

Gia blinked, her attention shifting to Zach.

Resignation shadowed his face.

She remembered Jennie's words. *Zach has a thing for you. Surely you've noticed.*

"I'm sorry." She winced at how inadequate her apology felt. Zach was a good man. But she'd never considered him more than a friend.

"Just don't end up with a broken heart."

"I won't." She'd be crazy to fall in love again.

Again?

Had she been in love with Vincente, or simply allowed herself to be seduced by his flattering attention and money?

Allowed herself to be treated like an object for his pleasure.

Right now, she hated him with a passion that ran soul deep.

Caleb had once again stepped into the role of her protector and, even though he could have died today, he wasn't running.

No one had ever done that for her. Ever.

This isn't about you, it's about his mother.

Caleb wanted revenge. She'd do well to remember that.

Still, it didn't change the fact that he was in danger because of her.

And she had one card left to play.

Her stomach cramped hard. Cold prickled her skin.

Zach's eyes narrowed. "What's wrong?"

"Cramp. Probably pulled something unloading supplies." She forced a breath. "I need to make a call for a patient. If you see Caleb, tell him I'll be right there."

She left the room, heart hammering, half expecting Zach to follow.

This plan to lure Vincente to the rez? Madness.

He would come with plenty of his soldiers. People would die.

Caleb.

Zach.

You know what you have to do.

She stepped into her office. Locked the door. Pulled her phone from her pocket.

It slipped from her sweaty fingers and clattered to the desk.

"Breathe." She closed her eyes, filled her lungs, and reached for sorely needed composure.

This was insane.

But not doing it was worse.

She tapped out the first nine digits of Vincente's number. Her finger hovered, shaking, over the last one.

All this time, silence had been her shield. Protecting herself and—she'd told herself—others. But wasn't that just an excuse?

Look at Caleb. His scars—both visible and invisible—were proof you could survive the jagged edges of life and come out stronger for it.

Her own scars were self-inflicted, a reminder she'd chosen fear and silence over courage and truth.

Enough letting fear keep her small. If this was a war. She'd fight too.

She pressed the final digit.

Vincente answered on the fourth ring. "Hello? Who is this?"

Of course he answered. Very few people had his personal number. He'd be curious.

Her heart beat like a bird desperately trying to escape its cage. "It's Abigail."

"Ah, Abigail. Or Gianna I should say. That's your real name, after all."

His purr raised the hairs on the back of her neck. "So many secrets, *mi amor*. So many lies."

She knew that tone. It never ended well for the other person.

"I changed my name before I met you. Don't take it personally."

"Are you ready to come home? You aren't safe, you know. My family doesn't like loose ends."

Her blood chilled. She was a loose end. One who put everyone around her in danger.

If she hadn't truly understood that before, she did now.

"As my wife, they wouldn't dare move against you." His voice dropped, menace threading his words. "I'll even overlook your association with Caleb Varella if you return to Miami immediately."

"That's why I'm calling. Leave Caleb alone."

Her voice was steady, even if her pulse wasn't. "He's no one. Just a stranger who stepped in. There's nothing between us."

Her shoulder blades itched. Not a lie. Not the whole truth, either.

At least on her part. Even if they parted ways today, she had a feeling Caleb Varella would haunt her dreams for a long time.

Gia bit her lip and marshaled her courage before continuing. "I won't let you kill another innocent man. If you don't call off your soldiers, I'll go to the police and tell them what happened that night."

The memory still haunted her. The guilt clawed at her insides. Rather than do the right thing, she'd run.

"I don't know what you are talking about, *querida*."

So smooth. She'd almost believe him if she didn't know better.

"You can stop pretending, Vincente, this phone isn't tapped. Leave Caleb Varella alone. Leave the Navajo alone. If you do, I'll keep my mouth shut. If you don't..." She left the threat hanging.

Silence. Then a sigh. "Listen to how you speak to me. Such disrespect when all I have ever done is treat you like a queen."

His voice turned ice cold. "Have you slept with him?"

"No." Only in her dreams.

"Make sure it stays that way. Varella will be safe—as long as he stays out of my business, and you return to Miami."

Liar.

"Give me two months. I have work commitments I can't just ignore."

The request was a long shot. Her contract was up in six weeks. If he actually agreed, she'd have two weeks to disappear before he expected her to return.

"Unacceptable. You will come home immediately."

"One week," she bargained. "I have patients here. People who rely on me. And if your men come near Caleb or anyone else, I'm going straight to the authorities."

She hung up before he could make any further demands.

One week.

To either run, or stay and agree to serve as Caleb's bait.

Because there was no way in hell she'd ever go back.

Her emotions already on a razor's edge, Gia lost all the air in her lungs at the sight of Caleb in exam room two.

Long legs dangled over the table, his black leather jacket slung across the metal chair in the corner. His sheer size and the aura of controlled power he radiated made the sterile white walls close in, shrinking her vision until it took in only white cotton, denim, and gold flecks in dark eyes that watched her too closely.

"What's wrong?"

The man missed nothing.

"Other than the fact you could have died today?" Her voice came out sharper than intended.

She gestured to his shirt, needing something for her hands to do besides shake. "Take it off."

"Yes, ma'am." His lips curved with lazy, lethal charm.

He tugged the t-shirt from his jeans and peeled it off, dropping it beside him on the table. "Look at you, giving orders like an officer."

Sculpted muscle flowed like water beneath his smooth tanned skin and dusky brown nipples. She'd think of a snarky comeback if she wasn't busy trying not to drool.

Her gaze dropped to the t-shirt. No red stains. That was a good sign.

"I'm a doctor." The reminder was for her as much as him and would have been more effective if she didn't sound so out of breath.

She'd seen plenty of bare-chested men. So what if this one had abs that looked carved from stone?

The box of examination gloves was mounted on the wall next to his shoulder. Caleb spread his knees just enough that she had to step between them to pull out a pair.

Sandalwood and spice teased her nose. His body heat warmed her—every inch of smooth, bare skin urging her lips closer.

She jerked back. The snap of the rubber on her wrists stung—a small penance for the thoughts she shouldn't be having.

Adrenaline let down from her conversation with Vincente. It had to be why she couldn't focus.

The scar on Caleb's neck caught her attention again. It arced from behind his left ear and widened to his collarbone, dangerously close to his jugular.

Her fingers itched to trace it. Somehow, it made him sexier. More lethal.

"Iraq." Caleb's voice was a low rumble.

He'd caught her staring. When she looked up, his gaze drifted down her body in a raw, sexual manner that shot lightning straight to her core.

Her thighs clenched.

His smile said he noticed that, too.

Mortified, she yanked her gaze away and tried to pull the tattered remains of her professionalism around her. Hard to do when she was standing between his thighs.

More scars marked his torso—some faint, some fresh. All illustrating a life familiar with violence.

She pointed to the black tattoo of a parachute, flanked by a set of curved wings, on his left arm. "What does this mean?"

"That I'm qualified to jump out of a perfectly good airplane." A flash of humor lit his eyes. "A buddy talked me into it the night we earned our wings."

So not on her bucket list. "Hard pass."

"It's not so bad."

His right arm also sported a tattoo—a crest with a dagger intersecting two crossed arrows. Beneath the dagger and arrows were the words *De Oppresso Liber*.

She tapped his biceps. "And this one?"

"*To free the oppressed*. It's the Special Forces motto."

"How fitting." He bled protector from every pore.

She motioned for him to turn. "Let me see your back."

The wound from the other night was healing well. No signs of infection. There were several small knicks on his neck. "Glass?"

"Hmmm."

"I'll take that as a yes. Hold on." She left the room and returned with a headlamp and magnifier. "I want to make sure you don't have any embedded in these cuts."

"It was tempered glass, Doc." A low, amused murmur that curled her toes.

She cocked a brow. "Are you telling me how to do my job?"

"Wouldn't dare."

Fortunately, none of the wounds were deep. She cleaned them and applied ointment.

"You smell good," he murmured. Husky, sensual.

Her fingers froze. "So do you."

Warm and earthy. Masculine.

She stepped back. Peeled off her gloves. But her heart didn't follow.

Vincente's men nearly took him from her today. She was done dancing around her attraction. If Caleb wanted her, she'd take whatever part of himself he offered in the time she had left with him.

Even knowing she'd get her heart broken.

No more keeping small.

He faced forward on the table, his gaze smoldering. "Thanks for patching me up. Again."

That rasp in his voice—dangerous, intimate—called to a feminine part of her that hadn't been awake in too long.

His hand brushed aside the hem of her medical coat and hovered.

He wanted to touch her—she could see it in his face. But he wouldn't.

She had to make the first move.

With a sigh, she stepped into the space between his legs.

Her palms flattened on his bare chest. Silk over steel. Warm. Solid. *Alive*. She couldn't help but shiver.

"You're welcome. Don't make it a habit."

The desire, the need coursing through her like an addictive drug, turned her voice into a seductive murmur.

His hand landed gently on her hip. The other cupped her head.

He leaned in.

Gia's eyes fluttered closed. His heart thumped beneath her hand. Her own beat wildly in response.

Warm breath caressed her lips.

His kiss was soft, a fleeting touch, then firm, insistent as he took control. When his tongue swiped across the seam of her lips, requesting entrance, she surrendered eagerly.

He tasted like safety and decadence, all rolled into a beautifully masculine package. Heat, need, and a growing urgency made her lightheaded. She clutched his shoulders, because if she didn't, the firestorm of desire blasting through her would leave her boneless at his feet.

She wouldn't ask if he cared for her or if his aim was to win her over so she'd agree to help him. It didn't matter anymore.

One week.

The plastic clip holding her hair clattered on the tile floor.

A hand fisted her hair. Pinpricks of fire danced on her skull. Teeth grazed her neck.

The past crashed into the present, vivid and cruel.

"Vincente, you're hurting me."

He'd wound his fist in her hair and yanked her head back far enough she was staring at bright blue sky while he drove into her from behind.

Her breasts bounced against the low concrete wall of the penthouse rooftop in rhythm with his thrusts. He'd ripped off her bikini top and flung it onto a chaise lounge, out of reach.

He bit her neck. Another mark she'd have to cover with concealer.

"You enjoy this as much as I do, querida." The hand that held her hip in a bruising grip traveled up her naked body to cup one breast. He squeezed. Hard.

"I love your breasts." Hot breath blasted in her ear. "Not plastic like so many women in Miami."

"Gia." Caleb's voice cut through her memory like a scalpel. Sharp. Commanding.

She blinked, shaken, as the present snapped back into focus.

His hands were gone. The desire in his face replaced by concern.

His eyes searched hers, seeing through clear to her soul. "Where did you go?"

"Sorry. I'm sorry." She'd ruined the moment.

"Hey." He caught her hands and gently placed them back on his chest. "Did I do something wrong?"

Humiliation shriveled her insides and blurred her vision. "It's nothing."

"Sweetheart." His voice was gentle. Soothing. "What did he do?"

She searched his face, finding no judgement. "He liked to pull my hair during…"

It was more than that, but the words stayed locked inside her throat. She hadn't minded rough sex, even a little kink. Vincente always took it past her boundaries.

As his cousin watched. She knew he did. Maybe Vincente's other men did, too. Because he liked to have sex where someone might see.

Caleb's voice roughened. "Next time, and there *will* be a next time"—a vow she felt clear to her toes—"we'll go slow. Promise me you'll let me know if I do anything that makes you uncomfortable."

The tears she'd been trying to keep at bay broke free and trickled down her cheeks. "I want to. Do it again. With you."

Even knowing she risked losing her heart. She wanted Caleb's hands on her.

Wanted him inside her.

"Please," her voice cracked, "I need you to erase his touch."

His gaze flared with heat and a promise that clenched low in her belly. "Oh babe, don't doubt it. I'm going to erase him from every inch of your body and every corner of your mind."

Light filled the darkness in her soul and firmed her resolve. It was only a matter of time before Vincente or one of Espina Negra's assassins caught up with her. Even if she only had a week left with this man, she wanted the memories to sustain her for as long as she had left.

Caleb caught one of the tears staining her cheeks with his thumb.

"Vincente Lopez Garcia is a dead man."

CHAPTER SEVENTEEN

CALEB WAS GOING TO kill Lopez. Jail wasn't good enough.

Not for what he'd done to Gia.

She had an inner core of steel that Caleb admired the hell out of. Like him, she'd escaped a troubled childhood and made herself into someone respected by others. She'd bent beneath her former lover's abuse, but she hadn't broken. Her soft, caring heart was as big as ever, as was her determination to serve.

He'd seen yesterday how she treated her patients—her persistence in arranging the necessary care, her lack of judgment when they didn't, or couldn't, follow her recommendations. Her job at the medical clinic might have started out as a refuge, a place to hide, but it was obvious she'd fallen in love with the Navajo people she lived and worked with. For her, leaving would be a tragedy, not a relief.

His hand still hovered over her cheek. And the way she cared for him...she didn't have to. He was trained to defend himself, yet she worried more about what her ex-lover might do to him than what Vincente would do if he got his hands on her again.

That landed somewhere deep. Unsettled him.

She was still vulnerable. Still healing.

He needed to remember that.

As much as he wanted her, wanted this—whatever it was—he'd let her control their intimacy until she trusted him with her body and her pleasure.

He sat there on the exam table, staring at her like an idiot long enough that she noticed.

Her brows furrowed. "What?" She glanced at his thumb, her hand lifting to her face. "My makeup's smeared, isn't it?"

A knock on the exam room door gave him a reason to look away before he said something foolish.

Gia leaped back, putting a professional distance between them while she scrubbed her face to rid it of tears. "Come in."

The door opened just enough for Jennie Tsosie to peer inside. "Zach needs to speak with Caleb as soon as you're finished."

Concern tightened her expression as her gaze lit on Gia's red eyes and splotchy cheeks. She turned a steely-eyed glare on him, clearly deciding he was the asshole in the room.

Guilty as charged.

"We're done," Gia said.

She busied herself cleaning up the medical supplies while he slipped back into his t-shirt and hopped off the exam table. He needed to talk to his cousin about his phone call earlier with Nathan Long. He needed a new place to sleep.

A shadow of fear hovered like a bad omen at the edges of his brain.

If those bastards had come after Gia instead of him...

She couldn't stay at her home either. Even though Ortega and his men hadn't come after her today, it didn't mean they didn't know how to find her.

"As soon as I'm finished with Zach, we're going home." *To pack.* He grabbed his jacket off the chair, the leather making a faint creaking sound as he shoved his arms into the sleeves.

"My patients—"

"Will have to reschedule. Your safety comes first. Always." He delivered his words on a knifepoint. Sharp and staccato.

Gia's head snapped back, surprise widening her eyes before anger narrowed them. "You're the one that got shot at. *Again.* Is avenging your mother's death worth dying for?"

Fire licked his veins for a different reason now. She believed this was only about his mother?

Two steps. He gripped the counter on either side of her body.

His lips brushed the shell of her ear. "This isn't about my mother." Words meant only for her to hear. "It's about you. Touching you is a privilege Vincente Lopez will never have again."

He brushed past Jennie and went in search of his cousin.

Zach was in the lobby, on his cell. As soon as he saw Caleb, he hung up and tossed a small black object.

Caleb snatched it out of the air on instinct. A key fob.

Zach leveled a glare. "Not a scratch, Cousin. I asked one of my friends to drive it here."

He made a beckoning motion. "Give me your hotel key. You know you can't stay there anymore. I'll get your stuff and check you out when I'm off shift."

"Thanks." Caleb pulled the plastic key card from his wallet. "I asked my colleague to find a safe house nearby for me and Gia to hole up in. Nathan's making sure the rental's under one of Dìleas's shell company names—no paper trail, no way to trace it. Once he gets back to me, we're out of here."

He'd had to fill Nathan in—about the ambush, the cartel connection, and the job in New York he wouldn't be able to take now.

The conversation replayed in his head.

"I made friends in all the wrong places. Got ambushed between Gallup and the rez this morning."

Nathan let out a string of low curses. "Garcia? Or should I say... Lopez?"

"The men who tried to abduct Gia. And they brought friends. Local muscle. Probably part of the biker crew Espina Negra's using to move fentanyl through the area." Caleb grimaced. "I may have stirred up some shit between Lopez and his new business partners using that rumor about Los Coyotes moving north. And I sent him a message through his errand boys to stay the hell away from Gia."

He braced for the lecture.

Instead, a low rumble, then a snort, and finally—outright laughter.

Caleb scowled at his phone.

What the fuck?

Nathan was still chuckling when Caleb brought it back to his ear.

"Welcome to the club, amigo. I cannot wait to tell Lachlan this one."

"What club?"

"The stupid-shit-we-do-for-the-women-we-love club. When's the wedding?"

Love.

The word hit Caleb like a sucker punch.

"That's not what's going on here," he snapped.

But the word stuck. Burrowed in.

Caleb shoved the thought away. "Just find me a safe house."

Zach's voice cut through the memory, sharp with irritation. "Grandfather called me. He already heard about what happened. I'm sure he's not pleased the police chief was the one to tell him and not us."

"We've been a little busy." Caleb followed his cousin outside to the cruiser.

Zach slid into the Tahoe and rested his arm on the steering wheel. His gaze appraised Caleb. "This attack on you changes things. Grandfather wants to know what you plan to do next."

"I'm here until this thing with Lopez is finished."

"And after that?"

Caleb glanced behind him at the clinic. "After that will depend on Gia. What she wants."

"Don't break her heart." Zach's jaw tightened. "She doesn't deserve that."

Caleb held his cousin's stare. "I won't."

An older-model Toyota four-door turned into the clinic. Caleb and Zach went still, their eyes on the occupants.

A Diné woman in her forties stepped from the driver's seat and walked around to help an elderly man from the passenger seat.

Caleb trotted to the clinic's glass entrance door and held it open for them before returning to his conversation with Zach.

"Get Gia's name and photo scrubbed from the clinic's website and black out her address in any public Navajo Nation records," he told his cousin. "I'll ask Nathan to scrub any identifying information he finds on the internet."

Zach touched the brim of his police ball cap. "I'll get on it and call you if I get any news on our suspects. Text me your new address once you have it."

Caleb waited for his cousin's cruiser to disappear from view before heading back inside.

Gia should be ready to leave by now. He needed time to rest. Regroup.

Plan his next move.

She was in her office with Jennie.

"Are you ready?" He took hold of her navy backpack. "The Jeep's out of commission so Zach lent me his personal vehicle."

"Maybe he'd need his car more if he took some time off and got a life," Jennie muttered.

A closer look at the nurse revealed no wedding or engagement rings. Gia hadn't mentioned Jennie having a husband or boyfriend, either.

Caleb suppressed a sudden grin.

Zach needed to forget about Gia. Nothing would ever happen between them. Jennie clearly had a thing for him, and maybe if Zach would just pull his head out of his ass, he'd see it.

"I'm sorry my problems have come to the rez." Gia squeezed Jennie's forearm. "When this is over, maybe you can convince Zach to do something fun in Gallup. You both need a break."

Jennie's smile turned wistful. "Yeah, maybe."

She made a shooing motion. "Go. Mister Nelson is here for a med check. If anything comes up I can't handle, I'll call you."

Outside, Caleb led Gia to his cousin's black Charger. The interior was spotless, the red leather supple beneath his fingertips. From the passenger side air vent, an air freshener gave off that unmistakable new car smell.

"Um, wow." Gia's eyes widened as she glanced around the interior. "Lots of black and red. I would have never figured Zach as a muscle car guy."

Caleb laughed. He'd thought the same thing.

The high-performance V8 engine came to life with a guttural snarl, its barely leashed power rumbling their seats like the car was begging to be set loose.

Nice wheels. He wasn't picky about his vehicles unless he was on a job, but he had to admit, this was a sweet ride.

"Zach told me he'd shoot me himself if I get so much as a ding on her." He glanced at Gia. "Jennie's got a crush on him."

She shifted in her seat to gape at him. "When did you realize that? I've seen them together tons of times, and I just now figured that out. And *crush* makes it sound like she's a teenager pining after the high school quarterback."

"I'm trained to notice the little things." He took his gaze off the road long enough to glance at her. "You should tell Zach he doesn't have a chance with you. Maybe it will give Jennie the opening she needs."

"Why should I tell Zach he has no chance with me?" Her voice held humor, but he'd seen the flash of vulnerability in her eyes.

"Because you're with me. And I don't share." Caleb cut his gaze back to the road as Gia let out a small gasp.

His fingers tightened on the wheel. "I didn't mean that the way it sounded. I'm not Lopez. I'd never mistreat you or force you to do anything you didn't want to do."

I'm not my father either.

He'd tried to protect his mother from his father when he'd gotten big enough.

And after, when the Phoenix police found Pops dead in a back alley.

"I know." Her words were quiet but held a ring of conviction, and damned if that didn't have him mentally thumping his chest like a caveman.

"But you aren't staying." She turned her face toward the window, gaze distant.

"I'm staying for as long as you need me."

Her eyes snapped back to his—wary, hopeful. "And then?"

He didn't know. The only thing he *did* know was that he wasn't ready to walk away from her.

Once Lopez was out of the picture, then maybe he'd figure out what a future with Gia could look like.

Trust, he'd learned, could be a weapon. He'd seen how his father had twisted his mother's love until it became a noose around her neck.

That would never be Gia's fate—not with him. He'd rather cut out his own heart than see fear in her eyes because of something he'd done.

She needed to see every day, with every action, that she was safe with him. That she'd always have a choice.

"You've gone awfully quiet." Gia's soft murmur jolted him from his thoughts.

"Just thinking."

"About what?"

He turned onto her street and pulled into her driveway. Scanning the area, he checked for unfamiliar vehicles. Movement. Anything out of place from this morning.

Nothing jumped out, and his sixth sense remained blessedly quiet.

Throwing the gear into Park, he reached over and trailed one finger down the soft skin of her cheek. "You."

Her eyes deepened to a midnight blue. "I'm what put that serious look on your face?"

He loved the way her voice got all breathless when he touched her, like she'd run up a set of stairs.

His lips gave a slight tilt. "I'm always serious."

Gia laughed. "True. You definitely have a poker face. How are you at cards? We could go to Vegas."

"Don't gamble. I like to make sure the odds are always stacked in my favor."

His gaze raked the front of her home. Windows and doors closed. No obvious signs of tampering. He'd have to take a closer look, of course. "I need to figure out how to stop Lopez without risking the people in this community."

"You shouldn't try." Her fingers slid along his forearm to cover his hand. She squeezed. "He only came after you because of me. You're not the one he wants."

The hunted look he'd seen when they first met slid into her eyes. "If I leave"—her grip on his fingers tightened when he shook his head—"*If I leave*, everyone here on the rez will be safe. You'll be safe."

Hell no.

"You won't be."

"Caleb, you could have died today. It's a miracle you didn't." Gia's eyes glistened. "I don't want anything to happen to you. I don't want anything to happen to the people I've come to care about."

His stomach did a somersault. When he'd first learned she was fleeing her ex, he'd thought the best thing for her was to leave. Then, when he realized who her ex was, he wanted her to stay.

As bait. Zach had been right to call him out.

"This is your home. You're needed here. The people have accepted you, and they don't welcome outsiders easily."

"What about you?" She paused, licked her lips before those big blue eyes peered into his soul. "Would you ever consider this your home? Will you allow yourself to get to know your family? They're good people."

He thought about his answer before giving it. He'd already staked his claim. Might as well be honest.

"If I were to consider staying here, it wouldn't be for the Blackwaters. It would be for you."

Chapter Eighteen

Gia's lips parted at Caleb's words.

Hope. That's what was causing her heart to take up all the room in her chest. Why she felt her body lifting, as if she was full of helium and would float to the sky if her seatbelt wasn't holding her in place.

Hope and the giddy feeling of being wanted. Valued. Despite her past.

Caleb wanted her.

Her stomach filled with lead, rooting her back in her seat. Giddiness morphed into nausea.

He didn't know she'd contacted Vincente. What if instead of protecting Caleb and buying herself time, she'd made things worse?

"Now that you will be my wife, there are some things you need to know about my business, querida." Vincente's hot breath in her ear, his arms banding her in a crushing grip.

"No." A denial. A plea. Even as Antonio's body splashed into the Atlantic and her scream floated away on the ocean breeze.

She only had a week with the man she was dangerously close to falling in love with before she had to make a terrible choice. Disappear and let down everyone here who needed her, or turn herself in and testify, where she'd eventually be forced to disappear anyway.

If Espina Negra didn't get to her first.

Because she wouldn't help Caleb avenge his mother if it meant confronting Vincente directly. No matter how skilled a soldier he'd been—still was—he'd lose.

And he didn't know the secret she still kept, the one she clung to in order to protect them both.

"I don't blame you, you know, for wanting to use me to put Vincente in prison after what happened to your mother." She gave a hard swallow. "I wish I had the courage to do it."

Car leather creaked as Caleb leaned in.

Gia stiffened. She didn't deserve this man. She didn't deserve happiness.

"Stay with me, Gia." He kissed her. Not a hard, possessive kiss that branded her as his. *No*, this was a gentle sweep of his lips against hers until the tension seeped from her body. "You're not running. That takes courage."

Oh, but she was prepared to run. Or turn herself in and put an even bigger target on her back.

Would Caleb understand the sacrifice she made for him? Or would he think her a coward, while whatever he felt for her withered in disgust?

She cupped his cheek. He was everything she'd always wanted and never had.

Home. Safety. Love.

His dark eyes softened. "I need you to pack."

Pack?

Her heart stuttered. "Where am I going?"

Was today at the clinic the last time she'd see Jennie? Her patients?

Not yet. I'm not ready.

"I'm waiting on a call from a colleague. He's finding us somewhere to stay. Somewhere Vincente's men don't know about. It's not safe for us here any longer." Caleb unlatched his seatbelt and stepped from the car, engine still running.

His hand disappeared into his leather jacket and came out with his gun. "Shift over into the driver's seat. Lock the doors. If you see anyone but me come out of the house or into the yard, get out of here and call Zach."

He peered at her through the open door, his bodyguard persona firmly in command. "Do you understand? No hesitating."

She bit her lip and glanced at the blinds covering her living room window. Was it her imagination, or were they ajar, like someone had separated the slats to peer out? "Maybe you shouldn't go in there by yourself."

"I know what to look for. If someone's been in your home, I'll know it before I enter." He waited until she'd switched seats, then circuited her home, returning to inspect the front door before he entered.

What felt like twenty minutes—but, according to the clock on the dashboard, wasn't more than five—Caleb reappeared.

He motioned for her to turn off the engine and join him. His gun had disappeared.

He looked good on her doorstep. Handsome. Capable.

Like he belonged here, among the rugged sandstone buttes and mesas that blazed orange and red during the golden hour—just after sunrise and before sunset—in this stretch of the Colorado Plateau.

With her.

A fantasy. She had a week to decide whether to run or turn herself in.

Either way, despite the promises she'd made, her time with Caleb was short.

Caleb's phone belted out the hard-driving bass drum that kicked off a Metallica song.

Nathan.

The former SEAL got his kicks assigning custom ringtones to everyone's company-issued phones. Caleb's was *"Desperado"* by the Eagles—not exactly subtle, but better than Danny's, which was *"Crazy Train."*

He ushered Gia out of the cold and into the warmth of the house, locking the door before answering. "Did you find a place?"

"It's not like there are a lot of options in no-fucking-where Arizona and New Mexico, amigo," Nathan said. "Especially on short notice."

Hell. "So you didn't find anything?"

A nearby hotel, then. Not the best option given the circumstances, but it would have to do.

Nathan snorted in his ear. "You insult me. Of course I did. I'm texting you the address. It's on the outskirts of Gallup and remote enough that if shit goes down, you won't have neighbors caught in the crossfire."

Caleb's shoulders loosened. "Thanks, man."

Gia stood in the living room, watching him.

He put the phone on mute. "Pack enough clothes for a few days."

Once she'd disappeared down the hall, he returned to his conversation with Nathan.

"What can we do to help?" Gone was the banter. Nathan's tone settled into mission mode.

"I appreciate everything you've already done. But this business with Lopez could get messy. I can't ask you guys to put Dìleas in a cartel's crosshairs."

"Caleb," Nathan growled. "I know you're just an Army grunt but listen up—we've got your six. Always."

Unexpected emotion clogged Caleb's throat. "Thanks, man. Send me that address."

Gia appeared, suitcase in a death grip that bleached her knuckles white.

He ended his call. "You ready?"

"Since I left Vincente, all I've done is run." She glanced around her home, her gaze deliberate as it moved from place to place.

Almost as if she didn't expect to see it again. It was in her body language.

Flight mode.

She wasn't going anywhere without him. "We aren't running, sweetheart. We're relocating to a safe base of operations while we figure out a plan."

Caleb's colleague had rented them a seven-hundred-square-foot adobe casita on the outskirts of Gallup. It sat down a long dirt road, about a half-mile from a contemporary two-story home made of brick, steel beams, and glass—likely the owner's place. That house, perched at the top of the drive, reminded her of the East Coast.

The adobe casita was all Southwest. Barbed wire separated the one-bedroom dwelling from a field of horses grazing on the few shoots of vegetation that hadn't gone dormant for the winter.

It was cute, secluded and—Gia thought—her last haven before she had to make a terrible decision.

Run—and lose Caleb forever. Stay—and watch him die. Turn herself in—and live the rest of her life looking over her shoulder.

No matter what she chose, she would never be free.

One week.

The clock ticking in her head felt like it had enough dynamite attached to it to blow her entire world to smithereens.

Caleb input the access code to unlock the front door. A click followed a soft whirr of the locking mechanism as the deadbolt slid back.

He glanced back at her and frowned. "Everything okay?"

"Other than you holding a gun?" A pointed glance at the Glock in his hand. She could deflect with the best of them.

"Better safe than sorry."

They stepped into the main living area with its bright white walls and rustic hardwood floors. The air inside was cool and smelled of pine-scented household cleaner.

"Cozy." Her mood lightened.

The space was just large enough to accommodate the burnt orange upholstered couch that reminded her of desert sunsets and two sand colored canvas side chairs that were grouped around a petrified wood slab coffee table. The sliding glass doors on the back wall provided a picturesque view of the horses and a distant butte.

"No drapes." Caleb didn't seem as enamored of the view as she was. "Gotta find some blankets to cover all that glass."

"Why? I like it."

He shifted on his feet. Looked away. "We'd be sitting ducks for anyone with a rifle and scope, especially at night."

Her stomach knotted. Sweat broke out on her temple, the bucolic scene ruined.

She moved to the corner, out of sight.

"Wait here while I clear the rest of the house." Caleb disappeared through the archway to their right.

"Kitchen," he called out.

He reappeared and crossed the living room to the other side of the casita. Opened the door there. "Bedroom."

His gaze narrowed on her. "Why don't you lie down while I unload the car and take a look around outside, before it gets dark."

Apparently, the dull throb in her temple hadn't gone unnoticed.

She trudged into the bedroom while the front door clicked behind her as Caleb went outside.

The bedroom and bathroom were modeled along the same clean lines as the living room. White walls, white tile. Even the duvet that covered the king-sized bed was white. The only splash of color was the hot air balloon shower curtain and a stack of mint-green bath towels.

Gia dropped her purse on the bed. Big enough for two. Whereas that orange couch in the living room?

Too small for anyone to sleep comfortably on.

She knew where she wanted Caleb.

In bed. With her.

But after what happened at the clinic, she couldn't trust her mind not to betray her and ruin everything.

"Worry about that later." It had been a day.

She slipped out of her ankle boots and stretched out on the bed, still in her jeans and purple knit sweater.

A ringing came from inside her purse.

Jennie had said she'd call if there were any issues at the clinic.

Gia fumbled for the phone, fingers digging past keys and a crumpled tissue until she wrapped her hand around the plastic case.

Ring.

A jolt ran through her.

Ring.

The last person to call her had been Vincente.

Ring.

What if he'd traced her number? Her heartbeat roared in her ears.

Ring.

How many was that now?

She darted a glance toward the bedroom door. Could Caleb hear?

Ring.

She turned the phone over with a slow, shaking hand.

The number wasn't one she recognized. Local area code.

A clinician from the regional medical center? A patient?

She hit the green button just before it went to voicemail.

"He—hello?"

A low, steady dial tone buzzed in her ear.

Gia dropped the phone on the bed.

By the time Zach pulled in, the last light had drained from the sky. Caleb opened the door to a gust of cold air that knifed through his shirt and carried the scent of snow. Steel gray clouds rolled in overhead, blotting out the stars.

He stepped back to let his cousin inside.

"Is that from my car?" Zach pointed at the gray tarp Caleb found in the Charger's trunk that was serving as a makeshift drape over the sliding glass doors.

"You'll get it back. Thanks for picking up my things." Caleb took his duffle and the garment bag containing his funeral suit from Zach's hands.

"Hi, Zach."

Gia's voice held a note of hesitation. Even before she spoke, Caleb had felt her behind him.

Zach stepped forward and tugged off his ball cap. His gaze lifted, and the second it landed on Gia, something in his face shifted. Softer.

Too soft.

Beneath Caleb's skin, tension gathered like a fuse burning short.

He'd seen that look before. Knew exactly what it meant. And every instinct demanded he knock it off Zach's face.

His fingers curled into his palms.

Awareness sparked in his cousin's eyes. Zach's gaze dropped to Caleb's hands and rose again, mouth twitching with a smug little smirk.

Asshole.

Behind Caleb, Gia moved. "Why don't I find a place for these?" she said, reaching for his duffel and garment bag.

A tightness pulled at her mouth. "I'm sure you two have some things to discuss."

As she retreated down the hallway, the sway of her hips snagged his attention—and held it. That bedroom had become her refuge since they arrived.

"You've got it bad, cousin."

His head jerked around to find Zach's smirk now a full-on taunting grin.

He opened his mouth to tell his cousin to fuck-off. Only...

The bastard was right. He did have it bad, and it seemed wrong to deny it.

"Any news?" he asked instead.

Zach's expression turned grim. "The guys who came after you managed to slip back under whatever rock they came out from."

"Ortega is getting help from the Aztec Kings."

"Probably. He has history with them." Zach's hat beat a rhythmic *thwap* against his thigh. "Not gonna lie, Cousin. Taking on a drug cartel and an outlaw biker gang at the same time may be biting off a bit more than we can chew."

Caleb peered at the closed bedroom door and kept his voice low. "It's the only way to keep Gia safe. I don't think this bastard has any intention of letting her go."

Men like Lopez didn't let people walk out of their lives. Carried out in body bags, yes. Leave unscathed?

He had a bad feeling Gia wouldn't be so lucky.

"So, it's about Gia now, not getting revenge for what happened to your *amá*?"

His head whipped around to glare at his cousin. "Can't it be both?"

Even as he said it, he knew the truth. If he thought there was a better way to keep Gia safe, he'd take it.

Abandon his plan. Let someone else take on Espina Negra.

For her.

A sharp twinge jolted his heart, sending his hand flying to his chest.

"You look like you just ran into an electrified cattle fence." Zach positioned his cap on his head. "Maybe you won't be putting us and the rez in your rearview so fast, huh?"

Hell. "My life isn't here." The words felt hollow. Performative.

A few days ago, he'd meant them with his whole chest.

Zach's grin faded. "Grandfather wants to hear from you. These guys came onto Navajo Nation land to try and take you out. You're our problem now."

As the front door shut behind his departing cousin, the bedroom door opened.

Caleb felt Gia's gaze caress the space between his shoulder blades.

"Maybe Vincente will leave us alone." He heard the tremble in her voice. The false hope she didn't believe. "The police are searching for his men. He can't afford the attention."

"He won't."

"But, maybe he—"

"He won't." Caleb turned. Gia had closed the distance between them. "Men like him don't stop until someone makes them stop."

Color drained from her face, the light in her eyes dimming. She sat on the orange couch. Tilted her head back. Closed her eyes. Shut him out.

But she couldn't hide the tremble on her lips.

That sensation crawled across the back of his neck. The sense that there were still things Gia kept from him.

Trust.

She was running from a man who'd abused her trust.

Was with a man who wanted to use her as bait.

Just as Caleb wanted to trust her, he had to earn her trust in return.

He sat next to her, his fingers itching to smooth over the waterfall of glossy hair hanging down the back of the sofa.

"Get some sleep. Tomorrow, we make a plan. Together." He gave up the fight and twisted a lock of her hair around his finger. The soft strands clung to the calluses on his fingertip. "If there's an extra pillow and blanket in that bedroom, I'll make do on the couch."

Her eyes opened. Their gazes locked. Held.

Need so strong it threatened to level him surged.

His vision narrowed to encompass only Gia. Her deep blue irises framed by thick black lashes that didn't need mascara to enhance them. The gentle slope of her feminine nose. Her full bottom lip. Even the curves of her ears were graceful.

His lips brushed hers. A gesture of comfort.

That's what he told himself, at least. And he wouldn't go any further. It had been a helluva day and there were too many unspoken issues to address.

Except her scent filled his lungs. Her lips tasted like prickly pear from the balm he'd seen her apply several times during the day.

It was becoming his favorite flavor.

"Caleb."

Her palm lifted to his chest, the feel of her warm skin against the thin cotton of his shirt jacking his muscles taut.

He wanted her hands everywhere on his body. "Get me that pillow and blanket, sweetheart, before I end up sharing that bed with you."

The rasp in his voice should clue her in on how close he was to kicking his good intentions to the curb.

She took her hand back, gave an unsteady nod, and rose from the couch. "I'll be right back."

Caleb removed his weapons—shoulder holster, the knife strapped to his ankle—and placed them on the coffee table.

He wanted Gia.

In his bed.

In his life going forward.

But when he put Vincente Lopez in jail—or in the ground—what then?

Would she still want him?

Or remember he'd been willing to use her as bait?

The thought gutted him.

Somewhere along the way, his feelings had moved from attraction and the impulse to protect, to something deeper that burrowed its way into every cell in his body.

Not simply need or lust. It was more.

It was respect.

Admiration.

Despite everything she'd lived through, Gia led with her heart.

Caleb braced his forearms on his knees. The weapons on the table—that's what he knew.

How to fight and how to protect. How to be a good teammate.

And yet, his whole damn life he'd been the kid peering in from the outside, watching people form connections he never let himself truly be a part of, always the outsider.

He told himself it was safer that way.

But Gia? Gia belonged wherever she went—because she made the people around her feel seen, understood, valued. She built communities. She didn't hold herself apart, afraid to care too much.

For just a moment, he let himself imagine what it would be like to be part of this community.

His grandfather was right. There were things he didn't know. Didn't understand about what went down between his mom and her family. He wasn't sure he could ever let go of the feeling they'd abandoned her. That they could have done more.

But maybe they could come to some sort of understanding.

Gia wasn't the only one who needed roots, even if he'd spent his life pretending otherwise.

"Caleb." His name. Soft and hesitant.

He raised his head. Gia stood at the bedroom door, empty-handed, her teeth worrying her lush bottom lip. She still wore her jeans and purple sweater, but she was barefoot, her toenails painted a dusky pink that matched the lip color she favored.

"I don't want you to sleep on the couch." She swallowed, gripping the doorframe as if steadying herself.

Her voice wavered, then steadied. "I want you to make love to me."

Chapter Nineteen

Gia's knees were quaking in anticipation, and she'd had to swallow twice to moisten her throat enough to get out the words that both scared her and made her feel more alive than she'd been in years.

Maybe her entire life.

Caleb sat on the couch, hands on knees, head bowed. But when she'd spoken, he'd lifted his head.

The hunger on his face, the flare of desire in his eyes...

Everything else in the room dropped away until there was only him.

"Are you sure?" The hungry rasp in Caleb's voice glided down her arms in a shiver

He was giving her an out.

Her heart stuttered. She bit her lip.

His gaze hooded. "You aren't sure."

He settled back on the couch into a casual pose.

Sort of.

Her eyesight wasn't so bad that she didn't see the rather conspicuous bulge in his jeans.

Damn you, Vincente, for making me doubt myself.

"I'm sure. It's just." Her face heated. "I'm afraid."

She swallowed hard, then forced out the rest. "I don't want what happened between me and Vincente to ruin this."

Caleb sat up straight, his face hardening. "Fuck Vincente."

He rose from the couch in one fluid movement. Disappeared into the kitchen. Returned with a white dinette chair and sat down, jean-clad legs spread, the evidence of his desire on display.

"Come here." His fingers beckoned. "You're in charge, baby. I won't touch you unless you ask me to."

Baby.

Her tongue swiped nervously over her lip. "What do you want me to do?"

"Touch me."

His smile was relaxed, his words a casual stroke of assurance. Calm. Non-threatening. "Wherever and however you want."

"Are you sure?" Her fingers flexed.

She knew just where she'd start. His firm, muscled chest. The one she'd had to force herself to assess with a clinical eye earlier. No exam gloves his time. And her tongue. She'd use her tongue to taste that smooth, masculine skin.

"Yes." His hot stare raked her. "You're in control."

A giddy feeling fizzed through her veins. The look on his face sparked a memory of who she used to be.

Bold. Playful. Adventurous.

She stepped forward. Her finger glided over his lips.

Caleb's eyes darkened to molten chocolate. But he didn't move.

She circled behind him. Brushed her fingers over the short strands of his thick, raven hair.

Bending her knees, she whispered a kiss on his ear, then slid down to allow her lips to follow the jagged line of his scar down to the neckline of his white t-shirt. Specks of blood marred the cotton from the earlier attempt on his life.

His chest expanded on a harsh inhale.

"Someone tried to hurt you." Anger. It flickered through her. She might have never met him. Now, because of her, he was in danger again.

She pressed another kiss to his scar. *Iraq*, he'd said.

"He didn't live long enough to succeed."

"Good." She didn't care if that wasn't an appropriate reaction from someone dedicated to saving lives.

Her decision to call Vincente had been the right one.

For Caleb. He thought because he'd been a warrior, that he could handle Vincente.

He was wrong. Vincente never acted alone. Never played by the rules. It wouldn't be a fair fight.

She pushed thoughts of her ex-lover away. He didn't belong here with her and Caleb.

Instead, she dedicated her entire attention to the man in front of her.

What next?

Chest.

Ah, yes.

Her hands slid over his shoulders, down his torso. She gathered cotton and tugged. "Take this off."

"Yes, ma'am."

His biceps flexed. The t-shirt landed on the floor.

Gia moved from behind the chair to drink in the glorious sight.

Defined pecs. Smooth skin and dusky nipples. The carved peaks and valleys of his abs.

A beautiful male specimen. Her fingers trembled, eager to touch.

She threw a leg over his lap and settled, straddling him. Leaning in, she inhaled sandalwood and spice.

His scent dripped over her like hot fudge over ice cream, melting her insides.

Caleb jerked.

She froze, waiting for rough hands to grab her hair. "Should I stop?"

"Hell no." His knuckles were white with the death grip he had on the edges of his seat. "I enjoy your hands on me."

"I enjoy touching you." A blush heated her cheeks as she admitted it.

She smoothed her palms up the corded muscles of his forearms to his biceps. He was all lean, hard muscle, his shoulders broad, his waist narrow.

Her attention shifted to the angles of Caleb's face, tracing the straight line of his nose, admiring the symmetry of his features. His lashes were sinfully long for a man.

Those lashes lifted, the lust burning in his gaze nearly knocking her off his lap.

Speaking of his lap.

An evil grin twisted her lips.

She ground the hot and needy part of her against the hard ridge between her thighs.

Pleasure shot from her clit to her womb and traveled up to her breasts. Enough to make her eyes cross and a gasp to escape.

Caleb's lips parted on a groan.

Who knew freedom could be so addictive?

More.

"Jeans off." Desperate. She couldn't get in a proper breath.

So much for sounding commanding.

"Then take them off."

His words made her shiver.

Not from fear. *No.* She wasn't afraid of Caleb. The dominance in his voice should have made her afraid. She'd grown to hate it before now.

But Caleb was different. His dominance came wrapped in protection rather than exploitation.

She slid from his lap.

His hips lifted.

Nerves made her fumble with his zipper, the sound of the teeth synchronizing with the hiss that tore from Caleb's lips. He kept his hips raised while she wrestled his jeans down, past his black boxer-briefs, and over his knees.

Boots need to go.

She tugged them off, taking his socks with them, then pulled his jeans the rest of the way to the floor.

Then she stood back and simply...admired.

The grip Caleb had on the chair brought his pecs and biceps into sharp relief. He was a Renaissance sculpture, only warm, with beautiful sunset kissed skin and blazing dark eyes that could see clear through to her soul.

And he was hers.

For tonight, at least.

It might be the only night she got. She wouldn't waste it.

Stepping between his splayed legs, she cupped one of his knees. Let her hand drift up his thigh, to the bulge filling out his sexy black briefs.

His hips arched on a groan that filled her with a heady sense of feminine power. "Let me touch you."

"Not yet." She stroked him.

He grew longer, thicker, harder beneath her touch, his hips jerking in small, uncontrolled movements. His head dropped back, exposing the smooth column of his throat. His Adam's apple bobbed on a hard swallow.

She had the urge to bite him there. An ancient claiming. Mark him as hers so that he remembered her after she was gone.

"I'd rather cut off my hand than hurt you," he growled. "I need you to understand."

Her brows furrowed. "I do."

"Then take your clothes off." A guttural growl. A command that demanded she obey. "I need to show you how good it can be. For you. For both of us."

She waited for her stomach to cramp. For anxiety to kick in and steal her desire.

Caleb's dominant nature wanted to be in control. Vincente had always taken control.

It didn't happen.

Instead, her breasts felt heavy, her skin sensitive.

She wanted his hands on her. Caleb's dominance felt...different. Like he was taking her with him, using his dominance for her pleasure, not solely for his own.

She was a partner, not an object for him to slake his lust with.

Slowly, her hands lifted. She gripped the hem of her purple knit sweater.

Inch by inch, she lifted it. Over her stomach, to her breasts. Past her head.

Caleb's eyes blazed with hunger. "Keep going."

The shirt dropped to the floor next to his.

She leaned in. Let her tongue follow the line of his jaw to his ear. "I feel like we should be playing strip poker."

"Too late. I'd win, anyway."

The rasp in his voice, as if he was hanging on by a thread.

She deliberately arched a brow. Taunting. "Who says you'd win?"

Flashing a sassy grin, she stood and stepped out of her slacks.

"Because I'm a competitive SOB and I always win." His heated gaze caressed every inch of her, leaving fire in its wake. "You are so fucking sexy. Take off your bra and straddle me."

"You want this off?" She ran her finger down the lace border of her black bra and licked her lips.

This brazen, wanton side of her she'd locked away in shame stretched her wings with a flourish. "What do we say?"

Oh yeah, that was a sexy purr in her voice.

If it was possible, Caleb's eyes grew even hotter. "Take your bra off and straddle me...please."

Her pelvic muscles clenched, sending more liquid heat to soak her already soaked panties.

Any thought of resisting his commands evaporated beneath an aching void she was desperate for him to fill.

She unhooked her bra and shrugged it off to join the rest of her discarded clothing.

Lifting her leg, she slung it over Caleb's thighs. His erection teased her swollen clit through the thin cotton barrier of their underwear.

She gave in and twisted her hips. Electricity traveled from her core to her breasts. She did it again.

"That's it, baby. Take your pleasure from me." Caleb's voice was strained.

Gia whimpered. The throbbing between her legs intensified. Demanded more.

She twerked her hips again. Shuddered.

Did it again and again.

Her eyes slammed shut. All that mattered was reaching that peak.

"Harder, baby. Take what you need."

Caleb uttered other words. Dirty, sexy words she barely heard.

Her nails dug into his shoulders. Her body coiled tighter.

Almost there.

The orgasm rose and swept her away. She cried out as it washed over her in wave after wave until the tide receded and her senses returned.

Oh God.

She'd just rode Caleb like a pony.

Her eyes flew open.

"You are so fucking beautiful when you come."

He snarled those words. His jaw was granite. His eyes wild.

But he still hadn't touched her.

She glanced down at the white-knuckled grip he had on the chair.

He ensnared her with his eyes.

Lust.

Need.

Admiration?

"I want your nipples beneath my tongue."

When Caleb didn't move to touch her, she cupped her breasts. Brought one rosy tip to his lips.

Warm, moist heat surrounded her sensitive flesh.

He suckled her, gently at first, then with powerful draws that hallowed out his cheeks.

Her hips jerked, attached by an invisible cord to his mouth. Her head fell back with a moan.

"So beautiful," Caleb muttered against her skin.

He transferred his attention to her other breast.

"*Caleb.*"

"Give me permission to touch you, sweetheart. I need to hear you say it."

"Touch me. Oh, God, please touch me."

If he didn't, she was going to go up in flames.

His arms caged her hips. His abs flexed against her inner thighs as he stood in one strong, fluid movement, taking her with him.

"Bedroom," he rasped.

She was too busy clinging to him to answer, inhaling his scent like it was a drug and she needed the high.

She licked the skin behind his ear.

He shuddered, slamming his shoulder into the bedroom door-frame.

Caleb reached out one long arm to rip away the duvet and top sheet.

Gia's back met the mattress, his body covering her.

He took her mouth, his tongue spearing between her lips to claim her. His calloused hands memorized every inch of her skin.

Shifting to his side, he tugged her panties down her legs, leaving her completely bare—in more ways than one.

Possessive. Dominant. So incredibly sexy.

"I want to taste you."

His gaze moved to the juncture between her thighs, but he made no move.

After a moment, Gia's brows furrowed. "Are you waiting for permission?"

"Yes." His eyes met hers, open and direct.

She parted her thighs.

"Don't touch me like I'm fragile, easily broken. I want to be touched like—"

Like I'm loved.

Only she couldn't say that. "—like a normal woman."

His face tightened. "You are a normal woman."

He moved between her spread legs. Lowered his head.

"I take that back." His voice was low, rumbly, and so hot. "You outclass any woman I've ever met."

He dragged his tongue through her folds to curl around her clit.

"*Caleb.*"

His name slipped out on a gasp before she could stop it—raw, breathless, stunned by the rush of pleasure.

"You taste like you smell—sweet desert syrup."

He licked and sucked, driving her mad with the sweetest kind of torture, until she was a mindless creature beneath him, responding only to stimuli.

A finger thrust inside her. Then another.

She dug her heels into the mattress for leverage and rode them hard.

"Come for me, baby." A command wrapped in a velvet whisper.

He kept pumping his hand. Rubbing her clit. Harder, faster.

Gia's body snapped like a rubber band.

Pulsating waves of pleasure crashed over her—a second orgasm, drowning her in bliss.

And freedom.

Yet she still ached with a need only he could fill. Her hands shot out to tangle in his short hair.

"I need you inside me."

Caleb stood. Shucked his briefs.

She sat up, her fingers itching to touch the part of him jutting arrogantly toward her.

He cursed under his breath, scanned the room. "Duffle bag."

Before she formed a response, he'd located it and returned with a foil wrapper in his grip.

"Let me." She held out her hand.

He dropped the packet into her palm.

She tore it open and sheathed him, taking her time.

His legs quivered. His chest heaved. "Tease."

Her hand froze until her brain processed his tone.

Not accusatory. Tight with lust, yes, but affectionate.

Another piece of Caleb found its way into her soul.

The second she'd finished, he pushed her against the mattress and positioned himself at her entrance.

Finally.

His lips caressed the shell of her ear, his warm breath causing goosebumps to pebble her flesh.

"Give me permission, Gia."

"If you don't get inside me right now, I swear, I'll—"

Caleb entered her in one savage thrust, sending the headboard into the wall and stealing the breath from her lungs.

"You feel so good." Braced on his forearms above her, his voice was strained. His face a mask of concentration.

Her body loosened, drew him in deeper.

Someone moaned. Him? Her? Both of them?

He pulled back partway, and the slow drag over her inner walls sent a ripple of pleasure through her. Another thrust. Retreat.

"Look at me, Gia. See who is pleasuring you."

"I see you."

How could she not? His eyes held her in his thrall, mirroring her pleasure. His arms sheltered her. His body claimed her.

She didn't feel used. She felt cherished.

The realization sent her flying into a third, impossible orgasm.

Caleb's hips churned, driving himself into her faster, deeper, without restraint. Then he stilled, coming with a hoarse shout before collapsing.

She held him to her, reveling in his weight, the damp heat of his chest, the way his heart thundered against her breasts, his gasps buffeting her ear.

The ceiling above her blurred as tears found their way to her eyes.

Just her luck. She'd finally found the right man at the wrong time.

Tell him.

About her phone call. Her secret. Everything.

"Stop thinking."

She jerked her gaze from the ceiling to meet his fierce, determined one.

"Just let yourself feel. You and me. Together. No one will take this away from us."

He scowled. "No one."

If only it were that easy.

She kissed him. Let her lips linger to warm his cool ones.

"Maybe if we keep our heads low and stay out of sight, Vincente will get bored and leave us both alone," she whispered.

It was a lie. She realized that now. He'd never let her go.

Not after what she'd witnessed.

Worse, to him, she was his possession.

If he couldn't have her, no one could.

And if Caleb stayed with her, he was still in danger.

One week.

Caleb nipped her ear.

"*Ow.*" She swatted his shoulder.

He hadn't hurt her, really. More like startled her. "What was that for?"

"You're still thinking too hard."

I'll show you hard.

She threaded her hand between them to wrap her fingers around him.

He pushed into her grip, a ragged sound escaping him as his body stirred back to life.

Just a little more time. More time to enjoy Caleb before he found out she was a selfish coward.

"On your back," she murmured, lips brushing his ear. "It's my turn to taste you."

"Hold that thought." Caleb rolled off her and jumped to his feet. "I gotta take care of this condom."

He disappeared into the bathroom before reappearing moments later and practically doing a swan dive onto the bed.

Gia laughed as the mattress bounced beneath her.

If only she could freeze this moment. Keep her and Caleb in a bubble where time had no meaning.

Her gaze wandered over the beautiful, naked man spread out on the bed. Shoving her thoughts aside, she lifted on one elbow and wrapped her fingers around him.

His erection lengthened, grew hard at her touch. He hissed and arched, driving himself deeper into her fist.

"Someone recovered quickly," she purred.

"I've got a gorgeous woman fondling my dick."

She dipped her head. Dragged her lips up his length before taking him into her mouth.

Warm, salty precum coated her tongue. She relaxed her throat and hollowed out her cheeks, alternately sucking and rubbing her tongue against the underside of his crown.

Caleb's hand brushed her hair. She tensed, waiting for him to take over.

"I love how you touch me."

She loved the way his voice sounded. Deep and raspy.

"Keep touching me, Gia. Everything you do feels good."

Her heart swelled. Warmth flooded her body.

She redoubled her efforts, alternately licking and sucking him in as deeply as she could until his breaths grew ragged, and his hips thrust in an erratic pattern that told her he was nearing the edge of his control.

Caleb's hands wrapped hers. "Sweetheart, if you don't want to swallow me, you'd better stop."

Like hell she would. He was hers. Even if she couldn't keep him forever, she'd leave her mark.

She lifted her head. "Please. I want to."

"Are you sure?"

"Yes."

He released his hold on her with a groan.

It didn't take her long to push him over the edge. He came with a shout, and she swallowed him down. Tasted him as he'd tasted her.

And, for the first time, took pleasure in the action.

"Damn." Caleb hauled her to his lips for a gentle, lingering kiss that squeezed her heart.

She tasted both of them, together, on her tongue.

He shifted to his side. Pulled up the covers so they could slide beneath.

A wall of warm, hard flesh pressed against her back. One arm burrowed beneath her neck and the other draped her waist.

A soft kiss brushed her shoulder. "You're amazing. Thank you."

She let out a contented sigh. This was what it felt like to be worshipped by a man. To be safe.

Only she wasn't safe. And neither was Caleb as long as he was with her.

Her post-sex high evaporated.

A heavy sigh gusted the back of her neck. "Babe, you're thinking too hard again."

She faced him. Stared into those beautiful brown eyes. Traced the lips that had caressed her, brought her pleasure.

Told her nothing but truth.

For the rest of her time with Caleb, she'd show him with her body and her heart what he meant to her. She'd do her best to encourage him to reconcile with his family.

So when she had to let him go, when he realized what a coward she was, a part of him might recognize her actions for what they were.

Love.

One week.

CHAPTER TWENTY

VINCENTE TOOK A SIP of tequila and let his free hand wander down the back of the girl bent over the teak executive desk in his office at Club Turquesa. She wore a hot pink sequined dress that barely covered her voluptuous ass—now hiked to her waist, her pink lace thong around her knees.

His phone rang.

He took another sip. Leisurely brushed aside her long brown hair, which had fallen over the cell phone resting on the desk. With the hundred-dollar bill plucked from his own wallet, he brushed away the faint dusting of white powder the girl had just snorted.

Whatever the call was, surely it could wait. He unzipped his trousers.

Glanced at the screen.

Ramón.

Fuck.

His appetite for pleasure gone, he zipped up his pants and slapped the girl on the ass. "I have business to attend to. Another time, *querida.*"

She gave him a pout from glossy pink lips—cosmetically enhanced—adjusted her panties and dress and slipped out to the dance floor.

The door opened again. Juan stepped in.

"Your father just tried to call me," Vincente said, not looking up.

He stared at the screen a beat longer, then sighed and dialed his uncle's number.

"Your men failed."

No greeting. Just straight to gloating, the *cabrón*.

Vincente's fingers tightened around the phone. He hit speaker so Juan could listen in.

"Why the continued interest in my affairs, *Tío*? I'm sure you must have better things to do."

Besides trying to make him look weak and incompetent in front of his father.

"I'm trying to look out for you, *Sobrino*. You'd be wise to take my counsel. Do you think to do business behind a jail cell if your *puta* goes to the *Federales*? Do you believe the Aztec Kings will not cut us out of our own business and side with Los Coyotes if they sense weakness?"

His uncle didn't wait for a reply. "Your father never had to reassure himself of his power. His enemies and friends alike fear *El Víbora*—and for good reason."

The fake concern made Vincente's teeth grind. So did the constant reminders that Tío Ramón thought him a pale shadow of his father.

Let the old man keep talking.

Once he took over the business, he'd squeeze Ramón's operation until his uncle had no choice but to surrender whatever scraps of power he still clung to, and spend the rest of his days drowning in tequila at the family compound.

Or better yet, he'd give Ramon's business to Juan. Let his uncle choke on the irony. See what he'd lost by mistreating his own son.

Vincente cast a sideways glance at his cousin.

Although...he'd have to take care if he did that. Power changed people. Made them disloyal.

He returned to the call with his uncle. "There is no threat to business. I'm in contact with the Aztec Kings. The other matter is personal. It's handled."

By the end of the week, Abigail—no, Gianna—would be back in Miami.

Not because he trusted her. He didn't. He'd already taken steps to ensure her compliance.

"Your whore hides on the Navajo reservation. Now she has a bodyguard—one who's beaten your men. Twice."

"I'm handling it," Vincente snapped. His uncle was goading him, trying to take the upper hand. He wouldn't give him the satisfaction.

"You mean you've let your men handle it. Maybe it's time you saw to this personally, no? To make sure it gets done right. It's what your father would've done at your age."

The dig slid beneath Vincente's ribs like a stiletto. Ramón never missed a chance to remind him he wasn't his father. That he was too soft. Too polished. Too comfortable in a life of privilege.

Which was a lie.

Just because he preferred Miami to Mexico didn't mean he wasn't focused on expanding Espina Negra's reach.

His gaze shifted to the framed photos on his office wall. There was the one of him with Miami's mayor, Sonja Ojeda, at her reelection fundraiser. The mayor was an important connection. He'd been quite generous with his support.

Strategic.

His father and uncle were stuck in the old ways. They built their empire with cunning, violence, and blood.

Vincente had a different vision—a twenty-first century one. Networking. Infrastructure. Innovation.

This new fentanyl, manufactured with precursor chemicals from China, was cheaper, more addictive, and easier to move. It was the future.

If they could dominate the US market, they'd crush every rival in Mexico—including the upstart Los Coyotes.

"Your concern is touching, *Tío,* but you're starting to sound like an old auntie." Vincente didn't bother to mask the sarcasm. "Maybe it's time you focused on your side of the business."

Trafficking in people and weapons. Messy. Outdated.

His uncle could play the old school *jefe* while Vincente built a modern enterprise. Expand product. Grow market share. Clean the money. Invest it in legitimate businesses. Repeat.

"*Papi* was pleased with the latest figures from my operation," Vincente added, a sheen of false warmth coating his words. "If I recall, yours weren't quite as impressive last month. Now, if you will excuse me, I'm a busy man."

He hung up, the sound of his uncle's furious sputtering music to his ears.

"You shouldn't provoke him like that." Juan stepped closer to the table, resting his hip on the edge. "My father can be as dangerous as yours."

"He's a meddling old fool who knows his days are numbered."

Juan shrugged. "Perhaps he's right about Gianna."

A huff of annoyance escaped Vincente. "I have a business to run. I look weak if I drop everything to run after a woman. Gianna will come to me because she has no choice. Not if she wants to keep her friends alive."

He met his cousin's stare. "But her defiance won't go unpunished. And as soon as she's back, her new companion will be dealt with. A reminder that actions have consequences."

Caleb Varella.

A slow burn of rage simmered in Vincente's blood.

Had the man touched what belonged to Vincente? Pleasured himself with Gianna? Had she welcomed it?

Red tinged the edges of his vision. The near constant burn in his chest flared hotter.

"What of the Aztec Kings?" Juan asked.

Vincente blinked. Refocused. "I've spoken personally to their leader. He assured me the rumors about Los Coyotes are untrue. Matteo vouched for him—said he wouldn't double-cross us this way. He understands the consequences."

Still, tension knotted his shoulders. If he was wrong, the fallout would be costly. Worse, his *tío* would be right.

That alone would be insufferable.

"Matteo's been in Phoenix for years now, attending to Espina Negra business. How well does he know the current Aztec leadership?" Juan shrugged and reached into the top left pocket of his white linen guayabera. He pulled out a pack of cigarettes. "A personal visit would allow you to shake this man's hand. Look him in the eye. The old way of sealing an agreement."

He pulled a cigarette out, offering one to Vincente in a wordless gesture.

Vincente shook his head. His vices were many, but the only tobacco he inhaled came from Cuban cigars, not cheap American shit.

The old ways.

At times, Juan still clung to tradition, like their fathers. Loyalty enforced by violence. Fear. Death.

Of course, his cousin *had* been the one to discover the DEA spy. Who'd encouraged Vincente to handle the matter himself, instead of taking care of the problem like he usually would.

Vincente's lips turned down. A messy business. He'd make it up to Gianna—once he'd brought her to heel.

Juan scraped the dial on his lighter and lit his cigarette, the tip glowing orange as he inhaled, then exhaled a stream of smoke. "You gave Gianna a week. Let Bembe watch the club and the restaurants for a few days. You and I take some men, visit the new distributor and bring Gianna home. Then all this will blow over, and my father will have nothing to gossip about."

Juan's gaze flicked to the modernist painting over Vincente's shoulder—splashes of red and yellow. It lingered there. "He'll sacrifice Gianna just to prove a point to you. Same as he did to me with Carlita."

Carlita had been lowlife trash compared to Gianna, but Vincente wasn't cruel enough to say that out loud.

He opened the center drawer of his desk and took out his acid reflux medicine.

Too much stress. He needed a distraction.

He tapped the monitor and brought up the feed to the main dance floor. Bodies pressed tight together beneath flickering strobes that pulsed like gunfire.

There she was—the brunette from earlier. Long, wavy hair. Pink sequined dress.

She and her friends danced without a care in the world.

"I'll think about it." Vincente gestured to the monitor. "Send that woman and her friends free drinks and access to the VIP area."

Tío Ramón, your days are numbered.

He gave his cousin a slow smile. One laced with promise. "Tonight, we enjoy ourselves."

CHAPTER
TWENTY-ONE

CALEB AWOKE WITH A hard-on, which wasn't unusual. After all, he was a healthy man of a certain age.

What was unusual was his erection lay trapped between his stomach and the silky cleft of Gia's ass—a reminder of where he'd been last night.

Deep inside her.

A faint glow of pale light lit the closed blinds in their rental bedroom of white, letting him know sunrise was on the horizon. Cool air clung to the room, tinged with the faint acrid scent of the electric heat kicking on.

He eased from beneath the covers, careful not to disturb her, grabbed his jeans, a fresh pair of underwear, and one of his new t-shirts—navy blue—and headed for the shower.

When he checked on her, Gia was still asleep, so he made his way to the kitchen to start the coffee.

The kitchen was as white as the rest of the home—cabinets, counter, table and chairs—the only color found on the adobe tile floor and the framed print of Monument Valley on the wall. Even so, this rental had more flair than his apartment in Northern Virginia.

What did that say about him?

Then there was Gia's home. A real home—not just a place to sleep. The homey touches she'd added in such a short time—the worn brown sofa, colorful throw rugs, succulents in pots with brightly colored blossoms, and the lingering aroma of a home-cooked meal.

Coffee dripped into the glass carafe as he stared at it, unseeing. Gia wanted to stay on the rez. Five days ago, the thought would have been a nonstarter. Now his carefully ordered life felt like a tangled mess of loose ends and conflicting truths.

Zach was growing on him—he could admit that much, even with the asshole's obvious infatuation with Gia. The man was a solid cop. A decent human being.

As for his grandfather? Caleb's sigh merged with the last hiss of steam from the coffeemaker. He still needed more answers about his mother's estrangement from her family.

Soft arms slipped around his waist.

Gia pressed a kiss between his shoulder blades. "I wondered where you went."

Turning to face her, he took in the sight of her wearing his white t-shirt from last night—nothing else visible but long, bare legs.

He dropped a kiss to her mouth, slow and lingering. "How'd you sleep?"

Her smile reminded him of the Mona Lisa. Full of feminine mystery. "Better than I have in a long time."

"Good. You needed it." He couldn't help arching his brow. "Must've been all the great sex."

Her cheeks pinkened. "Might have been."

She peered at him through her lashes and gave him a sly smile. "We may need to do it again to test that hypothesis."

Count him in as an enthusiastic participant. "Anything I can do to assist. After all, a hypothesis should be tested multiple times to account for different variables."

"Imagine all the variables we could try," she purred.

Purred.

There was no other way to describe the velvet brush of her voice across his skin.

The carnal look in her eyes made his dick stand at attention.

Breakfast could wait.

Gripping her waist, he lifted her onto the counter. Her shirt bunched in his hands, exposing her hips.

No panties.

Caleb forgot to breathe.

Lust rolled over him in a tidal wave and short-circuited any rational thought. His fingers curled around her thighs. Held them open.

"Look at you, sweetheart. So beautiful."

His voice came out a guttural rasp. Which was fitting because his instincts were all animal at the moment.

He swiped a finger down her slit. Gathered up her honey and brought it to his lips.

So sweet. His desert rose.

"*Caleb.*" Gia arched beneath his touch, exposing the smooth, pale column of her neck.

It was an offering he was powerless to resist. His mouth latched onto the soft skin. He nipped, then licked, branding her with his mark.

She shuddered. Pulled him closer.

Not enough room on the counter.

Not for what he wanted to do. He lifted his head long enough to scan his surroundings.

Table. Round with a pedestal base. Sturdy enough.

Scooping Gia in his arms, he carried her to the breakfast nook, beneath a window that looked out at open grassland and a grazing donkey.

He laid her out like a sacrifice. Dropped to his knees and hauled her to his mouth.

And feasted.

The sexy sounds she made, the way her hips moved, pressing herself against him. He was drunk with lust.

He thrust two fingers into her. *So tight. So hot.* Reveled in her gasp. Mimicked what he intended to do with his cock as he used his lips and tongue on her and in her.

Her hands fisted in his hair, sending pinpricks of pleasure pain over his scalp that he welcomed.

"Harder. Oh, God, Caleb. I need it harder."

Hell yes.

He'd give her the world right now.

She was so damn beautiful, splayed out like a goddess for him. And she was close. He could feel it. Hear it in her voice.

His fingers pumped faster. Stretched her. His lips suckled harder.

She came with a breathless scream, her inner walls tightening around him in pulsating waves that almost ripped his own orgasm from him.

He surged to his feet. Tore at the button on his jeans. Yanked down the zipper. His dick was in his hand and at her entrance—

"*Fuck.*" Even to his own ears, his voice was a snarl of pure sexual frustration.

Gia lifted onto her elbows and gazed at him with unfocused eyes. "What's wrong?"

"Condom."

The bedroom felt like it was a mile away.

"I'm on birth control." The desperation in her voice made his hips jerk. "And I'm clean. I got tested when I started my job at the clinic."

"I'm clean, too."

He wanted her so badly he was ready to walk over fire if that's what it took, but he wouldn't take this choice from her.

"What do you want me to do? I've got some in the bedroom."

Her eyes softened. "I want you. Inside me. Now. I trust you."

Holy hell, how this woman gutted him.

He drove into her so hard the table shuddered.

Without the barrier of latex, her inner walls gripped him flesh to flesh, the sensation so hot it made his eyes roll to the back of his head.

Her body softened, adjusted to his invasion, taking him deeper.

He lifted her. Spread her wider. Deepened his angle of penetration.

"Caleb. That feels so good."

Her moan of pleasure made him even harder. The prick of her nails on his biceps urged him on.

He took her mouth and let his control shatter, pistoning his hips in a frenzy of movement that shook the table and threatened a collapse.

Electrical impulses raced up and down his shaft. His muscles clenched.

Not yet. Not without Gia.

He reached between them. Rubbed her with quick, firm strokes.

"Come with me, baby."

Her walls tightened around him.

He rubbed harder. "Now."

Gia let out a keening cry as her orgasm took over, milking him.

Every molecule of his body converged to a singular point as he emptied himself into her in endless contractions that threatened to take him out of this world.

Mine.

Caleb's forearms hit the table. Still lodged inside her, his breath still ragged against her skin, reality settled over him like a heavy cloak.

He had just taken her bare. Nothing between them. No excuses.

His body was still humming with pleasure, but his mind raced.

The word that thundered through him moments ago—*mine*—hadn't faded. If anything, it felt more dangerous in the quiet aftermath.

He eased off her, pressing a lingering kiss to her collarbone before tucking himself back into his jeans.

"Gia?"

She stilled for a moment before answering. "I'm okay."

He heard the slight tremor beneath the words.

Her lashes pressed to her cheeks, denying him a peek into her soul.

Dammit. She still kept secrets from him.

God help him, he wanted her anyway. She was already too deep under his skin.

Caleb clenched his jaw. He'd spent years avoiding attachments for this exact reason—because once you had something, you had something to lose.

Turned out he was no better than her bastard ex, because he had no intention of letting her go.

"Tell me about your friends." Gia took a bite of the eggs Caleb scrambled while she showered and dressed.

She'd decided on her black jeans for a change, and topped them with a wool blend royal blue turtleneck. On her feet, she wore fuzzy socks to counteract the chill of the wood and tile flooring.

"Friends?"

He appeared confused at her question, and her heart broke a little.

From what she'd learned of him, he'd grown up in a troubled home, disconnected from his family and, like her, seemed to have shied away from cultivating deep friendships.

"There are a couple of guys I served with in the Army. My colleagues at Dìleas. My boss, Ryder Montague. I consider him a friend."

He smiled. A genuine smile that warmed her soul. "He lives in London with his fiancée, Nathalie."

"I've never had many friends." Gia gave a shrug that felt too casual, even to her. "It's hard to get close to people when you're living a lie."

Caleb's fork paused midair. His gaze sharpened, and she had the sense he'd read her too well.

"You're not living a lie anymore. Right?" His words were careful, measured.

Her breath caught. She forced a small smile.

"No. Not anymore."

It was mostly true. She wasn't pretending to be someone else. She wasn't hiding under a new name in a new town.

But the one secret she still held had the power to destroy everything good she'd started to build here. With the Navajo. With Caleb.

His stare unnerved her. "What aren't you telling me?"

She set down her mug. One day—soon—Caleb was going to discover it all.

Everything she'd done.

And hadn't done.

She wasn't ready for that.

The temperature in the room felt ten degrees warmer. She swiped at the perspiration dampening her hairline.

"You know I have reason to be afraid. Vincente is dangerous. Dangerous people answer to him."

"I do." His voice was steady. "But I also know there's something you haven't told me yet." Something in his eyes made her pulse hammer.

The sharp blast of a car horn jolted her.

Caleb was on his feet in an instant. He snatched his gun off the kitchen counter and peered out the front facing window. "It's Zach."

"What's he doing here this early?" She rose on shaky legs, grateful for the reprieve. Caleb had been moments from demanding answers she couldn't give.

"I don't know." His voice had dropped, edged with steel. "But it's not a social call."

He opened the front door, using his body to block the entrance. "Tell me you have good news and Lopez's band of merry men are in jail."

"There's been an accident." Zach's voice came from the other side of the door. "Jennie tried to reach Gia this morning, but she didn't answer her phone."

"Oh, shoot." Her stomach dropped. Doctor Lewis was back from his conference and on call last night, and after the way she'd reacted to the unknown caller, she'd left her phone on silent for her own peace of mind.

She tugged Caleb's arm, easing him aside so she could face Zach. "What kind of accident?"

"Some teenagers in the back of a pickup," Zach said. "The kid driving lost control, and the kids in the back went flying. Jennie's on her way from the clinic, she asked for you."

"Send someone else." Caleb's face was cold, his voice hard.

"Caleb!" He couldn't possibly believe she would turn down Jennie's plea for help.

Zach whipped off his cap, ran fingers through his hair, dislodging strands from the short ponytail he'd fastened at his nape.

"I get it. But Doc Lewis is at the clinic, he can't leave. Doc Chee is about to have her kid any minute—she's the one Gia replaced. The nearest medic unit is already engaged on a call."

He glanced at Gia before leveling a stare at Caleb. "We need her."

"I'll get my coat." Gia trotted to the bedroom and returned with her jacket and Caleb's.

Caleb let out a defeated sigh. "I was trained as a medic."

"Good, you can help." Zach jerked his thumb toward his Tahoe. "We'll take the cruiser."

Dust billowed as Zach gunned the Tahoe down dirt roads into the rez, Gia clutching the grab handle in the back seat to keep from shaking to pieces as the accident site came into view.

A pickup, caked in dried mud, lay on its side next to a rocky outcropping. Nearby an older model Toyota sedan sat askew, Jennie's red Nissan Frontier parked behind it.

Four teenagers—two girls and two boys—their faces pale and anxious, sat hunched by the side of the road. A fifth teenager—a boy—lay motionless beside the overturned truck, a woman kneeling beside him.

Jennie rushed over as soon as Zach braked. "I just got here."

She gestured with a quick nod toward the frantic woman at the boy's side. "That's Darlene Yazzie—her son was driving."

Gia was already moving. "Trauma kit?"

"I've got two in my truck." Jennie sprinted to retrieve them.

Gia handed Caleb one and grabbed the other. "You and Zach triage the others. Jennie and I will assess the boy."

She dropped to her knees beside the unconscious teenager and snapped on a pair of gloves. "What's his name?"

Jennie gently steered the sobbing mother back. "His name is Keough."

"Keough, can you hear me?" Gia checked his airway and listened to his chest.

A faint, high-pitched whistle. Lips tinged blue. Her fingers found the telltale shift in his trachea.

Collapsed lung.

She lifted the boy's eyelids to reveal a blown left pupil.

Her lips flattened. Traumatic brain injury. A quick physical assessment revealed a dislocated wrist and cracked ribs.

"Jennie, stabilize his head." Gia gave the boy's shoulder a hard pinch.

He responded with a faint moan, but didn't open his eyes.

She raised her voice. "Zach!"

He jogged over. "How bad?"

"Collapsed lung, possible brain trauma. Can you get a medivac out here?"

"On it." He stepped away, already radioing for air support.

Darlene choked out a sob and dropped to her knees next to her son. "One of the girls said a silver SUV came out of nowhere—cut Keough off. Made him swerve."

Gia's mouth flattened. "Someone will know who it was." Strangers didn't wander into this part of the reservation.

Caleb jogged over as she prepped a needle for decompression. "Need help?"

"Oxygen tank. Back of Jennie's truck."

Caleb returned with the tank as Gia inserted the needle into Keough's chest. A sharp whoosh of air escaped, the boy's breathing evening out slightly. Gia secured the cannula as his color improved.

The sound of rotor blades reached them.

Thank God.

They worked swiftly to stabilize Keough, loading him onto the medevac. His mother took off in her car for the hospital after assuring Zach she was in control and could drive.

As the helicopter lifted off, Gia turned to Caleb. "The others?"

"Two fractures, one concussion. No spinal injuries. They need to go to the clinic, but they'll be okay."

Relief loosened the knot in her chest. "You and Zach get the kids loaded in the Tahoe, Jennie and I will clean up." Empty wrappers and plastic caps littered the ground at both triage sites.

She admired the back of Caleb's jeans as he wandered over to the group.

Jennie bumped her shoulder. "Your bodyguard is hot *and* handy. You sure you don't want to keep him?"

Gia shook her head, fighting a smile.

"What?" Jennie's eyes twinkled. "You two aren't related. You could—"

She cut Jennie off. "Let's get these kids to the clinic." The things she'd done with Caleb were burned into her brain.

"Your face is on fire." Jennie gave a mock pout. "I want to hear every sordid detail later."

They made quick work of the cleanup. Gia walked Jennie back to her truck.

Jennie slid into the driver's seat.

Click. Click. Click.

She frowned. "Oh, come on."

Another turn of the key. Still nothing—just clicks.

With an exasperated glance at Gia, Jennie muttered, "I think it's the battery."

Zach had sauntered over. "Let me see." He motioned her out and slid behind the wheel.

Click. Click. Click.

"That's not the battery. It's the starter."

Gia eyed the Tahoe. Seven seats. Eight people.

One seat short.

Jennie must have been thinking the same thing. "I'll stay behind," she offered. "Richie Benally has to come tow Keough's truck."

She sighed. "I guess I'll have him tow mine, too."

Zach scowled. "You're not staying here alone."

"Then drop everyone off and come back for me." Jennie waved her phone and gave Zach a smirk. "I'll watch cat videos."

Gia hesitated, unease ghosting across her skin. "Are you sure you'll be safe?"

She caught Caleb's eye. His jaw was tight. Something felt...wrong. He looked as if he felt it, too.

Zach didn't look any happier.

"I'll stay with Jennie." Caleb leveled a hard stare at Zach. "You make sure nothing happens to Gia."

"Oh, for goodness sakes, look around." Jennie gave a half-twirl, her hands out, framing the buttes rising like sentinels nearby. "How much trouble could I get in? The Tohtsonis live, what, three miles from here? And the Sandoval farm is just over that ridge."

She made a shooing motion. "Go. Take care of those kids."

"I'll be back in an hour," Zach muttered.

"You worry too much." Jennie flashed a grin. "Richie will probably arrive before you do."

She gave Zach an arch look. "Maybe he'll buy me dinner."

Zach's eyes narrowed.

Gia climbed into the Tahoe, stomach unsettled as they pulled away. *She'll be fine.*

The unease nagging at Gia's brain was something different. Something Keough's mother had said to her.

What was it?

She stared out the window at her friend until Jennie and her red truck disappeared from view.

Chapter
Twenty-Two

UNEASE PRICKLED AT THE base of Caleb's skull as he sat next to Zach on the drive to the clinic. Bony fingers tapped out a message he couldn't decode.

Potholes forced Zach to move at a crawl, careful not to jostle the injured teens more than necessary.

Gia suddenly gripped his shoulder from the back seat. "Keogh's mother said there was another car involved. An SUV."

Zach muttered a low curse.

Caleb twisted, catching the eye of the girl cradling her fractured wrist. "What happened?"

The girl, Mckayla, hesitated, glancing at Zach. "We were out just having fun, ya know? Keough was on his way to pick up Zoey, his girlfriend, when this silver SUV flew up behind us."

"Silver, you're sure?" Caleb questioned. "Did you catch the model?"

The girl shrugged.

"GMC." The boy with the broken leg piped up. "It was on the grille."

Caleb's pulse ticked up. *Silver GMC.*

"Did you see the driver?" he pressed.

"Not really. It happened so fast. There was someone in the passenger seat." Mckayla looked at her friends for confirmation.

They nodded.

Zach called it in. "Dispatch, Unit One, we have a ten-fifty-seven, hit-and-run. Vehicle involved is a silver GMC SUV. Driver fled the scene."

He shot Caleb a grim look. "Be advised—it may be the same SUV from yesterday's drive-by."

Gia gasped. "Jennie."

They reached the paved road. Zach gunned the motor and tore off, sirens blaring, for the clinic.

"If they didn't circle back while we were there, they're long gone." Caleb didn't believe it, not really, but he said it anyway. "Any other units close?"

"No. We're spread thin," Zach said. He glanced at Gia in the rearview mirror. "Text Jennie. We don't want to alarm her, but tell her if a silver GMC shows up, lock her doors and call me."

Gia whipped out her cell, her thumbs moving rapidly over the screen.

The clinic came into view up ahead.

Caleb was out of the vehicle as soon as it stopped. He opened Gia's door. "She'll be okay." The words rang hollow.

"I sent the text." Her brows furrowed. "But I'm not sure it went through. Maybe now that we're on Wi-Fi."

Inside the clinic, frantic parents swarmed them. Fluorescent lights buzzed overhead as nurses converged on the chaos.

Caleb stepped aside while Zach handled the parents and Gia briefed the medical staff on duty.

Mid-brief, she glanced down at her phone, and her body visibly relaxed.

So did Caleb's—she must have heard from Jennie.

Once she'd finished her brief and let the medical staff take over, she returned to his side.

"Jennie texted back." Relief softened her face. "No silver SUV." Her phone dinged. She laughed and held it up.

> Guess who just pulled up. Remember the hot-
> tie delivery driver? Tell Zach to call me before
> he heads back. I may not be here…

"Feel better now?" Caleb didn't. The back of his neck still tingled.

"About Jennie? Yes." Her smile faded. "That these kids may have been run off the road by Vincente's men, no."

She shook her head. "It's got to be someone else, someone who lives on the rez. Why would his men be this far from the populated areas?"

Because they're hunting.

Time to set the trap.

Caleb shot off a text to Nathan.

> Situation here escalating. Need a favor.
> Lopez has to believe his deal with the Aztec
> Kings is unraveling enough to force a person-
> al visit. Manufacture some chatter between
> the Kings and Los Coyotes. Make sure it leaks.

Quiet whispers that would grow louder. Too loud to ignore. Too layered to dismiss with a single phone call.

And if Gia was the final nudge to get Lopez here?

Hell No.

That option was off the table. He'd give Lopez a reason—but it wouldn't be her.

His heart kicked hard. Sweat broke across his brow.

Now he got it.

Why Ryder broke protocol for Nathalie. Why Nathan and Lachlan had risked everything for their women.

"What's the matter." Gia was watching him too closely.

His phone vibrated. A reply from Nathan.

I'm on it.

Zach walked up to them. Tension carved lines into the corners of his eyes. "I can't get ahold of Jennie. I called Richie Benally, the tow truck driver. He hasn't reached the accident site yet."

"She texted me," Gia assured him. "The guy who delivered our medical supplies yesterday morning showed up. I think she's hitching a ride with him."

"Who is this guy?"

Caleb noted the way Zach stiffened. His sharp tone. Maybe his cousin wasn't as indifferent to Jennie as he'd assumed.

Gia's eyes widened. Her gaze shot to Caleb, suddenly wary. "I don't know. I'd never seen him before. Jennie said he was new. He seemed friendly, flirted with all the nurses."

Zach scowled. "She still needs to answer her damn phone."

"Let's go back to the site." Caleb needed to see for himself. Judging by the tic in Zach's jaw, so did he. "We'll double check she's not there, talk to the tow operator, then you can take us back to the safe house."

He and Gia were too exposed. They needed to lie low, out of sight, while he set his plan in motion.

By the time they returned to the accident scene, two tow trucks were there, the operators working to stabilize the overturned pickup so they could right it and get it loaded. Jennie's truck was parked in the same spot as when they left.

No sign of Jennie.

Caleb stayed in the Tahoe with Gia while Zach questioned the two men.

Frustration simmered on Zach's face when he came back. "Richie and Tristin, the other tow operator, said Jennie was gone by the time they arrived. Her truck's locked and she didn't leave the key—They looked everywhere for it."

Warning sirens blared in Caleb's head. "Take us back to the house."

"Why didn't she leave the key?" Zach held his phone to his ear, his lips thinning in a grim line. "She's still not answering her phone."

Caleb glanced back at Gia. "You try calling her."

After a moment, Gia's worried gaze met his in the rearview mirror. "She's not answering me, either. Maybe her phone died?"

She was reaching, grasping at straws. Caleb didn't blame her.

Maybe Jennie had her phone on silent and was too busy flirting with the delivery guy to notice. Maybe her battery *had* died. Maybe she was in a cell phone dead spot—God knows there were plenty on the rez.

There were too many reasonable explanations to get through before they considered foul play.

As they drove toward Gallup, Caleb scanned every vehicle on the road. When they arrived at the safe house, he and his cousin cleared the perimeter first, then moved inside while Gia waited in the Tahoe.

Once they were sure it was secure, Caleb ushered Gia indoors, then trailed Zach out to his cruiser.

"I'm heading to Jennie's," Zach said, his jaw set. "I'll let you know when I find her—if I don't strangle her first."

Caleb rested his forearms on the Tahoe's open window and met his cousin's stare. "I can get a trace on her cellphone faster than you can get a warrant to access the data."

"Thanks. I hope I don't need it."

"Call me when you hear anything. Gia's worried."

Back inside, Caleb followed the sharp clang of pans and rattle of cabinet doors into the kitchen.

"Lunch—you hungry?" Gia flew around the small kitchen, tossing bread, sliced turkey, cheese, and condiments carelessly on the counter. "We didn't get lunch—look at the time."

He stepped into her path and bent until they were eye level. "Gia, look at me." His voice was steady. "Let's not assume the worst, okay?"

Fear darkened her sapphire eyes to midnight. "Jennie always answers her phone. Her texts."

He had no response to give that would reassure her.

They ate in strained silence. Sat on the couch after. Waited.

Finally, Caleb's phone rang. *Zach.*

"Richie went back for Jennie's truck," Zach said. "He jimmied the lock. Her cell phone was on the floor, passenger side."

Hell. "And her home?" Caleb asked.

"I'm here now. No sign of her. I checked with the neighbors. No one's seen her come or go since this morning."

Gia's phone rang beside him. She'd barely let it out of her hands since they got back, checking it again and again.

She glanced at the screen—and a strangled sound escaped her throat.

The phone slipped from her hand.

"Hold on, Zach." Dread slithered between Caleb's ribs. "Gia, what is it, baby?"

"This is my fault." She shot to her feet. "All my fault." Her arms wrapped her waist. Her stare focused on something he couldn't see.

Caleb picked up her phone.

Insurance, querida, that you will return to me.

Attached to the text was a photo of Jennie Tsosie, one eye swollen shut, the other wide with terror.

Caleb held his own phone to his ear, grim. He steeled himself for what he had to tell his cousin.

"Lopez has Jennie."

Chapter
Twenty-Three

Guilt coated Gia's conscience—thick, ugly as tar.

Vincente hadn't believed her when she told him she'd return to Miami. But kidnapping Jennie?

She hadn't expected that.

She'd retreated to the bedroom after Vincente's message. Caleb filled the doorway now, solid and steady.

"It's not your fault."

"Stop making excuses for me." The words burst out before she could stop them. The anger felt sharp. Real. Almost...good.

Better than fear.

"Vincente tried to kill you because of me. They took Jennie because of me."

"Lopez is responsible for his actions, not you." Calm. Not a flicker of emotion in Caleb's eyes.

Damn him.

All it did was make her angrier—not at him. At herself.

"It *is* on me. Because I'm a coward."

His gaze narrowed. "How's that?"

Later, she could mourn what might have been.

He stepped all the way into the room. "What aren't you telling me?"

The composure she'd cultivated through med school and years spent treating patients had shattered the moment she'd learned of the attack on Caleb. She'd acted on impulse, ruled by fear.

"Vincente tried to have you killed." She paced the bedroom, hands tangled in her hair. "I called him that afternoon—threatened to expose him if he didn't back off."

If he didn't leave you alone.

But Vincente had found a loophole. He hadn't gone after Caleb again. Instead, he'd seized an innocent woman to force both Gia's silence and her return.

Caleb's jaw hardened, a chill darkening his eyes. "Expose him how?"

Guilt stabbed deep. Her breath hitched. Words clawed their way up, but she forced them down.

"Gia," he pressed, "if you have information we can use, I need to know. I can protect you."

"No, you can't." His face blurred through her tears. "Not from this."

Vincente kept proving, again and again, how futile escape truly was.

"You're hiding something." Caleb's voice carried an edge now. "Tell me."

She shook her head. Saying it out loud meant reliving it—the gunshot. The helplessness that had rooted her feet while a man bled out in front of her.

The chill in Vincente's eyes. Juan's laughter. The crew's indifference.

Caleb stepped in. Close enough that she could feel his heat.

He cupped her chin in his palm. "Whatever it is, baby, we're in this together."

His tenderness shattered her walls.

The truth she'd choked down and kept hidden for over two months spilled from her lips.

"Vincente...he shot him." The words wobbled out. "I saw him die."

The fingers on her chin tightened.

"So much blood." Her voice dropped. "It stained the white deck. I can still smell it."

A metallic, sweet odor. She saw blood, smelled it often in her practice. But this...Not even the stiff ocean breeze could wash it away.

She shut her eyes, too late to stop the flood of memory.

"I tried to help him. Vincente held me back—said Antonio was a DEA spy." Her laugh was bitter. "That this was an unfortunate part of his business and as his future wife, one I needed to understand."

Her throat swelled, nearly choking her. "Vincente's cousin, Juan, dragged Antonio's body to the railing...I watched him sink."

And she'd screamed, the wind ripping away her cries.

Silence stretched between them.

Caleb's hand dropped away. He exhaled, rough and quiet. "Jesus."

"I stayed a few more days. Tried to act normal, so he wouldn't watch me too closely. Made a plan. Then I took out as much money as I could from my accounts and hopped on a Greyhound bus headed west."

His lips thinned. "You were afraid."

"I was selfish." She swiped at her tears. "Vincente and Juan would be in jail now if I possessed an ounce of moral courage. Antonio's family doesn't know what happened to their loved one. Did he leave behind a wife? Children who will grow up without a father?"

It sickened her every time she thought about it.

Her Louis Vuitton suitcase sat in the corner. Reliving the memory brought back the suffocating terror, the helplessness.

A tremor shook her.

Run. A new name. Another city.

She could still do it.

But Jennie was out there.

Scared. Alone.

And Caleb was here.

Standing beside her. A rock who stood firm in the lashing rain.

Her fingers curled into fists.

She was done running. "I need to contact the DEA. Tell them what happened to Antonio."

There. She steeled herself for the condemnation. The disappointment that she wasn't the woman he thought she was.

Caleb's head tilted to one side. "Keeping the murder quiet, was that your leverage?"

"Yes."

"And he agreed to leave you alone?" The disbelief in his voice scraped against her already raw nerves.

She couldn't look at him. "I told him I'd return to Miami. By the end of the week."

"Over my dead body," he snarled.

Her head snapped up.

Caleb had that cold, hard look. The same one she'd seen the first night they'd met at the bar, when she hadn't known if he was on the side of the angels or darkness.

Her hand shot out, clutching his arm before she could stop herself, nails biting into his skin. "If you stay with me, that's exactly what will happen. Vincente will come after you. But I never had any intention of going back."

"What was the plan then? Run again?" Now his voice went dangerously soft.

Exactly as it had before he took out Vincente's men in a blur of movement she'd had trouble tracking.

A shiver crept up her spine. "Run. Stay and risk everyone I care about."

Including you.

"Or turn myself in, testify against Vincente, and end up in Witness Protection." Her mouth trembled. "I guess I'll end up in a new town with a new identity after all."

If she lived. And even if she made it into Witness Protection, what kind of life would she have without friends, a career?

Without Caleb.

How, in such a short time, had he come to mean so much to her?

He'd freed her. Emotionally. Sexually. She felt strong around him.

Cared for.

She squared her shoulders. "Clearly, he didn't believe me. I'm ready to go to the DEA," she repeated, "and tell them everything I know if it will save Jennie."

There would be questions. They'd tear apart her Abigail Winters identity. She might even lose her medical license. Watching a man die and staying silent—it had to violate the Hippocratic Oath, at least in spirit.

Caleb shook his head, rejection in every line of his taut body. "If you go to the authorities, Lopez will lawyer up and paint you as the liar—a woman who misled him about her true identity and then disappeared. Maybe he'll claim you stole money, and that's why you ran. He'll gaslight you. We'll never find Jennie."

"Then offer him a trade. Jennie for me."

His eyes flashed fire. "No way in hell."

Stubborn man.

She stepped in close, pressing herself against his chest to force his full attention. His muscles were hard, his fists clenched—but she didn't miss the sudden flare in his pupils at the contact.

"Listen to me. Vincente doesn't know about your estrangement from your family, and though he might suspect something between us, he has no proof. Tell him Jennie's your cousin. That you won't let family suffer for some outsider. Tell him it's me for her."

"He won't buy it."

"He will," she insisted. Her stomach bottomed out at the thought of being anywhere near her ex-lover again. "He's arrogant enough to believe it."

When his expression didn't budge, she threw out her trump card. "You can get justice for your mother."

Caleb spun away, raking a hand through his hair.

Gia held her breath. Waited.

He wheeled back around, jabbing a finger toward her. "As much as I'd like to avenge my *amá*, this isn't about her. This is about you."

His voice dropped, rough with emotion. "I won't sacrifice you."

Her heart fluttered at the look in his eyes. "It's the only way," she whispered.

Surely he could see that.

She saw the moment his eyes registered defeat. Then his gaze shuttered.

"I have a call to make."

The missing DEA agent.

Caleb stepped outside the cottage in nothing but his navy t-shirt and jeans, letting the bite of high desert winter air slap against his skin.

Maybe it would shock some sense into him.

Make that the murdered DEA agent.

Nathan mentioned the DEA had put a man in Lopez's Miami operation—an agent who vanished two months ago.

It could be the key to putting Lopez away for good, and a crippling blow to Espina Negra.

Exactly what Caleb had wanted.

But if Gia had to testify, she'd never know peace again. She'd spend her life in hiding.

And he'd lose her.

Fuck.

He couldn't do this. Couldn't use her, not after everything she'd survived. Not after she finally started to feel safe with him.

But there was no other way.

One of the horses grazing nearby nickered softly, its tail swishing. Caleb envied the animal's uncomplicated existence.

Zach, he could trust.

The rest of the Navajo Police? Gallup PD? Too many unknowns. Cartel informants were everywhere—and if Espina Negra didn't have someone in the area, the Aztec Kings did.

No, whatever plan he made had to be airtight. On a need-to-know basis.

Gia's life depended on it. Jennie's, too.

He scrolled through his contacts.

Stopped on Ryder's name.

His thumb hovered over the call button.

Old instinct kicked in—stay detached, be the steady one, never need anyone.

His childhood had wired him that way.

Military service and executive protection work had taught him the value of a team—had made him a damn good teammate, even.

But relying on others—*really* relying on them—had never come easy. Not unless it was part of the job.

He didn't need anyone.

Except now he did.

For Gia. For Jennie.

Because Gia was right. The only way to draw Lopez out and get Jennie back safely was to offer her as bait.

His fingers clenched around the phone, knuckles white.

He'd wanted intel from Dìleas, but hadn't wanted to draw the agency into his personal confrontation with a cartel.

Now he needed his teammates.

They had his six. They were his family. Always had been.

He just hadn't let himself believe it.

His jaw flexed. One sharp inhale, then he placed the call.

The phone rang once before Ryder picked up. "Caleb."

"I need help."

"Name it, mate." No hesitation. No questions. Just loyalty.

Caleb exhaled. "One of Gia's friends is missing. Lopez took her to force Gia's hand."

He hesitated, then pushed through. "There's more. That missing DEA agent Nathan mentioned? Lopez killed him. Dumped his body in the ocean. Gia witnessed it."

"Bloody Hell," Ryder muttered. "Lucas Caldwell needs to know."

Fuck no.

"Lopez is cartel royalty. He's got too many connections for me to believe this will end well if law enforcement gets involved."

Caleb had no time for the red tape of the FBI, even if Lucas Caldwell—godfather to Ryder's fiancée, Nathalie—had proven to be a valuable friend to Dìleas.

As far as he was concerned, his mission was simple: Vincente Lopez was a high value target. Eliminate the threat and disrupt Espina Negra—a terrorist organization in practice, if not in official designation.

"Lucas will be discrete," Ryder said.

"I need to get Jennie Tsosie back and make sure this asshole never comes near Gia again."

"Has Lopez given her a deadline?"

"End of week. But I don't trust it. Going after Jennie was an escalation we didn't anticipate."

He paused, choosing his words carefully. This wasn't just his boss. Ryder was a friend.

"Bring in law enforcement, and Lopez might kill Jennie. Gia would be next. If he wants her, he can come and get her himself. And when he does..." The fury in Caleb's voice iced. "I'll either get a confession or bury him."

Silence.

Long enough for Caleb to shuffle his feet, his shoulders tightening.

"You love her." Ryder didn't phrase it as a question.

Caleb opened his mouth to deny it, but no words came.

Ryder let out a quiet breath that was half chuckle, half resignation. "All the rules go out the window when we're protecting the women we love, don't they, mate?"

His voice hardened. "Keep your head down. Help is on the way."

CHAPTER
TWENTY-FOUR

NOW THAT CALEB HAD Dìleas on board, he needed to see his grand-father. Whatever went down on or near the Navajo Nation would need President Blackwater's consent.

He stepped back into the cottage, shook off the cold, and called Zach. Briefed him on the plan he and Gia had agreed to—lure Lopez to the reservation under the pretense of a trade.

Gia for Jennie.

In reality, they'd orchestrate a carefully planned trap.

To his surprise, Zach hadn't pushed back.

We need to get Jennie back. Unharmed.

Anger, determination, and something close to fear had edged his cousin's voice. Caleb had already sent him the photo of Jennie's bruised face.

After hanging up, he texted his grandfather.

> *Espina Negra has Jennie Tsosie. We need to talk.*

The reply came quickly.

> *My office. One hour.*

Caleb stiffened at the curt message.

Another text flashed across his screen, this one from Zach.

Grandfather wants to see us in his office.
Hope you're ready.

Zach was waiting outside when Caleb and Gia pulled up to the rust-colored stone building that housed the offices of the president and vice president of the Navajo Nation.

Caleb parked across the street, taking a moment before getting out. The structure blended into the landscape, rising organically in proximity to the sandstone formation that gave Window Rock its name.

Twin flags flanked the entrance—the Stars and Stripes on one side, the Navajo Nation flag on the other, its familiar rainbow arching over the outline of the reservation.

Above the double doors, the Great Seal of the Navajo Nation gleamed against the stone—fifty arrowheads encircling the four sacred mountains, livestock, and corn beneath a rising sun.

Caleb stared at it longer than he meant to. Sovereignty. Protection. Identity.

Symbols he hadn't grown up claiming—but maybe, finally, was beginning to understand.

Stress lined Zach's eyes. "Chief Nez has officers combing the rez. He's also notified the Sheriff's Offices in Apache and McKinley counties. The medical supply truck driver was a temp. He's vanished into the wind."

"We need Grandfather to let us handle this our way." Caleb tightened his hold on Gia's hand and followed Zach inside.

The president's office resembled a stately conference room. Polished mahogany panels reflected the soft sheen of overhead lights. Ben Blackwater sat at a long conference table, his phone pressed to his ear.

He barely glanced up before issuing a curt command. "Sit."

Caleb obeyed before he realized he'd done so.

Zach moved just as fast.

Gia took a more graceful seat beside Caleb.

Ben ended his call with a sharp sigh. "That was Chief Nez. No sign of Jennie. And until we have proof she's been taken across state lines," his mouth thinned, "or murdered, the FBI won't intervene."

"Gia has information that will help." Caleb cast a wary glance at his grandfather's aide and security detail. "But it needs to stay between us for now."

Ben motioned to the others in the room. "Wait outside."

Once the door clicked shut, he leaned back, the leather creaking beneath his shifting weight. "Tell me."

Caleb waited for Gia's nod before speaking. "Vincente Lopez murdered a DEA agent. Gia witnessed it—that's why she fled Miami. Now he's using Jennie as leverage to force her back."

Gia's voice wobbled. "I can turn myself in, tell the DEA what I saw. They'll arrest Vincente."

Caleb shook his head. "Lopez has high-powered lawyers. They'll discredit Gia, and the cartel will put a target on her back. We need to lure him here, and after we get Jennie back, we get him to incriminate himself, so Gia's not involved. On video. Once the footage of his confession is public, the Feds will arrest him, and his father's cartel will likely disown him to avoid the heat. He'll take the fall alone."

Plausible enough. What he didn't say was he expected Lopez to come with armed men, ready to kill.

And that was just fine.

Because he didn't plan on Lopez or his men leaving the reservation alive.

Ben's gaze shifted toward the closed door, his expression unreadable. When he spoke, it was low, forcing them to lean in.

"We've been tracking cartel activity on the reservation. Their reach is long. Their money fills too many pockets."

His face hardened. "I'd like to trust the Tribal Council and the police, but I can't guarantee we wouldn't have a leak. And there are rumors of a second cartel."

Caleb darted a look at Zach. "Los Coyotes?" A flicker of satisfaction filled him at his grandfather's nod. "I may have started that rumor to force Lopez into a personal visit."

His amusement vanished. "Too bad the asshole didn't take the bait before he grabbed Jennie."

His grandfather's disapproving stare had his mouth snapping shut.

"I won't let the reservation become a war zone," Ben said sternly. "And I won't invite more federal oversight."

"We won't involve them," Caleb replied. He wouldn't leave Gia's safety, or Jennie's to strangers. "We don't know what informants the cartel has in the FBI and DEA. Here, we control the meeting. We limit Lopez's access."

"Jennie is one of us." Zach's voice was taut with anger. "If we don't control this fight, Lopez does. And Jennie loses."

His gaze slid to Gia. "Gia loses, too."

Ben steepled his fingers, the silver and turquoise jewelry on his wrists and fingers catching the light.

He studied them quietly before finally speaking. "He won't come alone."

"That's why we dictate the terms." Caleb clung to his patience. "My friends have agreed to help. They're all former special operations guys. Experienced. We'll keep their presence low-key and control the operation from start to finish."

"What makes you think he will agree to your terms?"

This time it was Gia who spoke up. "He'll come because he believes he holds all the power."

She stretched out her hand in supplication to the man who wielded the authority. "He tried to murder your grandson, and he won't hesitate to hurt Jennie to force me to return to him. He needs to be stopped."

Silence blanketed the room.

Ben exhaled slowly. "This stays between us. The more people involved, the greater the chance someone whispers the truth in Lopez's ear."

His gaze lasered in on Caleb, then moved to Zach. "If you fail, the responsibility will fall on me."

Caleb shifted uneasily in his chair. He hadn't considered the risk to his grandfather's position, his family's safety.

"Report back when you have the details in place." Ben said. "I'm due at the Tribal Council chambers."

They stood to leave, but Ben stopped Caleb. "Stay a moment, Grandson."

Caleb stiffened. *Now what?*

He darted a glance at Zach, who shrugged.

Gia squeezed his arm. "We'll wait outside."

Once the door closed behind Zach and Gia, his grandfather spoke. "Don't let your anger make you reckless."

"I won't." But Caleb wouldn't deny it fueled him—his mother's death, the threat to Gia, Jennie's life hanging in the balance.

Ben gave a sharp nod, as if that settled the matter. Then he hefted a brown cardboard box from behind his desk. "This came today. Addressed to you."

Caleb took the box and glanced at the sender address.

Camila had forwarded his mother's belongings. All that was left of her.

"Whatever answers are in there, I hope they bring you peace." Ben's voice gentled. "We are your family, whether you recognize us or not."

Caleb's throat tightened. He didn't push back this time.

"We'll get Jennie back. And keep Gia safe."

Back at the safe house Zach stood, arms crossed, a glower creasing his forehead. The grim set of his eyes told her he didn't like the plan they'd made—but he'd agreed to it.

"We're not letting him touch you," Caleb said, his voice edged with danger. The tone raised the hairs on the back of her neck.

"But?" she asked, already knowing the answer.

His eyes were bleak. "We need him to think I'm willing to hand you over. You need to be there when this goes down."

"I know." She'd always known.

He took her hand, pulled her into his arms. "Trust me."

She melted into him, letting his strength calm her. "I do."

"Your phone." He cupped her cheek, studied her face. "Are you ready?"

Her throat too tight for words, she nodded and handed it over.

Caleb met Zach's eyes over her head. Whatever passed silently between them seemed to satisfy him.

"Let me do the talking." He tapped the number Vincente had used to send the photo of Jennie—bruised and terrified—and switched the phone to speaker.

It rang. Once. Twice.

Each chime cinched a steel band tighter around Gia's ribs.

On the fourth ring, Vincente answered.

"Ah, *querida*. Ready to return to Miami? I can have my plane there in a matter of hours."

Her soul shriveled at the smug confidence in his voice.

She pressed closer to Caleb, breathing in sandalwood, anchoring herself to the heat and muscle of his body.

"You want Gia?" Caleb's voice sliced the air, dripping menace. "Come and get her yourself, asshole. Where the fuck is my cousin?"

Rather than be intimidated, Vincente chuckled. "Señor Varella, I presume? I have no idea what you mean."

"I'm not in the mood for games. I saw the photo. You want Gia, you bring Jennie Tsosie back to the rez. Alive and unharmed."

"A trade then? Reasonable. But why should I believe you'd give up Gianna—she's quite stunning, no?" Vincente's voice dropped to a quiet snarl. "Have you tasted her sweetness? Sullied what belongs to me?"

Caleb's gaze locked on hers. His thumb slid down her cheek. "Here's what you don't know about the Navajo, Lopez. Jennie is family. We don't sacrifice family for outsiders. So yeah, I'll make the trade. No one has to die."

His voice was flat, cold. But pain dulled the gold in his eyes, and his grip on Gia tightened. "Gia said you wouldn't hurt her."

She gave a subtle nod.

He was playing to Vincente's ego—just like she'd told him. Vincente couldn't know she'd already told Caleb about the DEA agent's murder.

"Of course I wouldn't," Vincente said, smug. "She's to be my wife."

A growl tore from Caleb's throat.

Gia stabbed the mute button, praying the sound hadn't carried.

Another voice rumbled in the background of the call.

Juan.

"His cousin," she murmured. "If Vincente agrees to the trade, Juan will be with him."

Her stomach clenched. Juan had dumped Antonio's body in the ocean. Laughed when she'd screamed.

Vincente's voice returned. "Let me speak to Gianna. She is there with you, yes?"

A muscle ticked in Caleb's jaw. "You don't have to talk to him."

Sweat dampened her hairline. Her heart pounded in her throat. "I do. He needs to believe I'll go."

She took the phone off mute, forcing her voice to stay steady. "I'll return to Miami, but only if you release Jennie and promise no one else will get hurt."

"Very well, *mi amor.*" His false indulgence turned her stomach. "You and your soldier will meet me at a location of my choosing. No one else. Or the Indian woman suffers the consequences."

"I'm not stupid enough to walk into a trap," Caleb cut in. "Gia and I come alone. Day after tomorrow. Time and place are my choice. I'll be in touch."

He ended the call before Vincente could respond.

Gia sagged against him, adrenaline crashing, the taint of Vincente's voice still clinging like smoke.

"Now what?" Zach had been a silent witness until now, but the tension in his body betrayed the fury simmering underneath. He looked carved from stone, violence just beneath the surface. His eyes mirrored the guilt and fear Gia had seen in her own reflection ever since Jennie disappeared.

"Find me a location," Caleb said. "Isolated. No civilians. Lopez will bring men. Armed. We need ingress and egress mapped out—and a sniper in position. That's your specialty, if I remember. Day after tomorrow should be enough time for me to get my Dìleas teammates here and in place."

Zach nodded. "Set the trade for late afternoon. I'll scout in the morning, then we'll work the plan."

His gaze shifted to Gia. "You sure about this?"

Her smile felt brittle. "We need Jennie back. Alive."

"Which means we don't play by the book," Caleb said. "No local law enforcement. No Feds. Time is our enemy. So are loose lips."

Zach's jaw tightened. "I *am* law enforcement." He exhaled hard. "At least for now. I'll be in touch."

Caleb walked him out to the Tahoe.

Gia hovered near the door, the weight of their plan pressing against her chest like a boulder.

She shut her eyes, as if that might quiet the panic flooding her veins. Even with all their planning, Vincente wasn't stupid.

She had to be ready to go with him—if that's what it took to free Jennie.

And keep Caleb alive. Because she had no doubt Vincente wanted him dead.

The door opened, bringing a rush of cold air.

Strong arms wrapped around her. Sheltered her. Made her feel like she mattered.

If they survived this...

She would happily spend the rest of her life with this man.

The rest of my life.

She'd done it.

Fallen stupidly, hopelessly, madly in love.

She wanted everything.

To accept President Blackwater's offer and stay on at the clinic.

To live in this community, with the people she'd so quickly grown to care about.

With Caleb by her side, rediscovering his family, his roots.

If she could convince him to stay.

Did Caleb love her? She didn't want to know. Not yet.

Not when the answer might shatter her.

If he loved her—and she lost him—she shuddered.

Oh God.

"You're thinking too hard again." Caleb's voice rumbled against her ear, deep and low and steady.

Her future teetered on a knife's edge. In two days' time, she'd either be free—or back in Vincente's grasp.

She refused to waste whatever time she had left.

Turning, she cradled his face in her hands.

"I don't want to think," she whispered. "I want to feel. Make me feel."

His mouth crashed onto hers.

She met him with everything she had, clinging to him like she'd never let go.

Every stroke of Caleb's tongue erased Vincente. Erased fear. Erased the darkness closing in.

The world tilted as he swept her into his arms and carried her to the bedroom.

Clothes fell in a fevered trail.

His broad palm cradled her head as she sank into the mattress, the bed cool against her back, his body blazing hot above her.

Weight settled over her, solid and grounding, warmth seeping into her bones.

Lips traced fire down her throat. "Do you feel this?"

"Yes," she moaned. Shivers rippled through her.

He cupped her breast. Took her nipple into his mouth. Licked and nipped until she trembled.

Electricity coiled in her belly, radiating outward with every flick of his wicked tongue.

"Can you feel this, baby?" His voice was raw. Reverent.

Her breath hitched. "Yes, *Caleb*."

His hand skimmed down her stomach, over her hip. Found her center.

He thrust two fingers deep.

She arched. "I need—"

His tongue replaced his hand, teasing her with long, slow glides as her spine arched and her thighs quivered. Licking her like she was his favorite ice cream.

Ratcheting her tighter, inch by delicious inch.

"I love the way you taste," he growled. "So sweet. Like prickly pear."

"Please." He'd reduced her to begging. "I need you inside me."

He hovered above her, dark eyes wild and wanting. "Look at me. See me, Gia."

Her heart nearly exploded. She did see him.

Not the soldier.

Not the protector.

The man.

The one who made her believe in something more than survival.

"I see you," she whispered.

Something fierce and aching flickered in his gaze. Then he thrust into her—deep, possessive.

A sob tore from her lips. Not pain. Pure, aching rightness.

He was hers. She was his.

Heart and soul.

She clung to him. Scored his back with her nails. Tasted the salt on his skin. Drank in his groans.

"Mine." His grip tightened. His thrusts turned savage, relentless.

He slipped a hand between them.

She shattered—pleasure crashing through her like a tidal wave, her scream caught in the curve of his neck.

He came with her, hips jerking, body shaking, a rough groan breaking from his chest.

She held him as he collapsed, his weight grounding her, his heartbeat pounding against her breasts.

Proof of life. Proof of *them*.

But even as his warmth surrounded her, reality clawed its way back in.

Vincente always won.

And if he saw the truth in her eyes—if he guessed how deeply she loved Caleb—he'd kill him.

Just to watch her break.

CHAPTER
TWENTY-FIVE

VINCENTE FLUNG HIS PHONE.

It bounced, skidded across the glass table, then tumbled onto the plush white carpet. Rain lashed the floor-to-ceiling windows of his Miami Beach penthouse as an evening storm system rolled through southern Florida. Lightning forked from towering gray clouds to meet the churning aqua waves below.

Varella had hung up on him.

Pendejo. The disrespect.

Jaw tight, he leaned forward, forearms braced on his thighs, fingers interlocked to keep from smashing his fists through the table. "Do you think they're serious?"

Juan stood by the windows, staring out.

He turned with a shrug. "About exchanging your woman for the Indian girl? Does it matter? We'll bring enough men to make sure you get what you want."

What Vincente wanted?

So many things.

"I want Gianna returned to me and this *cabrón* left to rot in the desert, bones picked clean by scavengers," he snarled.

Varella thought he controlled the situation?

He'll find out who's the one in control.

He reached for his cortadito, thick with sugar and steamed milk. It was the wrong drink for the time of day, and with his heart already racing.

What he needed was liquor.

Or to fuck.

The cup clanged against its china saucer. "What about the Aztec Kings. Will they help us?"

Juan hesitated—so briefly it almost passed unnoticed. He dug into his pocket for a cigarette. His third this hour. He always smoked more when stressed.

His cousin disapproved of this business with Gia.

Too bad.

"I think we should leave them out of it until we've confirmed their loyalties." The tip of Juan's cigarette glowed a fiery orange, his mouth pinched at the corners.

"Then the meeting with them will have to wait until I've secured Gianna." Vincente watched for his cousin's reaction. "If it turns out they are disloyal, and I need to make an example of them, I will."

Smoke curled from Juan's mouth. "We can't wait too long." His words simmered with tension. "My father is watching. If it's more than a rumor and the Aztec Kings have gone behind our backs to Los Coyotes, he will go straight to your father."

"Tío Ramón." Vincente spat his uncle's name like a curse.

He stood, smoothing his hands down his linen trousers. "He's too ambitious for his own good and has too many rats who report to him."

Juan took another long drag of his cigarette.

Vincente's shoulders bunched under the weight of his cousin's stare.

"He's clever," Juan said. "And careful."

"He's waiting." Vincente's laugh lacked humor. "That's what he does best, isn't it? Looking for a mistake. Waiting to make his move."

At least Vincente had Juan at his side to counter Ramón's deviousness. Juan knew his treacherous father well.

Tequila.

That's what Vincente needed instead of coffee.

At the bar, he poured a glass of his finest tequila—Don Julio Ultima Reserva, an indulgence from an exclusive, invitation-only tasting during Miami Art Week.

He lifted the crystal tumbler to his lips. Toasted oak, caramel and dried fruit—the flavors teased his tongue as the liquor burned a path down his throat and warmed his chest.

"And if he does? Make a move?" Juan eyed him from the couch.

Vincente poured a glass for his cousin. "He won't succeed."

A bright flash lit the sky, followed by a sharp crack and a boom that vibrated the windows.

Juan sipped his tequila. "He thinks your doctor matters more to you than the business."

His glass halfway to his mouth, Vincente stilled. "I'm focused on what belongs to me."

"That's not how he sees it."

Temper, not tequila, flushed Vincente's skin and hazed his vision. "And how do you see it?"

Sharp needles of rain splattered violently against the glass.

His cousin's gaze drifted to the storm outside. "We are in a dangerous business. Enemies are often where we least expect them."

Vincente tilted his head. Was that a warning? There was an odd inflection in Juan's voice.

"Is there something you aren't telling me, *primo*?"

"Of course not." Juan crushed his cigarette, drained his tequila in one swallow, and stood. "You know everything. It's a matter of what you do with the information."

He'd had his liquor. Vincente set down his empty glass.

Fucking would have to wait.

"Pack your things," he told Juan. "Varella will not be the one to dictate a time for this meeting. We leave tomorrow morning."

Another flash of lightning cracked like gunfire.

"Once we have Gianna, we return to Mexico—to the family estate." Vincente turned toward his bedroom. "Then, we remind both of our fathers why *I* will keep Espina Negra the most powerful cartel in North America."

CHAPTER
TWENTY-SIX

HE LOVED GIA.

Love.

It was the first time Caleb let the word rise fully to the surface, even though it had been there, waiting, just beneath his thoughts.

He lay on his side and watched her sleep. Moonlight filtered through the blinds, casting the bed in pale stripes of silver and shadow.

They'd crawled out of bed long enough to eat dinner, made love again, then crashed. He'd been sleeping pretty soundly, in fact.

Until a hot, wet mouth on his dick blasted his eyes open. Gia knelt between his legs, hair cascading like rainwater over his thighs, sapphire eyes wide with hunger.

And fear.

No matter how many times he'd made her scream with pleasure, he hadn't been able to erase the shadows clinging to the edges.

He wound a strand of her hair around his finger and brought it to his nose.

Desert rose.

When was the exact moment he'd fallen for her?

Maybe it was when she walked into Lucero's Lounge with that scared-doe look.

Or when she slid into the seat beside him at his mother's funeral, refusing to let him sit alone.

Maybe it was when she took command at the accident scene—boss-lady energy in full force—yet still trusted him enough to back her up with his training.

Hell, all he knew was he wanted her.

Wanted her safe.

And he'd do whatever it took to make sure she stayed that way.

His fists curled, bronzed knuckles standing out against the sterile white sheets.

Those hands had worshipped her. Every inch of her softness and curves. He'd sunk his fingers into her wet heat and lapped up her screams when she came.

He flexed them now. Those same hands had killed—and would again, without hesitation, if that's what it took to protect her.

Would she look at him differently?

Her, with her healer's hands and gentle heart.

Him, with his warrior's fists and cold calculation.

Lopez wouldn't walk away from this alive. He'd make sure the drug lord didn't live to see the end of the week.

Restless, he slid out of bed, threw on his jeans, and slipped quietly into the living room so as to not awaken Gia.

His grandfather's words from earlier in the day lingered.

We are your family.

He'd learned, finally, the meaning of family—family were the ones who had your six, the ones you called when your back was against the wall, the ones you were willing to fight and bleed for.

His teammates at Dìleas. They weren't just people he trusted.

They were family.

Zach.

Despite the risk to his career, Zach stood with him, ready to help take down Vincente Lopez. His grandfather risked his position, too.

They saw him as family—even when he hadn't been ready to do the same.

Caleb's gaze drifted to the box his grandfather had given him—the one he'd set down in the corner when they'd returned to the safe house, too preoccupied with the call to Lopez to worry about what it contained.

The one with his mother's belongings.

He picked it up and carried it to the couch.

Just a plain brown box, like a million others delivered across the country every day. Unremarkable, with no hint of the weight it carried.

Digging out his multi-tool, he sliced through the tape.

Inside was a wad of white tissue paper. It had weight to it. When he peeled it back, a turquoise and silver squash blossom necklace emerged—nearly identical to the one someone had placed around his mother's neck in her coffin.

A pang pulled tight in his chest.

One of her prized possessions, given to her by her mother on her wedding day. He'd thought his old man had pawned it years ago. Somehow, she'd kept it hidden—protected it, even as his father stole whatever he could for coke, booze, or whatever the hell else he was chasing.

On impulse, he fastened the heavy chain around his neck. The silver felt cool against his skin. Then it warmed to him.

He reached into the box again and found a sterling silver cuff bracelet, set with five turquoise stones, similar to the ones worn by Zach and his grandfather. He slipped it onto his wrist.

Beneath old photographs and insurance papers, he found a stack of journals. The top one had a colorful floral design on its cover.

It took him a moment to recognize it as the same adhesive shelf paper his mother used to line their kitchen cupboards.

He set the journal on his lap. Stared at it. Seconds crawled by.

Read it.

But what if it confirmed everything he'd always believed?

That her family had turned their backs on her.

Or worse—

What if everything Lillie Blackwater Varella told him was a lie?

Lifting the cover, he saw his mother's light, looping scrawl.

At a glance, he could tell her mood when she wrote—on good days, the letters were big and rounded. On bad ones, when depression dragged her into a ravine she couldn't escape, her handwriting turned small and pinched, like her emotions.

The first entry was dated the day she met Julian Varella—an outsider working at a local construction job—at the Navajo Nation Fair. A teenage girl, flush with excitement, who'd caught the attention of a handsome man in his twenties.

Caleb skimmed through the entries. They were sporadic rather than daily, reflecting the highs and lows that apparently dictated when his mother felt the need to write.

Her parents' disapproval of the man she'd chosen.

The shock of finding out she was pregnant.

Her belief that the baby was her way out of reservation life.

And then, the slow unraveling.

The man she'd married wasn't Prince Charming.

He isolated her after Caleb was born. Got her hooked on drugs.

Threatened to have her declared unfit when she tried to leave.

Her mental health declined, especially after her mother died when Caleb was twelve. They'd fought constantly, but Patricia Blackwater had been her anchor. When she was gone, something in Lillie broke.

Not long after, they moved to Phoenix. Even as her family reached out, fear and shame kept her from going back.

The only bright spot left in her life was Caleb. She'd clung to him. Feared losing him. Feared her family might believe the lies—that she wasn't fit to raise her son.

Caleb closed the last journal and ran his fingers over the frayed cover.

It hadn't been his mother's family who cut ties.

It had been her.

And she'd regretted it.

He swallowed hard. Then again. Grief—raw and aching—pushed up from where he'd buried it for years.

If things had been different, he might have grown up knowing Zach. Might have had a relationship with his grandfather. Might have belonged—to his people. To the Diné culture he'd always kept at arm's length.

"Caleb?"

Gia. He hadn't heard her come into the living room.

She crept to the couch and sat beside him. "I woke up and you were gone."

Her fingers brushed his cheek and came away wet. Tears he hadn't realized he'd shed. "You opened your mother's box."

"I should have done more."

"You were a child." Her hand drifted to the necklace at his throat. "This is beautiful. Was it hers?"

"She was ashamed of what she'd become. Afraid of losing me."

Gia took his hand and squeezed. "It's not too late to get to know your family."

He kissed her—gently at first, then deeper, pulling her close, needing her warmth to quiet the storm inside him.

She was his refuge. Her sweet kisses softened his grief. Her hands smoothed up his arms and curled around his neck, anchoring him in the present.

He breathed her in, her scent like desert flowers after rain, and molded her softness against the hard edges of himself.

His mother would have liked her. Would've seen a kindred soul—someone who understood what it meant to survive violence and chaos and still find strength on the other side.

And he had to dangle her like bait in front of a cartel prince just to set her free.

The thought turned his blood to ice—then sent it surging through his veins like a fire hose, threatening to rupture the one organ he couldn't live without.

The one that belonged to Gia.

"Come back to bed," she whispered when they finally broke for breath. She twined her fingers with his and rose, gently pulling him to his feet.

He followed—willing, undone.

And then he made love to her again—slow and reverent, pouring every piece of himself into her.

Her soft, breathy cry as she came unshackled the boy he'd once been—watching life from the outside—and freed the man who could finally love.

He loved Gia. She was his family.

And, after reading his mother's journals, he owed his Diné family a fresh start, built upon the ashes of misunderstanding and regret.

All they had to do was get through the next few days.

Chapter
Twenty-Seven

A CAR ENGINE CUT through the quiet. Too close.

Caleb's eyes flew open. He found his gun on the nightstand, slipped out of bed, and crept into the living room to peer through the blinds.

Snow had dusted the ground overnight as he and Gia slept, turning the beige earth white and frosting the desert scrub. The sandstone buttes blazed brighter than usual in the early morning sun—vibrant red-orange and stark brown.

A dark blue SUV braked in front of the cottage. From it emerged a tall, shaggy blond wearing a red Hawaiian shirt under a brown Carhartt jacket, faded jeans, and white Nike high-tops.

I'll be damned.

Caleb ducked into the bedroom, tugging on jeans and a black t-shirt.

Gia had burrowed deep beneath the covers, her dark hair spilling over the pillow.

He kissed her cheek. "Wake up, baby. Get dressed. We've got company."

Not waiting for a response, he headed for the front door.

Outside, Danny Mayhew lifted both hands and flashed a grin full of pearly white teeth. His blue eyes twinkled with amusement.

"Don't shoot me, bro." He gestured to Zach's Dodge Charger. "That the car in the pic? Hella sweet ride. Looks like your taste is finally improving."

Caleb stepped outside and clasped forearms with his Dìleas teammate. "My cousin's—I'm borrowing it. What are you doing here?"

"The bosses sent me. Officially, I'm on vacay visiting family in California." Danny winked. "No law says I can't swing through and check on my buddy while I'm at it."

We've got your six. Always. Nathan's words.

Help is on the way. Ryder's voice in his ear.

Caleb cleared his throat, the sudden tightness unexpected. "Thanks, man. Come on in."

Gia stood in the living room in jeans and a navy sweater that made her eyes even bluer. With her hair in a ponytail and no makeup, she looked more like a college student than a seasoned doctor.

Mine.

"Gia, this is Danny Mayhew—one of my colleagues at Dìleas."

"Ma'am." Danny gave her a respectful nod, then shot Caleb a sideways look.

"Nice to meet you, Danny." Gia offered the former SEAL a polite smile.

The glance she sent Caleb brimmed with questions.

Understandable. Danny's tousled hair and surfer-dude vibe didn't exactly scream executive protection. But that laid-back exterior masked lethal skills—and gave him the advantage of blending into a crowd. A valuable trait in close protection.

"Danny's here to help," Caleb said. "He's former Naval Special Warfare."

That earned him a more appraising look from Gia.

"Navy SEAL?"

With a flourish that would've made a middle school drama teacher proud, Danny brought a hand to his chest and offered a dramatic bow. "At your service, ma'am."

Caleb didn't bother hiding his eye roll.

On duty, Danny was all business.

Off duty?

The guy flirted with anything female.

A smile teased the corners of Gia's lips, some of the shadows in her eyes lifting.

"I'm going to take a shower while you two catch up." She excused herself and disappeared into the bedroom.

"Very nice. I can see why you've stuck around." The frank appreciation in Danny's gaze made Caleb want to smash his fist into his friend's face.

"Keep your charm to yourself," he growled. "How'd you get here so fast?" He hadn't even called Ryder yet to tell him about the timeline he'd set for the meetup with Lopez.

Danny barked out a laugh, not the least bit offended. "Just finished a job and had leave coming. Ryder asked if I was game, so I booked a flight last night."

He grinned. "Don't worry—Lachlan and Nathan sent goodies."

Goodies. Weapons and gear.

"Show me." Caleb followed him out to the SUV.

Danny popped the cargo hatch. Tactical vests, hard-shelled gun cases, and a black duffel filled the back.

"SCAR-Heavy rifle, a couple of Glocks, plenty of ammo." He patted one of the cases. "None of it officially tied to Dìleas, by the way."

He unzipped the duffel and handed Caleb a radio with an earpiece, then held up a small brown envelope. "Tracker tags. Same model Nathan used on Emily in Paris."

Danny's grin faded. "Ryder filled me in. This feels familiar—bad guy wants your girl and he's willing to kill you to get her. We good on support? I'm assuming we can source anything else we need?"

"My cousin Zach can." Caleb peered inside at the flesh-colored trackers, then lifted the rifle from its case. "This isn't official Dìleas business. It could get ugly."

Not could. Would.

"Dude, you know me. I'm always up for a party."

Caleb shook his head. *SEALs.* There was a reason Green Berets were called the quiet professionals and SEALs...were not.

"Gia's ex is high-ranking in Espina Negra. He kidnapped one of her friends to force her return. I offered a trade—Gia for Jennie—but only if Lopez shows up in person to make the swap."

He met Danny's eyes. "I was going to call Ryder for backup. We'll need more triggers on target. Lopez won't come alone."

Danny folded his arms, leaning against the SUV. "I'm going to assume you're not actually trading one woman for the other."

"Not a chance. I want Jennie back, and I want Gia free of this asshole for good. Once Zach confirms the location, I'll text it to Lopez. The meet's tomorrow—late afternoon. He'll come armed, but he won't know the terrain like we do."

Danny's brow lifted. "So... what's the play? Capture and hand him over to the police?"

Caleb let his silence speak for him.

"Got it." Danny scanned the horizon. "If anyone's going to disappear, this is a good place for it."

Both men straightened at the sound of a vehicle.

A white Tahoe barreled toward them, tires flinging mud instead of dust thanks to the thawing snow. The temperature had begun to climb and was supposed to reach seventy, but as soon as the sun dipped below the horizon, it would plummet.

Danny's hand hovered over one of the Glocks. "You expecting anybody?"

"My cousin."

Zach parked behind the Charger and stepped out, dressed in desert camo pants and a tan T-shirt. His gaze flicked to Danny, narrowing.

"Danny Mayhew," Caleb said. "From Dìleas. He's here to help. Danny, my cousin, Zach Blackwater—Navajo Nation Police."

The two men shook hands.

Caleb gestured to Zach's outfit. "Take the day off?"

"A couple of days," Zach said. "I can't do what we're about to do in uniform."

The words hit harder than expected. Caleb hadn't fully let himself feel it until now—the risk his cousin was taking. The line he was crossing.

"Maybe you shouldn't be there when this goes down."

Zach's eyes flared. "Maybe you should go fuck yourself."

Danny barked a laugh. "I like this guy."

"You would," Caleb muttered, then turned and led them inside.

Gia stepped out of the bedroom, her damp hair pulled into a ponytail, wearing the same jeans and blue sweater—both hugging her frame.

Still no makeup. Still gorgeous.

Her expression tightened as she took in the three men in the cramped living room. "Do we have a meeting site?"

Even with fear in her eyes, she stood tall—ready to face Lopez again if it meant getting Jennie back.

It made Caleb's chest swell with pride.

She was tougher than she gave herself credit for.

Zach spread photos across the coffee table. "Aerial shots."

Caleb leaned in and tapped on one. A crumbling hogan of piñon logs and packed earth sat tucked in a valley between two plateaus.

"Isn't that Old Joe's place?"

The mud-thatched roof had partially caved in, exposing wooden beams. Scrub, cactus, and tumbleweeds pressed in on all sides.

"It was," Zach said. "He died there."

"So it's abandoned."

Caleb remembered the old man—Vietnam vet, hair-trigger temper, haunted eyes. The kind who only came into town for liquor and supplies.

He smirked at his cousin. "You actually went inside?"

"Hell no." Zach made a face. "I'm not trying to get cursed by a *chindi*."

Danny squinted at the photo. "Why won't you go inside? I mean, aside from rattlesnakes and a dozen other things that want to kill you."

"The Navajo believe when someone dies inside their home, their spirit can linger—unless their belongings and the dwelling are destroyed." Caleb kept his expression deadpan, though the corner of his mouth threatened to lift. "You're the Anglo. We'll let you use the hogan as cover."

A high, piercing howl cut through the stillness outside.

Caleb froze. His gaze found Zach's.

Coyote.

The trickster. The bringer of death.

Their grandmother would've called it an omen.

He forced the chill from his spine. Just a male during mating season, staking territory. That's all.

"Gee, thanks." Oblivious, Danny held up another photo—this one showing the sloping base of the plateau. "Guess I'm the dumbass in the horror movie going into the basement. I thought I was on overwatch."

"That's my job," Zach said. "My MOS in the Marine Corps was scout sniper."

"Damn," Danny muttered. "Here I thought with Nathan not being around, I'd get to be sniper for once."

Gia gave them all a wide-eyed look. "Hopefully, no one gets shot and we get Jennie back unharmed."

Caleb exchanged covert glances with Zach and Danny.

Yeah. Getting Jennie back unharmed?

That was the hope.

But as for no one getting shot?

That wasn't the plan.

"It's a perfect spot," Zach continued. "Isolated. Abandoned. There's a place for a sniper to set up on the eastern slope, and"—he pointed to a dry channel masked by sagebrush beside the home—"this arroyo is deep enough to provide cover for my guys to spring the trap when the time comes. As far as the cartel boys will know, only you and Gia will be waiting."

"Your guys?" Caleb asked.

"Roy and Ford. I spoke to them last night. They wouldn't miss this for the world."

Caleb frowned. "It's going to be dangerous. Did you tell them that?"

Zach met his gaze without flinching. "They don't like outsiders messing with our people."

A twinge of pressure settled beneath Caleb's sternum. He could accept the danger himself. Zach and Danny had trained for it. Dìleas would send reinforcements.

But civilians? Even with prior military experience?

All these men, stepping up. For Gia. For him.

Dìleas. The Diné. His family.

His throat tightened. He swallowed hard, breath hitching before he forced it steady.

To ground himself, he rapped his knuckles on the stack of photos. "Let's get this plan mapped out. Once it's solid, I'll text Lopez the coordinates. Set the meet for tomorrow afternoon."

When they wrapped, Zach gathered the photos and stood. "I've asked Roy and Ford to meet me at the site."

"I'll go with you," Danny said. "Then I need to find a hotel. This place"—he glanced around, sly—"is a little too cozy for my taste."

He squinted at Zach. "That Charger outside yours?"

A rare smile creased Zach's face. "She's a beauty, isn't she?"

"You should see my baby," Danny said. "A 2016 Mustang GT California Special in Deep Impact Blue. Coyote V-8 engine." He grinned. "I call her *Consuela*."

Caleb rolled his eyes for the second time since Danny's arrival.

"We'll grab breakfast and find you a room after the ground assessment," Zach replied.

Danny held up his phone. "You know how to reach me," he said to Caleb. He nodded to Gia. "Ma'am."

Caleb walked them to the door.

"Cousin." He clasped Zach's forearm—a warrior's gesture. "*Ahéhee.*"

"You're welcome, *shił na'aash*—my cousin." Zach held his stare.

Something passed between them. Respect. A flicker of the bond they'd once shared as boys.

A new one forming now, as men.

Outside, the snow continued to melt away. The next few days promised unseasonably warm February sun. Zach would have to contend with the glare on his sniper scope, but at least the wind wouldn't be a factor.

Caleb waited until the vehicles disappeared down the road before shutting the door.

"That bastard's bringing his Miami weather with him," he muttered, low enough that Gia couldn't hear.

She still sat on the couch, forearms on her thighs, her hair a glossy curtain veiling her face.

But he knew exactly what she was thinking.

"You're scared."

"I'd be a fool not to be."

He nodded. *True.*

"The thing is..." Her gaze lifted. "I'm not afraid for myself so much as for Jennie."

Her eyes glistened in the light. "And for you. Vincente will know we've been together the moment he sees us. He doesn't like anyone touching what's his."

His jaw flexed, rage coiling tight beneath his skin.

"You're not his. And if I have to kill him to prove it, I will." He already planned to.

Gia flinched.

Caleb stalked to the sofa. Lifted her to her feet. Folded her into his arms.

She shuddered. "I should have gone to the DEA right away." Her voice was muffled against his shirt. "None of this would've happened if I'd just done the right thing."

He smoothed a hand along her back, anchoring her. Soaking in the feel of her in his arms.

Everything in him centered on this—keeping Gia safe. Making sure she could live her life without fear.

A life that included him.

If she'd have him.

"When this is over," he said, the words slow and cautious. "Do you want to stay? Keep working on the rez?"

She raised her tear-streaked face. He saw the answer in her eyes before she spoke.

"I love it here, Caleb. I feel needed in a way I never have before."

His heart thundered in his ears, his throat dry as a desert. "What if I stayed? I'd still need to travel for assignments, of course, but what if I decided to make this my home? At least for a little while."

Surprise lit her face. Hope, too. Something that settled the last of his nerves.

"I'd love that. And your family would, too. They love you." She rose on tiptoes and pressed her lips to his. Her eyes softened.

"*I* love you."

The words hit Caleb like a grenade. Joy detonated in his chest.

"I love you, too."

Pleasure bloomed in her eyes and on her cheeks. "You do?"

He laughed. "Yeah, I do."

On impulse, he gave in to a bit of whimsy and swung her around the tiny living room.

So this was what it felt like to walk on the moon. His body felt so light, his boots barely touched the ground.

A shadow chased across her beautiful face.

Heart stuttering, he stilled and set her down, searching her face. "What's wrong?"

"I'm so happy." She caressed his cheek. "And that scares me. I don't want to lose you now that I've found you."

The shimmer in her eyes sliced through him like a blade.

"You won't lose me."

He kissed her, deep and sure, sealing the promise with everything he had.

But even as he held her close, a chill crept down his spine.

Life had just served him a bright future with an amazing woman.

With one giant caveat.

They had to survive.

Chapter
Twenty-Eight

Change of plans. We meet today. This afternoon.

CALEB STOOD AT THE sliding glass door of the safe house, phone in hand. He tugged the tarp aside, letting winter sunlight flood the room. Sixty degrees already—false spring, the kind that teased warmth before the temperature plummeted again.

Vincente Lopez's text had arrived an hour ago.

Clever bastard.

Lopez was trying to catch them off guard by moving the meeting up a day.

Too late for Dìleas to send more support.

He'd called Zach and Danny immediately. They'd raced over.

Zach, dressed in desert cammies and tan boots, sat in the beige armchair, his Marine Corps cap turned backward over tied-back hair.

"A private jet from Miami landed at Gallup Municipal," he said, ending a call. "Tail number belongs to Havana Sol Entertainment Holdings. Four men deplaned. My contact says at least two are muscle."

"If Lopez is bringing more than four," Caleb said, "he's hiring local."

"Aztec Kings?" Zach leaned forward, fingers laced. "Probably who Ortega used during the ambush. Same with the medical supply driver who grabbed Jennie—still no ID." He exhaled. "But I doubt they'll risk open conflict on tribal land. They don't want that kind of heat." His jaw flexed. "I've checked with every local agency—no signs of a cartel presence."

A beat passed.

"I find that hard to believe." His gaze met Caleb's. "You were right to keep this off law enforcement's radar."

Caleb dropped onto the orange sofa beside Gia, in jeans and a plaid button-down borrowed from Zach covering his tactical vest.

He rested a hand on her thigh—comfort for her, an anchor for him.

She sat curled into herself, legs tucked beneath her, wearing an olive button-down he'd handed her earlier to cover the vest Danny brought. Her face was pale, her silence stretched.

"Gia thinks Lopez will underestimate us," Caleb said. "Maybe he brings just his cousin and two enforcers."

Danny snorted from across the room. "We're never that lucky." He wore mission gear—tan pants, beige shirt, tactical boots, his shaggy blond hair pulled into a stubby ponytail.

"Only one road in, one road out." Caleb glanced at his cousin. "What about air?"

"No fixed-wing planes can land there," Zach said, scrolling through his phone. "A helo could squeeze in, but it's tight. Most in Gallup are med flights. Charter company's tiny—no flights scheduled today."

He looked up. "And the charter uses local pilots. If Lopez plans to kill you, I doubt he'll leave a civilian witness who's also his ride."

Gia flinched.

Caleb gave her thigh a gentle squeeze. "Have your guy at the airport watch every bird. Even med flights. I want to know the second one lifts."

Danny checked his watch. "We need to move if we want to be in position before Lopez and his boys roll in."

The three men stood.

Caleb turned to Gia, offered his hand, and pulled her to her feet.

He brushed a knuckle down her cheek. "You ready?" He kept his voice soft—she was close to the edge.

"Yes."

Shoulders drawn tight, face still pale, but her voice didn't waver.

His woman was a fighter.

He grabbed the envelope Nathan had sent—tracker tags. Flesh-toned. Flat. Barely visible.

"Turn around," he murmured.

She did. He parted her hair and pressed the tag firmly into place beneath her ponytail.

Then he kissed her. In front of everyone.

"Let's end this so we can start the rest of our lives."

Caleb steered Zach's Charger down a narrow dirt road, winding into a valley hemmed by twin plateaus. The track ended at a clearing, where Old Joe's hogan slumped on a gentle rise about fifty yards from the dry riverbed they'd seen in the drone footage.

Low mesquite, saltbush, and yellow-tipped cactus blurred the edges of the arroyo, perfect concealment for Danny and Zach's friends, Roy and Ford. The hogan looked even worse up close than it had from the air—sunbaked dirt crumbling off its sides, rotted wood exposed beneath, the door sagging on its hinges like a drunk mid-stumble.

Beside him, Gia twisted her fingers in silence.

"You doing okay?"

He'd asked her that too many times.

"I'm hot."

She had on the vest beneath her shirt. Dark sunglasses shielded her eyes. A black ball cap, embroidered with the Arizona state flag, kept her ponytail tucked out of sight.

"Me too."

Sweat already formed between the vest, his undershirt, and skin. He'd known worse—Iraq in full kit in one hundred twenty-degrees.

His Glock rode his belt beneath his untucked shirt, a folding knife in his pocket, Danny's conceal-carry Sig snug at his ankle. Armed as he could be without tipping Lopez off.

He'd be standing in the open with his balls hanging out, relying on Zach, Danny, and a pair of Army vets to watch his six.

And praying Lopez didn't give the order to open fire—with Gia or Jennie in the crosshairs.

Caleb parked behind the hogan and rolled down the window.

Mild air drifted in, laced with the mineral scent of lingering snow from the shadows and the sun-warmed tang of dormant grass and old hay.

A low-pitched, plaintive cry broke the quiet.

"What was that?" Gia's eyes rounded. "Sounds like a cow's in trouble."

"It's the call of a Capuchinbird."

"A bird makes that sound?" She narrowed her eyes. "Why are you grinning?"

"It's Zach. We learned the call from a nature documentary when we were kids. Drove our family nuts."

He opened the door. "We use it as a signal. You won't hear a real one unless you're in northeastern South America."

Zach stood nearby, Remington 700 slung casually across his shoulder, the black carbon barrel catching a gleam of sunlight.

Behind him, Danny, Roy, and Ford emerged from the arroyo.

Danny wore a Glock on his thigh and a SCAR rifle slung over his shoulder.

Roy and Ford sported lightweight camo and Winchester rifles—the same ones they'd used to fend off Ortega and his crew when they ambushed Caleb.

Danny joined Caleb and Gia by the hogan while the three Diné kept a respectful distance.

"There's a dirt road on the west side." Zach pointed toward the plateau, eight hundred yards out. "We're parked just beneath the ridgeline."

His finger shifted, tracing to a cluster of boulders halfway up the eastern slope. "That's where I'll be posted."

"Jennie and Gia will meet here." Caleb gestured to a spot near the right side of the hogan. "Keeps them close to the car and clear of any crossfire."

"Then what?" Danny asked.

Caleb turned to Zach. If it were his call, they'd already know the answer.

But this was Zach's territory. His call.

Zach huffed out a breath. "I know what you want me to say, but we need to do this by the book. If they don't put up a fight, we arrest them. Let the Feds handle it."

"And if they do?" Caleb asked.

"We shoot back. Then it's self-defense."

Danny barked a laugh. "Nathan's gonna be pissed he missed this. But with the wedding coming up, if he tried, Emily would cut his nads off."

Caleb was still adjusting to the fact that his bosses were unofficially backing the op. If it went sideways, Dìleas Security Agency risked blowback—an inquiry, bad press, worse.

But they backed him anyway.

Family.

"So, this is normal for you guys?" Gia's sunglasses hid her expression, but her tone dripped with incredulity. "Just another day?"

"Used to be." Caleb didn't miss war. He was proud of his service—but he'd seen enough hell for one lifetime.

Still, for Gia?

He'd walk straight back into the fire if it meant she stayed safe.

"I'm heading to my spot." Zach checked his watch. "Comm check once everyone is in position. Ford, get the drone up—we'll need eyes for the approach." With a wave, he peeled off toward the plateau.

Danny bumped fists with Caleb. "Good luck, brother."

Caleb watched them disperse. The quiet settled in again.

A chill crept down his spine, his sixth sense flaring.

Something didn't feel right. The coyote's howl from the day before echoed in his memory.

Just nerves.

He had more to lose now than on any combat op.

He brushed Gia's arm, needing the contact one more time before Lopez arrived.

Needing her.

A traitorous thought whispered.

What if this is the last time you touch her?

The last time he heard that smoky voice that hooked him the first night at Lucero's Lounge.

Her answering smile was subdued. "Now what?"

He swallowed the fear clawing at his spine. Let none of it show.

"Now, we wait."

CHAPTER
TWENTY-NINE

"WE'VE GOT INCOMING. ONE black SUV."

Ford's voice crackled through Caleb's earpiece, tight with tension. "I'm bringing in the drone."

"Roger that." Caleb stepped out of the Charger with Gia.

Her hand in his, they strolled around the hogan.

The muscles between his shoulder blades twitched—that familiar itch.

Good.

It meant Zach's rifle scope was trained just past him.

Four men.

Too easy.

Unease crawled up his neck, whispering of bad luck in this place of death.

He shoved it down.

Superstition.

Old Joe was long gone.

With Zach on overwatch, and Danny, Roy, and Ford concealed in the arroyo, the odds were stacked in his favor—unless the bastards showed up spraying bullets.

He was betting his life that Lopez wouldn't give that order until he'd secured Gia.

"Danny, when the vehicle pulls up, you and Zach train your rifles on the doors facing me. If you catch a barrel rising, you know what to do."

Gia, the only one without comms, tensed beside him and squeezed his hand hard. He rubbed his thumb over her knuckles in a soothing gesture.

"Jennie's in that SUV." Zach's terse voice rasped in his ear. "Don't fire unless you have a clear shot—and you're good enough not to miss."

"I'm good enough," Danny answered, calm and cool. Mission mode.

Caleb turned to Gia. "Stay behind the hogan. Close enough to hear us. Out of sight. When I give the signal, get Jennie and run for the car."

The key fob was on the console. She just had to gun it out of there.

He didn't want her or Jennie sticking around to see what happened next.

She nodded once, then surged forward to press a hard, desperate kiss to his lips. "Be careful."

As she jogged off, she turned back and mouthed, *I love you,* before disappearing.

He swallowed the words he wanted to say in return. Not with four men listening on comms.

Dust plumed in the distance, the incoming SUV's growl filling the silence.

Caleb stood his ground, arms loose at his sides like a big, juicy target, waiting.

The vehicle rolled to a stop. Dark tinted windows obscured the passengers inside.

His pulse slowed, muscles primed.

The front passenger door opened first. A man stepped out—brown hair streaked with blond, white slacks, a pale blue striped shirt with a white collar beneath a gunmetal gray blazer.

Juan. The cousin.

"Where's Gianna?"

The sneer in Juan's voice made Caleb's jaw tick.

"Where's Jennie?"

The rear door opened.

A burly man stepped out next, dressed in jeans and a tight black tee that showed off thick, veined muscle, a brown leather shoulder holster and 45-caliber handgun nestled beneath his armpit.

The man who emerged behind him was in his thirties, with neatly groomed, dark brown hair, tailored beige trousers and a white linen guayabera shirt.

He removed his sunglasses slowly, revealing a cool, assessing stare. "Señor Varella."

Vincente Lopez Garcia.

"Lopez." Caleb resisted the urge to reach for his weapon. "Where's my cousin?"

The bodyguard yanked Jennie from the SUV by the back of her scrubs, jamming a gun to her temple as she stumbled to find her footing.

Caleb's temper flared. "That's unnecessary."

Jennie's right eye was darkening into an ugly bruise, her lip freshly split.

"You okay?" He gentled his tone for her.

"Yes." Her gaze darted past him, searching.

Lopez flicked his fingers. "We've kept our deal. Where's Gianna?"

"Gia, come here," Caleb said, his eyes never leaving Lopez.

She stepped from behind the hogan.

He recognized fear when he saw it—and it clung to her now like a second skin. He ached to reach for her, offer comfort. But he couldn't. Not yet.

Not until she and Jennie were safe.

"Jennie." Gia's voice cracked at the sight of her friend.

"Don't—" Jennie started, but the bodyguard silenced her with another jab of the barrel.

Caleb's fingers twitched.

That bastard dies first.

Lopez stared at Gia, his expression twisting in displeasure.

"Take off the sunglasses, *querida*."

Gia lifted them slowly, resting them on the brim of her cap. She met his gaze without flinching.

Lopez gave a single nod and turned his attention to Caleb.

"I'm still surprised you returned her to me."

Caleb let his face go flat. Cold.

"Gia makes her own decisions. Jennie is Diné. What would you do to protect your family?"

"I'd make the necessary sacrifices." Lopez's smile didn't reach his eyes. "Come, Gianna. We'll put this behind us."

"Not so fast." Caleb gestured to the marked spot he'd shown Gia earlier. "Gia waits there. As soon as Jennie reaches her, then she'll walk to you."

A flash of irritation tightened Lopez's jaw. He glanced at Juan, who gave a nod.

The bodyguard shoved Jennie forward.

"Slowly," Juan warned.

"Go," Caleb murmured to Gia, "and remember what we talked about."

Every cell in his body screamed to pull her back. Shield her. Order Zach to take out the armed bodyguard while he dealt with Juan, then Lopez, and then the driver. Dump the bodies in Old Joe's hogan and let the scavengers feast.

Instead, he let Gia go.

Jennie reached her. The women embraced, Gia whispering apologies.

"Come, Gianna." Lopez's voice cracked like a whip. "Our business here is finished."

"We've got a helo." Zach's sudden warning crackled through the comms, sharp in Caleb's ear.

The *whop-whop-whop* of rotor blades thundered, closing in fast.

"Incoming!" Zach shouted.

A helicopter crested the ridgeline. Two men dangled from the sides, AR-15s leveled, raining gunfire down the slope where Zach lay positioned.

"Gia, now!" Caleb roared, drawing his weapon.

He couldn't focus on the threat from the sky.

His vision narrowed to the bodyguard pulling out his .45.

Training took over.

One shot.

Crimson burst against the SUV's window.

He didn't wait to see the man drop.

Gia.

She was dragging Jennie toward the car.

Not fast enough.

The SUV's driver jumped out, closing the distance.

Caleb raised his weapon again.

Fired.

Two down.

"I'm pinned," Zach gritted out. "Dammit." A sharp grunt of pain followed.

"Fuck!" Danny's voice over comms. "Taking fire from above!"

A bullet whizzed past Caleb's shoulder like an angry bee.

Gia and Jennie hit the dirt, arms covering their heads as gunfire shredded the air.

Caleb sprinted toward them.

Almost there.

Something slammed into his back—hard.

He dropped to a knee, spun as he fell.

Juan.

The son of a bitch.

Rotor wash churned the sand into a blinding haze as the helicopter descended, obscuring the field.

Another round smashed into Caleb's chest.

The impact crushed the air from his lungs.

His back hit the ground.

Matteo Ortega jumped from the helo, spraying bullets and keeping Danny and the others pinned as Lopez scrambled aboard.

"*Caleb!*" Gia's panicked face hovered above him.

A boot came down—hard—crushing his hand and sending his gun skittering.

Juan grabbed Gia by the ponytail, knocking off her hat and glasses.

She screamed, kicking and flailing, as he dragged her toward the waiting helicopter.

No.

Caleb rolled to his stomach, body throbbing, vision swimming, lungs seizing.

Gia.

She was all that mattered.

Weapon.

He dug his boots into the ground and lunged, fingers closing around the stock.

Jennie appeared beside him. "Let me help—"

"Get down," he wheezed.

Gia fought for all she was worth—until Juan raised his hand and struck her.

Hard.

She slumped.

Caleb's heart thundered.

No shot. No fucking shot.

The bastard was using her as a shield.

All his training. All his combat experience. And he couldn't do a damn thing.

Emilio, Ortega's sidekick, rounded the helo, laying down cover fire while Juan and Ortega hauled Gia aboard.

Then the bird lifted.

"Got a bead on the rotors." Zach's voice was faint, slurred.

"Don't take the shot." Caleb slammed his fist into the dirt. "They have Gia. Dammit!"

Defeat, bitter and tasting like ash, coated his throat as he watched the helicopter streak across the sky.

How many times had he sworn she'd be safe?

His vision blurred.

She'd trusted him.

Heavy footsteps pounded the dirt. Danny dropped to one knee beside him. "Bro, you okay? I'm so sorry." He extended a hand.

Caleb gripped it, let Danny haul him upright.

A grunt tore from his chest.

Jesus.

Getting hit in the vest felt like taking a sledgehammer to the ribs.

He dropped back to his knees.

But it beat being dead.

"Take Jennie," he rasped. "Go to my cousin."

Jennie's face drained of color. "Zach?"

"I'll live," came Zach's voice through the comms—strained but steady. "Plugged in the shoulder. Think I stopped the leak."

He coughed, followed by a grunt. "Just need a ride."

"Go," Caleb growled. His control hung by a thread.

Danny hesitated, eyes flicking over Caleb like he wanted to argue.

He turned to Jennie. "Come on."

"My truck's got four-wheel drive," Roy called. "I'll get as close as I can. Ford will help you get Zach to the ridge."

Danny glanced back at Caleb. "I'll be back for you."

Caleb didn't answer. He stayed where he was, kneeling in the dirt as the others moved out.

The afternoon sun mocked him, bright and clear.

It should be dark. Storming.

To match his heart.

On your feet, soldier.

Gia needed him. He had to get his shit together.

He scrubbed a sleeve across his face, swallowing the roar rising in his throat—the one that threatened to echo through the canyon and split him apart.

Gia was gone.

He'd sworn he'd protect her.

And he'd failed.

Gia blinked back furious tears as she sat wedged in the back of the helicopter between Juan and the cartel soldier with the thick, drooping mustache—the one who'd found her in Lucero's Lounge.

The roar of the rotors, the thrum of vibration through the cabin, the stink of sweat and cologne from the men boxing her in.

Her face throbbed from Juan's backhand.

Caleb.

Juan had shot him. At least twice.

How badly was he hurt?

And Zach?

Danny. Roy. Ford. Jennie.

Had any of them survived that hail of gunfire?

Her gaze, veiled beneath her lashes, swept the cabin.

She wouldn't cry.

Not in front of these monsters.

Wouldn't give them the satisfaction.

Vincente lounged across from her, flanked by the sullen young soldier she'd once labeled Pink Cap. Juan had called him Emilio.

Vincente's cold brown eyes burned into her.

"You've caused me a lot of trouble, *querida*." His voice was low, dangerous. "This will not go unpunished."

He ran a hand over her head, catching her ponytail in his fingers. With a painful yank, he ripped the elastic band free.

Her hair spilled across her shoulders.

"That's better."

He stretched the band until it snapped, then dropped it to the metal floor.

"Your nurse friend almost died because of you. If you'd come to me willingly, none of this would've happened."

The dig struck home. Exactly as he'd intended.

She refused to look at him.

Guilt, fear, panic, and hate all brewed in a toxic stew that would show on her face. She couldn't risk antagonizing Vincente any more than she already had.

Not if she wanted to stay alive and find a way to escape.

Find her way back to Caleb.

To think she'd once believed she was in love with this monster.

Caleb had shown her what love truly meant.

He'd accepted her, even when she lied. Admired her skills as a doctor. Called her brave. Protected her. Cherished her.

Vincente's version of love was twisted. Ugly.

He didn't want a partner—he wanted a prize. Someone to control. An obedient wife and mother to his children. Her career was a hobby to him, something to keep her occupied until marriage, not a calling.

A shiver skittered across the base of her skull, hunching her shoulders. She reached up, rubbing the back of her neck—then froze.

The tracker.

Tucked beneath her hair, nearly forgotten. But now, its presence pressed against her skin.

If it stayed hidden, Caleb—or someone from Dìleas—could find her.

If Vincente's men searched her, she'd have to think fast. Fake a panic attack. A seizure. Anything to keep their hands off her neck.

For now, her best chance was to play along. "Are we returning to Miami?"

Vincente's laugh crawled over her skin like a spider, raising the hair on her arms.

"We're going to my family's estate in Mexico." Hard fingers gripped her chin, forcing her to meet her ex-lover's soulless eyes. "It'll be a long time before I trust you enough to bring you back to Miami. You'll have to prove your loyalty to me first."

His hand slid down her throat, across the curve of her breast, pausing there.

"And to my men."

Revulsion rolled through her. She shrank from his touch.

"I'm not your whore, Vincente. If you have so little respect for me, why go through all this to get me back?"

"Ah, but you are," he sneered. "You let that soldier touch you, didn't you?"

She turned away, only to meet Juan's leering gaze.

Slap.

Her head snapped back from the force of Vincente's hand.

"Didn't you!"

She curled into the seat, away from Vincente's flushed face and trembling hands.

Mercy wouldn't come from him. Not now.

She shut her eyes. Prayed.

To God. To every angel. To anyone listening.

Please. Let me escape before they reach Mexico.

After Antonio, she'd realized what Vincente's hospitality empire truly was—a front for cartel operations. A way to play the respectable citizen and climb the social ladder in Miami while importing poison that killed thousands.

She'd done her research. Vincente's father—*El Víbora*—ran the cartel from a fortified compound in rural Sinaloa. Not even the Mexican government dared raid it.

"You should have shot Varella in the head," Vincente snapped.

Gia's eyes flew open.

"Head shots on the run are difficult, cousin," Juan said, unbothered. "I was more concerned with securing your prize."

Prize. The word made her stomach turn.

"He killed Leo and Javier," Juan added. "Gianna will say she came willingly. Varella's got dead bodies to explain."

Blood. Bone. The spray on the SUV window. The way Caleb had moved—precise, deadly.

He'd killed for her.

Her stomach lurched. Bile rose. She clamped a hand over her mouth.

Juan's explanation appeared to do little to soothe Vincente's temper.

"We should have brought more men." He turned on Mustache Man. "Matteo, the Aztec Kings say they aren't working with Los Coyotes, but I don't believe them."

The cartel soldier threw up his hands. "*Jefe*, they insist they are working only with Espina Negra. And they cannot risk conflict with the Navajo if they want to distribute your product there."

"We'll keep an eye on them," Juan cut in. "For now, you can tell your father that everything is under control. We'll be landing soon in Albuquerque."

"*Dios,*" Vincente snarled. "Albuquerque? We left the plane nearby. We need to be out of American airspace as soon as possible."

"I understand, *primo*, but that soldier and his friends will alert the authorities in Gallup. Our plane has already left for Albuquerque, where this helicopter flew in from to avoid any spies watching the Gallup airport. Range is limited without refueling. Our pilot will have the jet ready for departure to Mexico without delay."

Albuquerque.

Inside Gia, a tiny flame of hope ignited to carve a circle of light out of the darkness.

She had one last chance. Once they landed, she had to act—fast.

Because once they got her on that plane, it was over.

Vincente thought he'd won.

He was wrong.

Caleb was alive. He *had* to be.

She'd get free.

Or die trying.

Chapter Thirty

Caleb managed to get his breath back.

He hobbled around the outside of the dilapidated hogan, stretched to keep from stiffening up, and compartmentalized the pain, because there was no way in hell he was sitting out Gia's rescue.

He'd stripped off his shirt, tactical vest, and undershirt, letting sweat evaporate in the dry desert air. A swollen red patch, roughly the size of his fist, decorated his sternum, and the ache in his mid-back told him he had a matching one there.

The vest had done its job, though. The sun beat down on his bare shoulders, and though his naturally tan skin could take more than some, he'd burn if he stayed uncovered too long.

Flies swarmed the two corpses, the stench of blood and brain matter churning his gut, dragging him back to war memories he'd rather leave buried. He yanked the tarp from Zach's car and dragged the smaller driver toward the bodyguard. Pain flared through his torso and shoulder with every strained movement, but he gritted through it, covering both bodies.

It didn't take long for Danny to return, jogging down the side of the slope from where Zach had taken up overwatch. The SEAL was out of breath and sweaty, the black duffel slung over his shoulder stuffed with the SCAR rifle, their handguns, and ammunition.

"Roy and Ford are taking Zach and Jennie to the hospital," Danny said. "Zach took a hit to the shoulder, got some shrapnel to the face, but he'll live."

Thank God.

Relief lightened the pressure in Caleb's chest. He and his cousin had a relationship now—one he intended to hold on to.

He winced as he slid back into his shirt. "Where the fuck did that helicopter come from?"

"Not Gallup. Zach called his contact while we were dragging him to Roy's truck." Danny nodded at the bodies. "What do we do with them?"

"Leave them. We don't have time. They aren't going anywhere."

Danny beat him to the Charger. "You better let me drive."

Caleb didn't argue. "Can we track the helo?"

"I fired off an SOS to Nathan. Helicopters don't have to file flight plans, but if anyone can locate it, Nathan can." Danny tossed the duffle into the trunk and slid behind the wheel. "He hasn't responded yet."

He started the engine and hit the gas. The muscle car leaped forward. "Any idea where Lopez might take Gia?"

"My money's on Mexico. I don't think he'll risk Miami." Caleb stifled a groan when the Charger hit a pothole. "Either way, they'll have to refuel or switch aircraft somewhere."

If Lopez secreted Gia over the border, it would become exponentially harder to bring her home. He needed to find her—fast. "How quickly can we get a plane?"

Danny shot him a side-eye. "Dude, you just took a couple of rounds. You may not be leaking, but you're in no shape to mount a rescue operation over the border—especially an unsanctioned one."

"I'll go alone if I have to." Caleb's jaw flexed. "I'm not leaving her with that bastard."

"You'd never make it into the compound," Danny said grimly. His phone chirped.

He glanced at the screen and passed it to Caleb. "Damn. Nathan works fast."

Caleb read the message.

> Intel says Lopez headed to Mexico through Phoenix airport. Plane waiting for you at Gallup.

He looked up. "Danny, better to ask forgiveness than permission. Let's see how fast this car goes."

They made the fifty-minute drive in thirty and were escorted to a ramp area where a Gulfstream waited, engines humming.

As they approached, the cabin door dropped to unfold air stairs. A tall, dark-haired man in a navy suit stood just inside.

Caleb's stomach knotted.

FBI Assistant Director Lucas Caldwell.

What the hell? If the Feds were involved, his hands were tied.

Lucas looked as happy as Caleb felt. Then again, Caleb wasn't sure he'd ever seen the former Army colonel turned Fed smile—unless his goddaughter, Nathalie, or her mother, Vivienne, were in the room.

"Lopez has a hostage on board—Doctor Gianna Barone. My priority is to get her back, unharmed, before he can take her to Mexico," Caleb said as he and Danny mounted the stairs.

He ducked his head to step into the cabin—and stopped short.

Lachlan Mackay, founder and president of Dìleas Security Agency, sat in one of the plush tan leather seats, dressed in black trousers and a crisp white button-down.

Across the aisle, Nathan Long hunched over an electronic tablet, his usual uniform of a black metal band t-shirt and faded jeans making him look more like a roadie than a corporate VP.

In the seat facing Lachlan was Ryder Montague, head of executive protection, and Caleb's direct superior. The last time they spoke, Ryder had been in London. Like Lachlan, Ryder wore dark trousers and a button-down—his in pale pink.

"Sorry we're late, pal. But we're here now." Lachlan's emerald gaze swept over Caleb, his Caithness accent slightly thicker than usual. At first glance, the former British SAS officer looked like he belonged on the cover of *GQ*—until you noticed the white scars on his temple and chin, and the hard glitter in his eyes.

Caleb blinked furiously, swallowing hard against a swell of emotion. "Thanks." It was all he could manage. Anything more and he might choke on the words.

His colleagues—his *friends*—had come.

"Let's get moving," Lucas said. "I have a joint FBI and DEA task force at the Phoenix airport. They're waiting to execute an arrest warrant for Vincente Lopez Garcia for the murder of DEA agent Antonio Cardenas. Doctor Barone will need to testify as a material witness."

"I want in on the assault team." Caleb carefully lowered himself into one of the plush leather seats, his body stiffening.

He ignored the Assistant Director's glare. No way would Caldwell leave him sitting on his hands while Gia was still in danger. The Feds could have Lopez, as long as he got Gia safely back.

Nathan chuckled. "Come on, Lucas. You've got an elite international special operations squad right here."

Caldwell's glare shifted to the big Texan.

"If we could track the helicopter, we'd know exactly where they were headed," Ryder added.

Track.

Caleb straightened, pulse spiking. "Nathan, how close do you need to be to track one of those skin tags you gave me?"

Nathan side-eyed Lucas, lips pursed. "Well..." The word dragged out slow.

Lucas sighed. "I have to use the latrine."

He headed for the back of the plane, passing the lone male flight attendant in a navy-blue uniform, who lingered at a discrete distance.

"The smallest dual-frequency GPS tags officially on the market are the size of a credit card or key fob." Nathan lowered his voice. "What I've got? Same tech, military grade, in a microchip. Off the books. Not even the government has these."

"Meaning?" Caleb pressed.

"Meaning if you tagged her, and she's still wearing it, I can track her anywhere she's in GPS or satellite range." Nathan swiped and tapped on his tablet. "I gave you three tags. Two are pinging at the safe house. The third," he paused.

Frowned.

Swiped again.

Caleb's shoulders went rigid. "What is it?"

Lucas reappeared just as the flight attendant stepped forward. "Gentlemen, the pilot needs you seated for departure now."

The plane started to taxi.

Nathan looked up. "She's still in the air." He glanced at Lucas. "But she's not heading toward Phoenix."

"That can't be right," Lucas snapped.

Nathan angled his screen. "She's tracking toward Albuquerque."

Lucas whipped out his phone.

"Gentlemen, please," the flight attendant tried again.

"You've confirmed Vincente Lopez Garcia is heading to Phoenix?" Lucas said into the phone, then listened, his eyes narrowing. "And you've got eyes on the aircraft. The N-number matches the one that left Miami this morning."

Another pause. "I'll be there in an hour. Do *not* move in until I give the order."

He hung up and motioned to the flight attendant. "Tell the pilots to stand down."

Lachlan was already moving to relay the message. By the time he returned to his seat, the plane had rolled to a stop.

"Lopez isn't going to Phoenix." Caleb's leg bounced up and down, his fingers tapping the armrest on his chair.

Every minute that slipped away took Gia further from him.

"I know." Cold anger radiated from Lucas. "But the head of the joint task force insists Lopez's plane is sitting in a private hanger at Phoenix Sky Harbor and ATC monitored chatter has a civilian helicopter heading to Phoenix from this direction."

He pulled a leather wallet from his suit jacket and stalked toward the cockpit.

Caleb rose, swallowing a groan as his body protested, and followed.

"Contact the tower." The Assistant Director flashed the pilots his credentials. "I need the call sign and N-number of the plane that landed this morning from Miami. I also need the flight plan the pilots filed before the plane left Gallup."

The captain checked Lucas's ID, glanced at his co-pilot, and picked up the mic.

A moment later, the tower came back with the details. The plane's N-number matched the flight that left Miami, but the flight plan—revised shortly before the plane's departure—listed its destination as a small general aviation airport outside Albuquerque.

"I need to deplane. Immediately," Lucas told the captain.

He returned to the group, Caleb on his heels. "The Phoenix task force has been compromised. If I loop them in, someone could tip off Lopez."

Lucas scrubbed a hand over his face. "I can't authorize a hostage rescue without proof that Doctor Barone is at the Albuquerque site—and that she's being held against her will."

"We have eyes on her," Caleb gritted out. His fists clenched. "In real time with the tracker she's wearing."

"Using technology that technically doesn't exist, Sergeant?" Lucas snapped, invoking Caleb's former Army rank. "I can't get a warrant with that—especially when my own damn agents insist she's headed to Phoenix."

The flight attendant unlocked the cabin door and engaged the automatic air stairs.

Lucas clasped Lachlan's shoulder. "Officially, I'm advising you to return to DC."

He dropped his hand to grab the overcoat draped over his seat. "Unofficially, I'll send a team as soon as I can. But it may be too late. Be careful. And good luck."

"Where are you going?" Caleb asked.

"To charter a flight to Phoenix. Lopez's mole expects me there. If I don't show, they'll know I'm onto them." Lucas's mouth set in a cruel line. "I need to unearth a traitor."

Caleb watched the Assistant Director descend the stairs, then turned to Lachlan. "We need to leave for Albuquerque. Now." Tension pulled his muscles taut, his temper balanced on a razor's edge.

Lachlan met Nathan's eyes.

A nod.

Then to Ryder.

Then Danny.

Two more nods.

"Go tell the pilots to change the flight plan," he instructed Caleb. "To Albuquerque International Sunport, not the smaller airport—we don't want to alert Lopez."

The to Nathan, "Driving time between the Sunport and our target?"

More swipes on the tablet. "Twenty-six minutes," Nathan told him.

Lachlan nodded. "Get us two SUVs for when we land."

"Weapons?" Caleb asked. "I've got my Glock and Danny's backup Sig."

"I've got a Glock and the SCAR-Heavy rifle," Danny added.

Caleb's shoulders tightened. "That's not enough."

A faint smile twitched Ryder's lips. "We may have packed extra luggage."

Caleb sank into his seat, relief making his legs weak.

The adrenaline crash left every muscle throbbing. No matter how hard he tried, he couldn't shake the fear that they'd arrive too late and Gia would be gone.

Over the border.

Out of reach.

He took out his phone and sent a text to his grandfather before he had to turn on airplane mode.

> *Zach and Jennie are at the hospital. Lopez has Gia.*

Something Ben Blackwater likely already knew.

Caleb had gotten his cousin shot. Put his grandfather in a terrible position.

And the two dead cartel soldiers he'd left behind?

He'd have some explaining to do.

> *Keep everyone away from Old Joe's. I'll be back as soon as I have Gia.*

A lump formed in his throat.

> *I'm sorry.*

The realization hit hard.

He cared what his grandfather thought of him.

> *I'll see you soon.*

The plane lifted, engines roaring as the earth fell away beneath them.

"How long?" he asked the flight attendant.

"To Albuquerque? Forty minutes. We'll barely be up before we're coming down again."

Two foil packets landed in Caleb's lap.

Danny settled across from him. "Snagged those from the first aid kit. Figured you could use them."

"Thanks." Caleb opened the water bottle in his seat's cup holder and swallowed the pills.

"You good, bro? Even with a vest, two rounds hurts like a mother-fucker. Sure you don't want to sit this one out?"

Caleb glared at his friend. "I'll rest when I'm dead. That plane isn't leaving with Gia on it."

Danny held up his fist. "Hooyah to that."

Despite the pain, the fear, the burn of urgency, Caleb smirked and bumped knuckles with Danny. "It's *hooah*, you squid."

CHAPTER
THIRTY-ONE

GIA LEANED PAST JUAN just enough to peer out the helicopter window at the dark gray strips of tarmac cutting through the dusty brown desert. Albuquerque's urban sprawl lay farther east, the late afternoon sun dusting the granite peaks of the Sandia Mountains in pink as it slid behind the horizon at her back. Closer to the airport, the barren, rugged slopes of Petroglyph National Monument stretched like a moonscape.

Sweat beaded along her hairline. This wasn't Albuquerque's main airport. It was much smaller, and from the air, far more isolated.

As in, middle of nowhere.

Her plan to escape into a crowded terminal crumbled. She fought to stay present, resisting the protective pull of numbness.

Caleb hovered in her mind. A constant presence.

What if he was—

No.

He'd been alive when Juan dragged her away. She refused to believe anything else.

Whatever happened to her, she had to believe Caleb would survive.

Her hand strayed to the collar of her shirt. The vest was stiff and hot, her skin underneath sticky with sweat. She wanted it off. But Vincente and his men either hadn't noticed or didn't care that she still wore it.

Maybe it would keep her alive long enough to escape.

The helicopter touched down in front of a sand-colored building. Its bay door lifted, revealing a sleek, white private jet beneath a two-story ceiling of steel beams and corrugated metal walls.

The jet faced out, and in the cockpit, she could just make out the silhouettes of the pilots.

Vincente yanked her forward by the arm. "Let's go."

She stumbled from the helicopter, crouching instinctively as the rotor wash whipped her hair across her face, the *whomp* of blades overhead deafening.

Vincente dragged her toward the plane, Juan and the two cartel soldiers falling in behind them.

Think, Gia. Stall.

"I have to go to the bathroom." She shouted over the din.

"There's one on the plane." Vincente's tone was flat. Final.

Behind her, the helicopter lifted, rising into the sky.

Cool air hit her face as they entered the hangar.

The silence slammed into her. The rap of shoes on concrete echoed like gunshots.

"Why is the plane still in the hanger?" Vincente's sharp voice rang through the cavernous interior.

"I thought you'd prefer to board Gianna without prying eyes." Juan appeared unruffled by Vincente's anger. "In case she's not cooperative. I'll have the pilot radio for a tow to the ramp. We'll be ready to depart as soon as we're aboard."

Panic clawed up Gia's throat.

Her heels scuffed against the smooth concrete. She tried to plant her feet. Resist.

She couldn't get on that plane. She *couldn't*—

A sudden jolt threw her off balance.

Vincente had stopped.

His grip on her arm tightened.

An older man strolled from behind the jet—graying hair, a short-sleeved light blue shirt untucked over beige linen trousers, brown loafers polished to a shine.

Two men dressed in black from their tops to their cowboy boots accompanied him, menace radiating from every pore.

"Vincente, *sobrino*."

Gia's heart skipped. *Sobrino.* Nephew.

She peered at the man from beneath her lashes.

Shorter than Vincente. Rougher, despite the expensive clothes. Less urbane. His dark eyes were windows into his soul, devoid of mercy.

Cruel. Remorseless. Cunning.

Her stomach pitched. Lightheaded, she fought to stay upright.

He made Vincente look like a choirboy.

If she remembered her research correctly, this was Diego Lopez Becerra's brother.

Juan's father.

If the brother who wasn't in charge was *this* terrifying, she might not survive meeting Vincente's father—the man at the top of the Espina Negra cartel.

She glanced between Vincente and Juan. Both had stilled, the tension in the hangar thick enough to suffocate.

Vincente's face remained composed, but his eyes snapped with anger.

Juan looked...resigned. It struck her then how little she knew about him—only that he was Vincente's cousin and loyal soldier.

"Tío Ramón." Vincente dropped his grip on her arm, flicking a quick glance over her at Juan before returning his focus to his uncle. "What are you doing here?"

"Juan, close the door." Ramón gestured impatiently. "We conduct our business in private."

Vincente stiffened.

Beside her, Juan flexed his fingers and took a subtle step back, his gaze sweeping the room. Without protest, he pressed a button on the wall.

The hydraulic metal panel hummed and groaned as it descended, closing them in with a final clang that made Gia flinch.

Whatever was happening now felt even more dangerous.

A laugh that felt vaguely unhinged bubbled up in Gia's throat.

More dangerous?

As if being carted off to a cartel kingpin's estate wasn't already bad enough?

"I'm pleased you've finally decided to clean up your affairs." Ramón's cruel gaze slanted to her. "Although why she still breathes is a mystery."

The words stole Gia's breath. Her pulse pounded.

A muscle ticked in Vincente's jaw. "She will be returning with me to Mexico. As my guest." His voice hardened. "I expect her to be treated as such."

"A guest?" Ramón arched a brow, his grin oily. "Perhaps you will offer her services to your father—a minor concession for the time you've wasted dealing with her."

"Perhaps." Vincente shrugged. "Not that it concerns you."

Gia's stomach cramped. A violent shudder rolled through her.

He wouldn't...

The look he gave her held no warmth. No regret. It was as if, as Ramón had put it, she was a concession to be offered in a business transaction.

Her knees threatened to give out.

He would.

He'd already threatened to give her to his men.

"I don't have time for this." Vincente's voice lowered, now encased in ice. "If you wish to discuss matters further, you can accompany me on my flight—or get out of my way and allow me to run my operation as I see fit."

He turned to Emilio. "Put her on the plane."

Then to Juan, "Open the hanger door."

Emilio gripped Gia's arm and hauled her across the hanger.

I can't get on.

If she did, her life was over.

Even if Vincente didn't kill her outright, she'd be a captive—punished, used, and from the sounds of it, lent out to others whenever he felt like it.

Panic overwhelmed her attempt to stay rational.

She fought back—kicking, scratching, resisting.

Cursing in Spanish, Emilio tightened his hold, cutting off the blood flow to her arm. He caught her flailing hand and yanked it behind her back, forcing her up the narrow air stairs into the jet's cramped cabin.

Pain shot up her shoulder. She twisted toward Vincente, one last desperate plea forming on her lips.

Ignoring her, he turned to Juan. "I told you it would come to this." Violence laced every syllable.

"Yes." Juan stepped back.

Reached behind his back. "You did."

Gia stilled at the sudden edge in Juan's voice.

A prickle of warning danced across her skin.

Vincente faced his uncle. "*Tío*, this is the last time you interfere in my business."

Juan's hand reappeared.

It held a gun.

But he didn't aim it at his father.

Shock rooted Gia in place.

Juan? But he and Vincente were like brothers.

Terror clawed up her throat. If Vincente died here, in this hangar, so would she.

"Vincente!" she shouted.

He turned, looking up at her standing in the plane's doorway.

Then his gaze shifted to Juan.

Puzzlement, disbelief, shock...

Each emotion flitted across his face in rapid succession.

He lifted his hand. A plea. "Juan, *primo,* what are you doing?"

The silenced shot sounded like a muffled crack, but it echoed in the cavernous space of the hangar.

Emilio froze, his grip on her arm going slack.

For a moment, nothing made sense.

Then Vincente's knees buckled. He collapsed in slow motion, his body thudding against the concrete floor.

The smell of gunpowder—sharp and acrid—hit her nose. Then the horribly familiar metallic tang of blood.

Gia screamed as her world slammed back into real time.

Her gaze flew to Juan.

For one brief second, regret tugged at the corners of his mouth.

Then his expression shuttered.

"I wasn't sure you would do it." Ramón's calm delivery shot ice through Gia's veins.

"My loyalty is to you, *Papá.* It always has been." Juan stood rigid, but Gia saw the slight tremor in his fingers, the quiet exhale that slipped past his lips.

He swung toward Matteo.

Lifted his weapon again.

She thought she heard him murmur, *Lo siento, amigo*, before he fired again.

Gia's knees buckled, as if the bullet that struck Matteo had torn through her instead.

Emilio yanked her inside the cabin and let go.

"¡Dios mío!" His hands plunged into his hair as he paced the aisle before collapsing into a seat, his gaze unfocused.

Up front, the two pilots sat frozen.

"Call someone," she hissed. "You have a radio. Use it."

The pilot glanced at her, fear and regret clouding his eyes. He reached back and slid the panel shut, separating the cockpit from the cabin.

"You've got to be kidding me." She had the urge to kick that panel in. Drag them from their seats and—

Then what?

She didn't know how to fly a plane or even work the radio.

There was only one option left.

"Hey!" Gia marched over to Emilio and shook his shoulder. "Listen to me. We have to get out of here before they kill us, too."

"Shut up!" he hissed. He was staring out the cabin window where Vincente and Ortega bled out on the hanger floor, his leg bouncing with nervous energy.

"Emilio. Bring out the woman." Juan's voice. Taunting. "Maybe we'll have some fun with her, yes?" Any hint of remorse he'd shown had vanished.

Gia clutched Emilio's sleeve, frantic. "Look what they did to Vincente. To your friend. They'll kill us both. They can't risk Vincente's father learning his own flesh and blood betrayed him."

Dead.

Vincente was dead.

She should have felt safe. Relieved.

Instead, she was caught in a family betrayal that would spill more blood before it was over.

The enormity of it hit her like a wave.

A sob escaped. So did the truth.

She'd thought staying silent would keep her safe.

How wrong she'd been.

"No, *puta*. They'll kill you." Emilio's voice rang with a false bravado that clashed with the fear in his eyes.

Not for her. For himself.

He shoved to his feet and grabbed her roughly, dragging her toward the open cabin door.

Gia planted her hands on the doorframe, feet braced at the top of the stairs.

She stared down at Juan—at the man who'd so cruelly betrayed his cousin.

Hate and fear coiled in her chest. She'd never liked Juan—with his snide remarks and inappropriate stares—but Vincente had trusted his cousin implicitly.

Now his blood stained the floor. Just like Antonio's had soaked the deck of Vincente's yacht.

The scent of copper and iron turned her stomach.

This time, there was no ocean nearby to swallow the bodies.

"Vincente's father will kill you both when he finds out. And he will."

It wasn't a threat. It wasn't a plea.

Just a final parting shot. A curse she prayed would come true.

Because the best she could hope for now was a quick death.

Ramón's sneer reeked of arrogance and disdain. "My brother will believe his son died in a trap laid for him and his men by you and that soldier you've been fucking. I will take great pleasure informing him that *my* son avenged Vincente's death by killing you."

He turned to Juan. "Deal with her. Then we leave."

Juan's leering smile made her want to claw his eyes out. "Vincente promised me a turn with you. All those times I saw your lips wrapped around his cock. Bent over while he took you and I could only watch..."

He glanced at his father. "We've got time, don't we, *Papá*?"

Ramón's backhand landed with a brutal crack, knocking Juan sideways. "Are you as dimwitted as your cousin? You think this is a game?"

For a flicker of a second, something dangerous burned in Juan's gaze.

"Once the Federales realize Vincente's plane isn't in Phoenix, they'll trace its path here," Ramón continued. "We need to be over the border before they do. Now, finish it."

"Emilio, *vámanos*," Juan barked. Color flared in his cheeks as he glared after his father's retreating back.

He made an impatient movement with his gun.

Emilio gave her a shove.

She shook him off.

Held her head high

Edged one foot down the metal stair.

She'd die with dignity, not dragged kicking and screaming to meet her fate.

I love you, Caleb. And I'm so sorry.

Chapter
Thirty-Two

THE SUN DIPPED OVER the horizon, casting the mountains in shadow. A fiery band of orange bled into pink, then cooled into the deep blue of the evening sky.

Caleb eased from the back seat of the rental SUV, exhaling against the throb in his chest and back. The over-the-counter pain meds Danny had given him dulled the worst of it.

He adjusted the new tactical vest Ryder had handed over to replace his compromised one.

The air was crisp but not biting. They'd parked, tucked beside a cluster of sagebrush, a quarter mile from the small general aviation airport. Lengthening shadows cloaked their approach.

During the flight, they'd reviewed aerial photos of the facility, and decided security consisted of badge access for vehicles at the gate and a five-foot perimeter fence that was easily scaled.

For once, something was going their way.

Lachlan had opted for handguns—easy to conceal if spotted and easier to explain to law enforcement—but a disadvantage if Lopez had cartel muscle toting semi-autos.

Nathan was the exception. His new toy—a disassembled precision long range AR-15—rested in the backpack slung over his shoulder.

Once they pinpointed Gia's location, he'd take position on a nearby rooftop, the gunner of last resort. If Caleb and the others failed—if the plane left the hangar—it would fall to Nathan to make sure it never reached the runway.

Stars blinked to life in the deepening sky as they crossed open ground, angling away from the runway zone and the control tower's line of sight.

The airport was quiet. At this hour, sparsely populated. A few workers moved between the maintenance hangar and fuel depot.

Nathan tracked Gia's tag to a small metal hanger at the far end of the compound, wedged between larger rectangular buildings built to house multiple aircraft.

After testing their comms, Danny crouched low and crept toward the target hangar.

His whisper crackled in Caleb's ear. "No movement outside. Bay door's a single panel hydraulic—no way to lift it from out here. Only other access is a standard pedestrian door at the back, right side. That's our way in unless we wait for them to open the bay."

Caleb lowered his gaze to his boots. Even with his poker face, the fear pressing against his ribs was hard to mask.

Not for himself. Not for his team—all former special operators.

For Gia.

"One entry point," he murmured. "No intel on the number of hostiles. No idea what they're carrying. No sightline inside. We're packing pea shooters, and don't even have flashbangs."

"Did someone say flashbang?" Nathan unzipped a side pocket, pulled out a black cylinder the size of a shaving cream can.

"Christ." Lachlan gave a quiet chuckle. "The lad and his toys."

Caleb took the flashbang, tested its weight, let it settle in his grip.

Their best shot at a dynamic entry without getting shredded on the threshold. "I could kiss you right now."

"Steady, amigo." Nathan grinned. "I'm taken."

Lachlan checked his weapon, pocketed an extra mag. "Let's get into position."

Caleb did the same.

Ryder followed suit.

Nathan assembled his rifle with quick, practiced movements. Slinging the backpack over his shoulder, he eyed the roof of the adjacent hanger. "Give me a boost."

Lachlan and Ryder braced him as he leveraged onto the sloped metal surface, moving with surprising speed for a man his size. He motioned for the rifle.

Lachlan turned to Caleb. "You take point. I'm secondary. Then Ryder. Danny handles cover and flashbang."

Caleb led the way to the rear of the hangar. They stacked against the white metal door.

He pressed his ear to the siding.

Voices—male, low, indistinct.

The back of his neck prickled.

Something was off.

He didn't know what. Just the need to move burned through him, pressing from gut to brain.

"We go in. Now."

Losing Gia wasn't an option.

Not now. Not after finding love. After discovering family.

He wanted a future with her.

He deserved that.

So did she. Even more than he did.

They were survivors.

Lachlan squeezed his shoulder.

Ryder stacked in.

Danny shifted to the opposite side. Tested the knob.

Unlocked.

His eyes met Caleb's. A slight nod.

Ready.

Danny twisted the handle and cracked the door an inch. Pulled the pin.

"Flash out."

The flashbang sailed inside.

A sharp *boom* rattled the hanger.

Shouts. A woman's scream.

Gia.

Caleb flowed into the room, weapon raised, slipping into his training as effortlessly as pulling on a robe.

Blood.

Sickly sweet and metallic.

Death.

Body parts exposed to air that shouldn't be.

Two men in black crouched over another, reaching for weapons.

Movement at the plane's cabin door—a male.

A body sprawled in the center of the hangar, blood spreading across a white shirt.

A flash of surprise. *Lopez?*

Another body slumped near the plane's nose.

Ortega.

Caleb's mind processed the carnage in an instant, but one detail took precedence.

Gia.

By the plane stairs.

Eyes wide with fear.

Clawing at the arm locked across her throat.

A gun pressed to her temple.

Caleb shoved down the fear clawing at his own throat.

Fear would get Gia killed.

Two shots cracked from his team.

The men in black dropped.

Caleb kept his weapon trained on his target.

Juan.

The cousin. Gia was his shield.

Behind him, Lachlan covered the open cabin door.

Whoever had been there vanished deeper inside.

To his left and right, Danny and Ryder cleared the hangar.

"Let her go." Caleb's voice was cold, thrumming with rage he didn't bother to hide.

Juan's grip didn't loosen.

"Why would I do that?" His voice was steady, but sweat glistened under the overhead lights. "She's my ticket out."

A figure stepped forward. Older, five-eight. Graying hair.

Cold, dark eyes flicked over Caleb and his team like they were nothing more than lint to be brushed away.

"Open the hanger door or she dies."

Mexican, judging from his accent.

Caleb's response was instant. "If she dies, you die."

The man gave him a shark's smile. "If I live, she lives."

Juan held the gun, but this man was in charge.

Caleb studied him. He appeared unbothered by the dead men at his feet—two of whom had been his protection.

A killer. The kind who gave orders, not took them.

Not *El Víbora.*

Caleb had studied Diego Lopez Becerra's photos. But the resemblance was there in the remorseless eyes, the straight-edged nose, the cruel line of his mouth.

The brother.

Ramón Lopez Becerra.

"No hostiles outside. I'm in position." Nathan's voice was calm and steady in Caleb's earpiece. "Let him think he has the upper hand."

"Chaos," Caleb said, using Danny's SEAL team call sign. "Open the door."

Danny backed to the wall, found the controls.

The hangar filled with airport noise as the door lifted.

"Hello, fellas," Nathan's voice returned. "Looks like you had fun without me. Eyes on the target." A pause. "No shot."

Caleb gave the faintest nod.

Juan was too close to Gia for a clean head shot.

He glanced at Vincente's body.

Eyes open. Frozen in surprise. Crimson blooming on his once pristine shirt.

Relief punched through Caleb.

Someone beat him to it.

Whether or not Gia admitted it, if he'd killed her ex, it would've always lived between them.

Caleb's gaze shifted to Ortega.

Had Lopez and Ortega turned on each other? A Wild West standoff?

Maybe the rumors he'd seeded—about the Aztec Kings courting Los Coyotes—had done the trick.

Only...no weapons near the bodies.

His attention snapped back to Ramón.

Cold bastard.

The uncle kills the prince to usurp the crown.

"You killed your nephew," he said.

"Juan did." Gia's voice, quiet, unsteady, cut through the chaos.

It was the first time she'd spoken since he heard her scream from the other side of the door.

Caleb imagined Lopez's last moment—betrayed by the person closest to him.

Time to push Juan.

Make the bastard focus on him.

Shift that gun off Gia.

Step away. Give Nathan the shot.

He let his lip curl. "Did you do it for yourself?" He arched a brow. "Or for Daddy?"

"Shut up!" Juan's gaze darted to his father.

Caleb smirked. "Yeah, we know who calls the shots. It isn't you. Killed your cousin just to be Daddy's lapdog."

"*Callate a la verga!*" Juan flushed red, eyes glassy. His grip on Gia loosened.

That's right, you bastard. Come after me.

"Enough." Ramón's sharp command snapped Juan back.

The senior cartel leader climbed the boarding stairs and turned. "I'll have the pilots start the engines."

He eyed Lachlan, Ryder, Danny, then Caleb. "If any of you interfere—including whoever's outside—she dies."

"Caleb." Gia's desperate plea twisted his gut.

He half-stepped forward.

Juan jammed the gun harder into her temple.

The plane's engines rumbled to life.

"It's okay, baby." Caleb forced his voice to remain calm. But inside, rage clawed at him.

If Gia got on that plane, she wouldn't come out alive.

The right turbine began to spin.

"SUV inbound. No headlights," Nathan barked through the comms.

Outside, a car engine growled closer.

Danny and Ryder took up positions by the hangar door.

Lachlan stayed beside Caleb, weapon steady.

The left turbine whined to life.

There was no more time.

Juan hauled Gia toward the stairs. "Come on, *puta*."

"Gia," Caleb shouted over the din.

"I love you," she cried, eyes shining. In them, a last goodbye.

His heart nearly cracked.

Fight. He mouthed silently. Desperately. *Fight baby.*

Her eyes widened.

Then narrowed.

Fear became determination.

Gia exploded—kicking and clawing like a hellcat.

Juan cursed in Spanish, trying to choke her off as he dragged her up the stairs.

Caleb edged closer.

"Not hostiles. Repeat—not hostiles." Nathan was shouting in his ear. "Hold your fire!"

Too late. Juan was nearly inside the cabin.

"Nathan—wide left. Now."

A *plink*, then the soft *pffit* of Nathan's suppressed AR. The bullet plowed into the lowered cabin door.

Juan jerked. His grip on Gia slackened.

She dropped—dead weight.

Caleb fired. Then surged forward, yanking Gia to him as Juan crumpled on the stairs.

"You're okay, baby, you're okay," he murmured as she sobbed against his chest.

His body shook. His heart hammered. "I love you."

He held her too tight, but he couldn't let go. Not yet. Not ever.

Four men in tactical gear stormed into the hangar, long guns raised

"FBI! Weapons down!" The lead agent—burly, with close cropped black hair and a military bearing—barked the command.

Caleb instantly shielded Gia.

"Weapons down, lads," Lachlan said quietly to the Dìleas team, making sure the order didn't carry to the Feds.

Caleb released Gia, moving to comply, then froze.

Movement at the plane's doorway.

Ramón.

He glanced at his son's body, then at Caleb.

No rage. No grief. Just cold calculation.

The boarding stairs began to retract, Juan's body tumbling onto the concrete.

Caleb held Ramón's stare until the closing door hid him from view.

The plane's engines revved. It rolled forward. Agents scattered from its path.

Hell no.

Ramón Lopez was not getting away.

Caleb grabbed Gia's hand and strode to the team leader.

The man pulled out a wallet from his tactical vest and flipped it open to show his ID. "FBI Special Agent Terrell Walton—Assistant Director Caldwell sent me."

Lachlan leaned toward Caleb and murmured, "Former Special Forces. Served under Lucas's command back in the day."

"Ramón Lopez is on that plane—*El Víbora's* brother," Caleb said. "He ordered his nephew's murder."

Walton's eyes flickered in surprise. "How many on board?"

"Ramón." Caleb recalled the shadowed movement at the cabin door. "At least one other." He looked to Gia, who trembled, skin cool, eyes unfocused.

"Gia, baby." He brushed a knuckle down her cheek. "Did you see anyone else?"

"Pink Hat," she murmured, then straightened. "Emilio. The younger one who tried to take me from Lucero's." Her voice steadied. "Two pilots. No one else."

Walton relayed the information to his team and snapped out orders. "Keep that plane from the runway!" He surveyed the carnage inside the hangar. "Jesus."

Police vehicles flooded the tarmac, strobes flashing red and blue. An armored SWAT vehicle rolled in behind them.

"One of the dead men is Vincente Lopez Garcia," Caleb added, tucking Gia closer. "He kidnapped a Navajo Nation tribal member to trade for Doctor Barone. When that failed, he took Doctor Barone at gunpoint, intending to fly her to Mexico."

He didn't mention the two cartel soldiers left behind at Old Joe's place. No need to answer questions they didn't want asked.

"So the guy Lucas Caldwell had an arrest warrant for is in there." Walton exhaled sharply, hands braced on hips. "Jesus," he muttered again, shaking his head.

Lachlan extended a hand to Gia. "Doctor Barone, Lachlan Mackay. 'Tis a pleasure to meet you. Pity it's under these circumstances."

"Nice to meet you." Gia offered a tired smile. "You're Scottish." Pink bloomed on her cheeks. She rubbed her forehead with a sigh. "I guess you know that."

"Aye." Lachlan grinned. He and Caleb exchanged a look.

Nathan appeared out of the dark, his rifle and backpack conspicuously absent. He joined Ryder and Danny as SWAT surrounded the plane.

"We've got them boxed in," Walton said.

He turned to Gia, his tone softening. "Doctor Barone, I know you've been through hell. My vehicle's right here if you need a breather." He gestured to the dark blue, government issued SUV beside the hangar.

"Thank you, but I'll stay with Caleb." Gia glanced toward the hanger. Shuddered. "I'm not going back in there."

The agent cast a pointed stare at Lachlan and Caleb, his voice sharpening. "You gentlemen can take a seat somewhere out of the way. You've had enough excitement for one night."

Gia, Caleb, and the Dìleas team watched as the standoff dragged on.

Finally, the plane's door opened. Ramón emerged first, head high. Even from a distance, Caleb could see the arrogance in his posture.

Unapologetic. Untouchable.

He wouldn't stay that way. Not when Diego Lopez learned who orchestrated his son's death.

Emilio followed, then the pilots.

Walton returned after Ramón and the others were cuffed and led away. Disgust pulled his features tight. "The bastard's son is dead, and all he said was to call his lawyer. Cold son of a bitch."

Caleb checked his watch. *Nine p.m.* "Gia needs rest. We'll get a hotel and give our statements in the morning."

Walton shook his head. "Doctor Barone's coming with me to Phoenix. Tonight. Assistant Director Caldwell and DEA agents from Miami want to question her first thing in the morning about the missing agent. She's a material witness."

"Am I under arrest?" Gia asked, her voice monotone.

Caleb tightened his grip on her hand.

"No," Walton said. His voice softened. "But you may want a lawyer."

"I'm going with her."

Caleb had just gotten her back. He wasn't letting her go.

Walton glanced at the hangar, now bustling with crime scene techs. "You all are coming with me."

He turned to glare at the men from Dìleas. "There's five body bags being loaded into the medical investigator's van. You have some explaining to do."

Lachlan sighed. "I'd better call Sophia in case we need a lawyer, too."

"Shit," Nathan muttered. "Emily's going to kill me if I end up in jail and screw up this wedding."

"Never mind Emily," Ryder added. "Admiral Dane is the one you need to worry about."

Caleb tuned them out. He feathered his lips over Gia's ear. "Are you ready?"

If only there was somewhere quiet he could take her.

Just to hold her. Feel her heartbeat against his bare skin.

"Ready as I'll ever be." Gia stepped back, smoothed her jeans, and squared her shoulders. "If I'm going to have a life again, I have to stop running. No more secrets. Mine or Vincente's."

"You'll get your life back sweetheart, I promise."

One way or another, it was a promise Caleb intended to keep.

CHAPTER
THIRTY-THREE

PHOENIX, ARIZONA, SPRAWLED ACROSS the Sonoran Desert—a desert metropolis where February days hovered in the seventies, pleasantly balmy. In the summer, the city turned into a furnace, heat rising past one hundred degrees for days on end.

The morning after Albuquerque, Gia stood on the steps of the concrete and glass government building that housed Phoenix's FBI field office. The sun warmed her skin, but it couldn't chase away the chill of nerves.

The people waiting for her inside would decide her fate.

A hand pressed to her back.

"Ready?" Caleb's lips brushed her hair. "Everything will be okay."

She shut her eyes, absorbing his strength.

Last night, they'd slept in an FBI safe house with an agent posted in the living room. The men from Dìleas had been housed elsewhere, also under watch.

She'd spent the night in Caleb's arms, wondering if it would be their last.

Her lashes lifted. It was time to own her choices—to tell the government everything. Every sordid detail of life with Vincente. Every moment of that horrible night on his yacht.

She would fight for her freedom.

For a life with Caleb.

"I'm ready." She stepped through the glass doors.

Inside, the blast of air-conditioning hit like an arctic wind, and she was grateful for the long-sleeved button-down and jeans she still wore from the day before. After clearing security, their FBI escort led them to a waiting area lined with framed photographs of Phoenix and, at its center, the FBI seal and motto, *Fidelity, Bravery, and Integrity*.

Caleb's friends were already there.

Last night's introductions had been brief. Now, after some sleep, she recalled what she'd learned.

Danny, the adrenaline junkie with shaggy hair and a love of muscle cars. He had an amusing fashion quirk—Hawaiian shirts in eye-searing colors and vintage bowling tops.

The dark-haired Scot, Lachlan. The founder of Dìleas. Handsome but intimidating, until he'd shown her a picture of his wife, Sophia. The love on his face had softened the edge of his ruthlessness.

Nathan—the giant. A harder-edged version of Thor. Terrifying until he'd smiled. His lazy Texas drawl and icy blue eyes had turned warm with humor. He'd ribbed his friends, shown her a picture of his fiancée, Emily, and offered an amused, "Welcome to the family."

Family? The word lingered.

She couldn't help but wonder what it would be like to be a member of this circle of men and the women they loved.

Then there was Ryder—Caleb's direct superior. Blue-eyed with wavy brown hair and a quiet reserve. Caleb had warned her not to compare him to Superman, despite the obvious resemblance to the British actor. He, too, had shown her a picture of his fiancée when she'd asked.

This was Caleb's family.

Not by blood, but by brotherhood.

A brotherhood she couldn't ask him to leave.

Even if the government absolved her, she likely had no job to return to on the rez. Not after the chaos she'd brought to their doorstep.

"Doctor Barone?" Special Agent Walton appeared in the doorway. "Come with me."

Gia wiped sweaty palms on her jeans and stood. She'd waived her right to have a lawyer present—she didn't want to delay the meeting. And she had nothing to hide. She was prepared to tell them everything.

"I'm going with her." Caleb gripped her hand.

"Caleb," Ryder warned.

"She's not going alone." Caleb's jaw was tight, his chest out.

Walton stared, then sighed. "Fine. Assistant Director Caldwell can deal with you."

He led them down the hall to a windowless conference room—stark and impersonal, with bare walls and a white-tiled drop ceiling. Four men and a woman sat around a long table in conservative suits, their ID badges clipped to pockets or lapels.

Caleb's arm circled her waist.

A tall man with dark hair silvered at the temples rose.

He was the one in charge, she decided quickly. Even Caleb had straightened to attention.

"Doctor Barone, I'm Assistant Director Lucas Caldwell with the FBI," he said.

He gestured to the others. "Special Agents Martinez and Lowell from the DEA's Miami Division, Special Agent Mia Anderson, FBI, Phoenix Field Office, and Special Agent Zamora, DEA, Phoenix Division. You've already met Special Agent Walton."

His sharp blue gaze locked on her. "We'd like to ask you some questions about Vincente Lopez Garcia and DEA Special Agent Cardenas."

Chin lifted, she faced the agents in the room. "Vincente murdered Antonio Cardenas. Said he was a DEA spy. I witnessed it. That's why I ran."

Her tongue swiped over dry lips. "I know I should have gone to the police or DEA right away, but...I was afraid."

Caldwell's gaze shifted to Caleb. "You need to wait outside."

Caleb's eyes narrowed. "That's not happening."

The Assistant Director didn't blink. "You and your colleagues have official statements to give to Special Agent Walton about yesterday's events."

His voice lowered. "I pulled strings, son, with the Attorney General to have the US Marshal's Office deputize Dìleas Security Agency personnel as federal agents. If I hadn't, you'd all be facing federal charges."

Gia's breath hitched.

The risk Caleb and his friends had taken for her...

No one had ever done that before.

She blinked back sudden tears and touched Caldwell's sleeve. "Thank you."

His expression softened for the briefest moment before turning steely again. "Your meeting is down the hall, Sergeant Varella. Special Agent Walton will escort you."

"I'll be fine," Gia promised Caleb, though her pulse hammered.

His gold-flecked eyes met hers. He placed a swift, hard kiss on her lips. "I'll be right outside when you're done, sweetheart. I'm not going anywhere."

With one last look leveled at Assistant Director Caldwell, Caleb left.

Gia turned back to the government agents. Their badges gleamed under the ceiling lights, their expressions unreadable.

She drew a long breath. Held it.

Caldwell gestured to a chair. "Have a seat."

Caleb followed Special Agent Walton to a second conference room, where Lachlan, Nathan, Ryder, and Danny were already waiting.

Danny slid a paper cup across the table. "Coffee?"

Nathan took a sip from his own and winced. "Gotta be a retired senior chief making this swill."

Lachlan glanced up from his phone and addressed Agent Walton. "Mind giving us a few minutes, pal? I still have a business to run, and something needs my team's immediate attention."

"Immediate attention, huh?" The agent's tone dripped with skepticism. But after a brief hesitation, he shoved back his chair. "Ten minutes."

The door clicked shut behind him.

Lachlan nodded to Nathan, who pulled out a palm-sized black box, pressed a button, and set it on the table.

"There," Lachlan said, "now we can talk."

He cast a pointed look at Caleb and Danny. "How many bodies need to be handled?"

Caleb stared into his coffee. "Before Albuquerque? Two. We'll see how the Navajo Nation Police deal with it."

And how his grandfather handled it with the police chief. The Diné didn't like the Feds in their business.

But this hadn't been Diné business.

He'd called his grandfather last night. Filled him in on what had happened in Albuquerque. That he and Gia were headed to Phoenix with the FBI. He'd also checked in on Zach, who was due to be released from the hospital tomorrow.

Lachlan exhaled and rubbed his temple. "How many more bloody favors am I going to owe Lucas Caldwell? He already has naming rights to my firstborn."

He gestured between Caleb and Danny. "Make sure your stories match with everyone who was there, just in case."

Caleb nodded. Since they were all together, he figured now was the time to bring up a decision he'd made.

He just wasn't sure how.

"I want to continue working at Dìleas," he began.

"But?" Lachlan asked. He and Ryder shared a look.

"I'm staying in northern Arizona. At least for now." Caleb scrubbed a hand along his jaw. He met the eyes of each man at the table. "This is where I need to be."

Silence stretched, ratcheting up tension at the base of his skull.

Lachlan and Ryder held another wordless exchange—battle-hardened shorthand from their SAS days.

Caleb shifted. If they cut him loose, it would hurt. But Gia came first. He'd figure something out. Maybe he'd join the Navajo Nation Police, work alongside Zach.

Finally, Ryder spoke. "As long as you're willing to travel for assignments, I don't see why it matters where you call home, mate. Actually," he glanced at Lachlan, "we could talk with Gia and your grandfather about using the clinic for medical visits that need...discretion."

Amusement flickered in his bright blue eyes. "You wouldn't be the first in this firm to rearrange your life for a woman."

"Christ," Lachlan groaned. "Here we go again. Another one of us making a bloody fool of himself."

"You started it," Nathan drawled.

"Whatever this virus is, keep it to yourselves." Danny mock shuddered. "I like my freedom."

"Don't say that too loudly," Nathan warned. "Karma's listening."

Relief loosened the knot in Caleb's chest. "Thanks."

A knock at the door.

Nathan pocketed the audio jammer as Special Agent Walton poked his head in.

"Your ten minutes are up."

After giving their statements, Walton dismissed them. "You're free to return home. Assistant Director Caldwell knows where to find you if we need anything else."

Fortunately for Caleb and Danny, Walton focused his questions on everything that happened after they landed in Albuquerque and postponed any inquiry into events on the rez until he could coordinate with Navajo Nation authorities.

Caleb checked his watch. Over two hours had passed since Gia went in.

He saw his teammates off as they left for the airport, then resumed pacing the waiting room, his gut twisting with thoughts of what Gia must be enduring—reliving the DEA agent's murder, recounting her time with Vincente Lopez Garcia. The Feds would throw everything at her, press her for every detail they could use against Espina Negra.

All Caleb wanted was to take her home. To her trailer on the rez.

Hold her until that haunted look faded.

Until she stopped checking her rearview mirror.

Until she no longer flinched at every touch.

His phone rang. He fished it out of his pocket, brows lifting at the name on the screen.

Carson Elliott.

The Phoenix detective investigating his mother's death.

Felt like a lifetime ago.

"Detective Elliott."

"Mister Varella. I canvassed your mother's neighbors like you asked. One of them remembered seeing her the morning of her overdose—talking to a man outside her apartment. He handed her a small white paper bag. Looked like it came from a pharmacy." A pause. "About five-eight to five-ten. Salt and pepper hair. Distinctive mustache."

"Manuel Ortega," Caleb growled. His mother had reconnected with his father's sleazebag friend.

"His employer says he's out of town. I plan to question him when he returns."

"Don't bother," Caleb said flatly. "He's dead. Gunned down last night in Albuquerque. The FBI can confirm."

"Huh. Well, one bad guy down," the detective said. "Unfortunately, plenty more to take his place." A beat passed. "Again, I'm sorry for your loss. I hope this gives you some closure."

Caleb ended the call and looked down at the silver and turquoise bracelet on his wrist—the one from the box of his mother's belongings.

Closure.

Vincente Lopez and his cousin Juan were dead. Ramón Lopez was in custody. And if Diego Lopez ever learned the truth about who ordered his son's murder, Ramón wouldn't stay alive for long.

If closure meant letting go of the vendetta and building a future with Gia, then yeah.

He had closure.

Footsteps echoed down the hallway.

Agent Walton appeared. "They've finished interviewing Doctor Barone."

Caleb's shoulders loosened. "Is she free to leave?"

Walton hesitated. Sympathy flickered in his eyes.

"No."

Gia stood outside the conference room with a female federal agent—her name escaped her—while the agents inside decided her fate.

Fatigue pressed down on her like a weight. She fought to stay upright.

She'd told them everything. In excruciating detail.

How she'd met Vincente. What little she'd seen of his business dealings. The people they'd dined with—names when she knew them, faces picked from photographs when she didn't. Times. Places.

The first time she met the man the DEA identified as their agent, Antonio Cardenas.

The night Vincente murdered him on the yacht.

How Juan dumped his body overboard.

Then the questions had turned personal.

How Vincente had charmed her. When the relationship became twisted. Controlling. Her childhood. Her ties to known Mafia figures in New York.

Why she'd taken the name of a dead child and forged a new identity.

Shame burned her throat. Pricked behind her eyes. By the end, she wanted to curl up in a corner and disappear.

"Gia."

Caleb.

She hadn't heard him approach. Something in her expression made his face tighten.

"It's going to be okay, baby."

A sob broke free—sudden and sharp. She bit her lip and pressed her face into his chest.

Warm. Solid. Safe.

He smelled of sandalwood, spices, and home.

His palm swept in slow circles across her back.

She wanted to sink into him, disappear into his strength, and never let go.

"I love you, Gia," he murmured against her ear. "Whatever happens, we face it together."

He cupped her face, a crooked smile stealing her breath. "You're my family."

The love in his eyes rocked her.

"I don't know what I did to deserve you," she whispered, "but there's no one I'd rather spend my life loving than you."

The conference room door opened.

Lucas Caldwell filled the threshold. "Doctor Barone, step inside, please."

Caleb's fingers laced with hers. "I'm coming with her." There was no negotiation in his tone.

"Suit yourself—if Doctor Barone allows it." Caldwell held the door.

Gia clutched Caleb's hand and followed him in.

The agents inside said nothing, their expressions blank.

Her throat tightened.

Caldwell waved them to their seats and took his own. "After reviewing your testimony—and given that the men responsible for Special Agent Cardenas's murder are deceased—we won't pursue charges for misprision of felony or accessory after the fact."

A low roar filled Gia's ears. She caught snatches of Caldwell's words—fear for her life, the power imbalance in her relationship with Vincente, her service to the Navajo community.

Chairs scraped. The agents stood.

AD Caldwell gathered his files, stacking them neatly into a black leather briefcase.

"What about Espina Negra?" Caleb asked. "If your mole leaks our identities..."

Gia's heart stuttered. She'd assumed with Vincente and Juan dead, and Ramón in jail, she was safe.

"The mole worked for Ramón. Now that Ramón's in prison, I expect him to peddle his services to Diego." Lucas's expression hardened. Gia recognized that look—the cold, flat stare she'd seen in Caleb's eyes the night at Lucero's. "And I'll be waiting."

The click of his briefcase echoed in the silence.

"As for retaliation, Diego's likely already put a death order on Ramón. Even if he ends up in federal supermax, he won't last. With two top lieutenants gone, the DEA expects Espina Negra will fracture. Rival cartels will move in. Diego will have his hands full."

"So, that's it?" Caleb's gaze slid to Gia, then back to Caldwell. "No retaliation?"

Lucas held his stare. "No guarantees. But Gia was never a threat to Diego. And you? You didn't kill his son. You just happened to be in the way of those who did."

The door whispered shut behind him.

The empty conference room, once suffocating, suddenly felt as cavernous as an arena.

It was over.

She could stay Gianna Barone.

No more hiding behind false identities.

No more running.

No more flinching at shadows, seeing danger in every stranger's face.

Relief should have flooded her.

Instead, she felt...nothing.

She searched Caleb's face, needing something solid to anchor herself to.

Warm fingers closed around hers. Tugged her to her feet.

"Gia." His voice was steady, solid. "You're free. It's over."

"Over."

She tested the word. Let it settle on her tongue. Waited for it to take root in her brain.

"Now what?"

He brushed a kiss over her lips. Squeezed her hand.

"I have one thing left to do here in Phoenix. Then we go home."

CHAPTER
THIRTY-FOUR

AFTER GRADUATING FROM THE Green Beret Qualification—or "Q"—course, an intense, months-long Special Forces training pipeline, and earning his Green Beret, Caleb had moved his mother from the crime infested South Side neighborhood he'd grown up in to a modest one-bedroom apartment in northeast Phoenix.

That was where he took Gia after leaving the FBI office and renting a car at the airport.

The place was nearly empty—only his mother's bed and dining table remained. A donation truck would collect them in the morning. At Caleb's request, Camila had offered his mother's friends whatever they wanted. She'd donated the rest, sending everything important in the box his grandfather had passed along.

Gia stood beside him, just as she had the day of his mother's funeral, when he'd sworn never to return.

Only he'd stayed.

For Gia.

And in doing so, he'd found love. Reconnected with his family. His roots.

Gia twined her fingers with his. "Do you need more time?"

He shook his head, giving the apartment one final glance. "Let's go home."

They made the five-hour journey back to the Navajo reservation, winding through the Tonto National Forest. The day was beautiful—sunny and warm, cooling to jacket weather as they climbed into the Colorado Plateau.

One hand on the steering wheel, the other resting on Gia's denim-clad thigh, Caleb drove while she dozed in the passenger seat. Her hand covered his, thumb grazing his knuckles in a slow rhythm.

By the time they reached Window Rock and continued north, the sun had dipped beneath layers of golden haze, the clouds ablaze with orange fire.

Tomorrow would be busy—he'd arranged a meeting with his grandfather while Gia met with the medical clinic's director. Then visits to Zach and Jennie.

He reached Gia's home and parked the rental behind her old SUV.

Gia smiled. "It's not much, but it's home."

The first time she'd said those words, she'd been self-conscious. Now her voice held something different.

Peace. Belonging.

Home.

He liked the sound of it.

Inside, everything was as they'd left it a few days ago—the worn brown sofa, the colorful rugs, the dark wood dining table. Gia's scent lingered strongest here, that desert floral note that clung to her skin and hair.

She stood in her living room, gaze drifting over the space. "I keep thinking this is a dream. That I'll wake up and Vincente will still be hunting me."

She turned, the ghostly remnants of fear clinging to the edges of her expression. "And you were just a fantasy I made up to survive."

Caleb stepped in close, brushing his knuckles along her cheek. "If it *is* a dream, don't wake me up."

He kissed her—not so much in hunger, but in release. The moment built slowly, like trust.

When they pulled apart, the shadows of fear had faded, but worry still lingered in Gia's eyes.

"What if I don't have a job anymore?"

He tugged her into his arms, kissed the top of her head. "You do."

She pressed her face to his chest. "How do you know?"

"I just do."

He trusted his grandfather. And he knew Gia was too valuable to lose. She'd had a long, emotionally draining couple of days. Her mind was spiraling, reaching for worst-case scenarios.

He had just the distraction in mind.

His lips brushed the shell of her ear. Tasted her skin.

She shivered, and his body tightened, the need to mark her as his a primal call in his blood.

"Are you hungry?" she murmured. "I know we had a late lunch on the road but—"

Her voice broke off as he kissed her throat. His hands slid up from her waist to cup her breasts. "Not for food."

Last night he'd held her while an FBI agent slept in the next room, his need to feel her fall apart beneath him, scream his name, kept on a tight leash.

She was alive. Safe. Her tormenter on a metal slab in the morgue.

Tonight, he'd show Gia exactly what she meant to him.

She moaned, tipping her head back to give him greater access.

He nipped the sensitive skin. Soaked in her breathy moan. Peeled her shirt over her head.

Her bra was plain, flesh-toned

Her body? *Breathtaking.*

He kissed each breast, inhaling a heady mix of desert flowers and hotel body wash.

She held his head to her chest, fingers delving in this hair.

"Bed." Her voice was ragged with need.

It went straight to his groin.

Twining his fingers with hers, he led her to her bedroom.

They undressed in haste, too desperate to explore, to build passion that already raged like molten lava.

His fingers shook. This woman wanted him. Loved him.

He dipped between her thighs. Found her slick and ready. Her hips rocked to meet his touch, soft mewls falling from her lips.

"Caleb, I need you. Now."

A few firm strokes and she shattered.

His own control broke. He positioned himself and thrust.

So tight. Hot.

Her inner walls milked him as her orgasm crested. He soon followed, the tingle spiraling from his toes upward to explode through him, hard and fast, as he poured himself into her, body, heart, and soul.

Gia owned it all.

"I love you," he groaned, the words dragged from the deepest part of him.

Gia traced his damp skin as he caught his breath. Her voice was soft, eyes clear, the fear haunting them gone.

"I love you, Caleb—I didn't think I deserved this kind of love."

He hadn't either. But now that he had it, he'd fight to keep it with his last breath.

"I'm going to prove you wrong." He kissed her deeply, tasting her, anchoring himself in her. "Every day. Every night."

And when he made love to her again, he drifted to sleep with her wrapped in his arms, his vow tattooed on his soul.

The next morning, Caleb met his grandfather at the tribal park beneath the Window Rock sandstone arch. The day was bright, the winter air cold but not bitter. He wore his leather jacket over a white Henley and black jeans.

Ben Blackwater stood near the Code Talker monument, dressed in a dark blue suit, traditional beaded necklace over his light blue dress shirt, turquoise and silver jewelry adorning his wrists and fingers. His gaze was fixed on the bronze statue of a kneeling World War II Navajo Marine.

Caleb's throat tightened. His grandfather was a man of honor. A leader. He saw that now. And, at long last, he was proud to be his grandson.

He walked up the path. Nodded to the security detail.

"Grandfather."

Ben turned. "Grandson." He patted Caleb's shoulder. "Walk with me."

They strolled the paved circular path of Tribal Park, passing beneath angled steel sculptures that honored Navajo war veterans.

"Have you seen your cousin?" Ben asked.

"Not yet. Gia and I plan to visit him this afternoon." Caleb paused. "What about...the situation at Old Joe's place?"

His grandfather's gaze lifted to the sandstone arch. "Chief Nez interviewed everyone. His official report states you and Zach were lured there by a false lead and ambushed. You acted to save Jennie and prevent Gia's abduction."

Two women walking along the path greeted Ben as they passed. Caleb nodded respectfully.

"Of course," Ben continued, "the FBI could still open their own investigation."

"They won't," Caleb said. "They've got bigger problems than two dead cartel soldiers."

"Hmm." Ben sighed. "After this, I may have to endorse the chief for president when my term ends."

Caleb's lips curled.

Politics were the same everywhere.

"So, this cartel leader who was after Gia—is he dead?" Ben asked.

"Yes. And Espina Negra has no further interest in her."

Caleb squinted into the sun, then glanced at his grandfather, an uncharacteristic flutter of nerves striking him. "Which means Gia's presence isn't a threat to the Navajo. She'd like to stay."

"We need her," Ben answered without hesitation. "I'll speak to the medical director."

They stopped walking. Ben's gaze turned warm, holding a flicker of hope. "And you, Grandson?"

Caleb's throat swelled. The past couldn't be undone, but it didn't have to define his future.

"I'd like to stay, too."

Ben's expression remained neutral, though Caleb swore the elder's eyes misted. "I'm glad."

"I'm sorry, Grandfather." Caleb's apology had layers to it. "I read Mom's journals. I understand now."

Silence.

Then, "I should have tried harder." The sadness in Ben's voice—and on his face—finally pushed Caleb to acknowledge his grandfather's pain.

"You did the best you could. So did she."

"And so did you." Ben's voice was gruff. "I'm proud of the man you've become."

His grandfather's praise hit a part of him long buried.

Caleb blinked back sudden tears.

Ben gestured to the silver and turquoise bracelet peeking from beneath Caleb's sleeve.

"I gave that one to Lillie." He smiled. "I have others, when you're ready."

They'd come full circle, back to the Code Talker monument.

"I have duties to attend to," Ben said. "Perhaps we can have dinner together soon?"

"I'd like that." Caleb turned to go.

"Grandson," his grandfather called.

He looked back.

"Welcome home."

His throat too tight to speak, Caleb simply nodded.

CHAPTER THIRTY-FIVE

LATER THAT AFTERNOON, CALEB and Gia drove to Zach's hogan.

Gia's happiness lit up the car as she chattered about her meeting with the clinic director, more animated than he'd ever seen her.

"I explained everything and assured her there's no longer any threat to me or her staff." She grinned. "She's keeping me on."

A familiar red pickup sat parked beside Zach's cruiser and Dodge Charger when they arrived.

"Jennie's here." Gia unbuckled her seatbelt.

Caleb smirked. "Maybe she's nursing him back to health."

They exchanged a knowing glance as they walked to the hogan and knocked.

Jennie flung open the door. The swelling in her eye had gone down, the bruising now a mix of purple and yellow.

"Oh, thank God!" she breathed, dragging Gia inside and wrapping her in a fierce hug.

Caleb followed, chuckling.

Zach lay sprawled on his cowhide sofa, bare-chested in jeans, his left arm in a sling. A white bandage peeked out just below his shoulder.

He started to rise.

"Sit," Jennie ordered. "You just got home from the hospital."

Zach sank back, grumbling. "Didn't know you were this bossy."

But Caleb caught the amused glint in his cousin's eye—and the way Zach's gaze lingered on Jennie, not Gia.

After Gia greeted Zach, the women drifted into the kitchen, chatting about his recovery.

Caleb settled onto the cushion beside his cousin. "I saw Grandfather today. Chief Nez cleared us."

"Not before he tore me a new one for bypassing procedure and involving civilians," Zach grumbled. "But yeah, he came through."

He lifted a brow. "And the Feds?"

Caleb recounted what had happened in Albuquerque and their summons to the FBI Field Office in Phoenix.

"Assistant Director Caldwell's a friend of my bosses at Dìleas. When he realized his task force was compromised, he had the US Marshal's Office deputize us to give us legal cover."

Zach glanced toward the kitchen. "And Gia?"

"She's in the clear. Vincente Lopez Garcia and his cousin are dead. Diego Lopez's brother tried to engineer a coup—he's on his way to supermax, but he won't last long. Right now, Gia and I are the least of the cartel's problems."

"So now what?" Zach studied him. Like their grandfather, his face gave nothing away.

"Gia is staying here. So am I."

A smile tugged at Zach's lips. His eyes gleamed with mischief.

"Navajo Nation Fair's in September. There's an open bull riding competition. Bet I can stay on longer than you."

Caleb snorted. "I rode Northern Alliance ponies in Afghanistan. If I survived those demons, I can handle a bull."

"Absolutely not." Jennie marched over, arms crossed, leveling them both with a glare.

Gia caught his eye, shaking her head with mock-disapproval, though she bit her lip, trying not to laugh.

Caleb and Zach looked at each other—and grinned like fools.

It was mid-afternoon by the time they left Zach and Jennie and drove to the cemetery.

Caleb held Gia's hand as they stood before the fresh mound of earth that marked his mother's grave.

"I brought you home, Mom." His throat closed up.

Gia squeezed his fingers and rested her head on his arm, lending him her strength.

The grief he'd buried beneath his need for vengeance bubbled to the surface. His chest heaved. He looked to the sky as tears blurred his vision.

It wasn't a day for sadness. Not anymore.

He had something special planned.

"I brought you home," he repeated, his voice stronger this time. "And I've decided to stay. See, there's this girl—"

Gia gave a quiet laugh, softening the edges of his sorrow.

He told his mother his secret, his silent words consigned to the wind, certain she'd hear and approve.

Wish me luck.

"Have you been to Canyon de Chelly yet?" he asked Gia.

She shook her head. "I haven't done much besides work and go home. I was too afraid."

"Come on, let's go for a drive."

An hour later, Caleb parked at an overlook on the South Rim.

The late afternoon temperature dipped into the low thirties, but the wind was calm. They hiked the half-mile paved trail.

When they came to the viewing platform, Gia gasped.

Towering sandstone cliffs blazed red and orange in the fading light, carved by ancient rivers, tectonic shifts, and time. The iconic red stone spire of Spider Rock soared from the canyon floor below. Shadows spilled into the valley, casting a blue haze over the cottonwood and juniper trees.

"It's beautiful."

He smiled at the wonder on her face, pride swelling in his chest—as if he'd somehow been responsible for this miracle of nature.

Caleb pulled Gia into his chest, wrapping his arms around her for warmth. Snowflakes drifted through the air, landing in her hair and on his shoulders.

"Spider Rock," he murmured. "My grandmother used to say this is the sacred home of Spider Woman, who wove the universe, taught my people to find beauty and balance."

He turned her in his arms to face him.

"You've brought beauty and balance into my life, Gianna Barone."

He took a breath. Dropped to one knee.

"Marry me. Build a future and a family with me."

For a beat, she simply stared, wide-eyed.

Then her smile bloomed—warm as a desert sunrise. Her eyes shimmered with tears.

"Yes to all of it. I love you, Caleb."

He stood, and they kissed as the last sunbeams set Spider Rock ablaze in a fiery burst of red.

Gia drew back slightly, her fingers curled in the front of his jacket. Her voice was soft, sure.

"I spent so long looking over my shoulder, afraid of being found. Afraid to want too much. But I'm done running, Caleb. I'm choosing you. This place. Our life."

Tears fell, glistening on her cheeks. Happy tears. "For the first time in a long time...I'm not afraid."

He'd spent a lifetime on the outside—never letting anyone in. Never letting himself belong.

Now, he'd found a love he never dared dream of.

A family he hadn't known he'd needed.

And a bond with his teammates—his brothers—he finally understood.

For the first time, Caleb saw his future.

And it was more than he'd ever dreamed possible.

THE END

If you liked Caleb and Gia's story, please consider leaving a review on Amazon.
Stay tuned for Danny Mayhew's story in book 5, Missile Strike, coming soon.

GLOSSARY OF DINÉ BIZAAD TERMS

Ahéhee'	Thank you
Amá	Mother
Shicheii	My Maternal Grandfather
Shidá'í'	My Maternal Uncle
Shił naa'aash	My Cousin (Father's Sister's Son)
Shimá	My Mother
Shimá Sáni'	My Maternal Grandmother
Shimá yázhí	My Maternal Aunt
Shinálí	My Paternal Grandfather
Tódich'íinii	Bitter Water Clan
Yá'át'ééh	Hello. Literal meaning: it is good.

BONUS FREEBIE

Want to know how it all began for the men of Dìleas Security Agency?

Sign up for my newsletter at cssmithauthor.com and I'll send you the prequel novella, The Mission, for free!

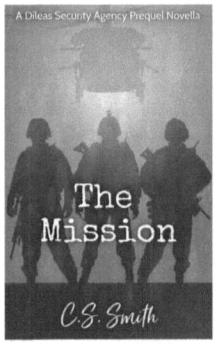

ALSO BY C.S. SMITH

Acknowledgments

The idea for Fatal Misstep came to me on one of my trips to and through Northern Arizona. The Navajo Nation, or the Diné as they call themselves, is the largest federally recognized tribe in the United States, larger than the states of Rhode Island, New Jersey, Connecticut, and Delaware combined, with over 27,000 square miles of land in Arizona, New Mexico, and Utah. If you've been to Antelope Canyon, Horseshoe Bend, Canyon de Chelly, Monument Valley, or Navajo National Monument, you've been on Navajo Nation land. If you've driven Interstate 40 from Gallup to Flagstaff, you've driven through the southern edge of the Navajo reservation and probably didn't even realize it. Most people who visit the area know very little about the Navajo people, their history, and their culture.

I set my story in and around the Navajo Nation to shed a small light on a part of the country and a culture most people know little about. But let me be clear: this is a fictional story. My characters are completely made up, as are the scenarios I placed them in. The role of Fatal Misstep is to entertain. It is neither to inform nor educate the reader on the complex history and culture of the Navajo people.

If you are interested in knowing more about the Navajo, I recommend the following websites:

Navajo Nation Official Website

The Navajo Times

Discover Navajo

Smithsonian National Museum of the American Indian: The Navajo Treaty of 1868

Some Interesting YouTube Channels:

Daybreak Warrior

Navajo Grandma

Navajo Traditional Teachings

A great fiction suspense thriller: Shutter (A Rita Todacheene Novel), written by Navajo Native Ramona Emerson.

One final note: I use the term Indian in my story rather than Native American because the US government and Navajo Nation official websites use the term Indian. The Navajo I spoke with when I visited also used the term Indian. I used the term in my story not to offend, but to reflect the reality of its usage.

Whew! That was a long one. It would be impossible to name all the websites I scoured, the books I read by Navajo authors, the countless YouTube videos I watched by native Navajo on everything from culture to language, and the Navajo I spoke with when I visited Antelope Canyon and Window Rock. But I thank everyone who has educated others on their culture, either through educational sites, personal stories, or through works of fiction.

I'd also like to thank my Green Beret resource, Rodney, for his help in explaining the organizational structure of an ODA, the role of each soldier in an ODA, and helping me choreograph some of the action scenes in this story.

Any and all mistakes are mine alone.

About the Author

Heat, Heart, and Heroes -- Steamy Romantic Suspense

C.S. Smith parlayed her degrees in government and national security studies into various careers as a policy analyst, export manager, and director of a city government committee on global connectivity. Her love of spine-tingling romantic suspense can be traced to her formative years in Washington, DC, surrounded by intrigue and good-looking men in uniform—including the one she married.

A native New Englander who has spent over half her life in North Carolina, she has joined the ranks of empty nesters, leaving only her husband and "faux" Golden Retriever at her mercy.

For more information, please visit cssmithauthor.com or connect with her on social media:

a amazon.com/author/c.s.smith

f facebook.com/CSSmithAuthor19

O instagram.com/c.s.smithauthor/

www.ingramcontent.com/pod-product-compliance
Lightning Source LLC
Chambersburg PA
CBHW030241120726
47903CB00005B/1573